To: K.

Ho! WARM REGARDS,

John

SAND TRAPPED

A Novel

by

John J. Gratton

This is a work of fiction. All names, characters, and incidents are purely imaginary, and any resemblance to actual events, or to persons living or dead, is coincidental.

§§§

I want to express my appreciation to all the men and women of all police forces for their perception, bravery and dedication. The fabricated detectives in this story do not portray the actual ability and performance of any police officers I have known. I sincerely hope I have not offended any law-enforcement officer.

Published by

Fairway Press
P. O. Box 1876
Fairfield Glade, Tennessee 38558

Printed by

Lightning Source
1246 Heil Quaker Blvd.
LaVergne, Tennessee 37086

Book Cover Design By

Jon Weaver
Crossville, Tennessee

ISBN: 978-1-4243-4189-4

Acknowledgements

My thanks to the many who encouraged me in this endeavor, especially to Jacqueline, Beverly, Debbie, Jeff…and my granddaughter Kristin, who said, "This thing is awesome, Papu…get it published!"

I also want to thank author Paul Leighty for his guidance and advice, and Mary Greene, copy editor, for her assistance in getting this ready for print. This would not have been possible without her.

And, last but not least, thanks to Ellie, my loving wife and faithful companion.

Dedication

This book is dedicated to all my golfing buddies. They'll understand...

ONE

Ever been locked up in an Alabama jail? Probably not. Let me tell you, it's not exactly "Sweet Home" as the song implies.

I guess this one in Gunter is pretty much like any other jail in Alabama—or anywhere in the country, for that matter. However, I'm not really sure. You see, I—Buddy Bowers—am not an expert on jails. In fact, this is the first one I've ever been in, around, or near.

Jeez, with a murder rap pinned on me, you'd think I would deserve something better—like the big jail in Huntsville.

WHAT THE HELL AM I TALKING ABOUT????
I don't deserve a bigger or better jail! I don't deserve to be in jail—period! I was framed! I'm innocent! INNOCENT!!!!

Uh-huh, sure. That's what all the incarcerated say. And that's what you're thinking about me, right? Well, not so fast.

Want to find out how I was trapped?
You're about to.

Let me digress a bit: Every year our golfing group goes on a golf outing. It's a different place each time. This year it was to a golf resort near the little town of Gunter, Alabama. Gunter is close to Huntsville, if you're not familiar with that part of the country. Usually we take along our wives. Unfortunately—for me, that is—we did not invite them this time. *Unfortunate* may be too weak a word.

I'll explain. You see, after our first day of golfing, we gathered at the 19th hole—a place where we divvy up the prize money, puff up our chests after a good round, or complain about the putts we missed. And, of course, we consume a few beers. *A few?* Gross understatement.

I had my share of the grog—and maybe a bit more than I should have imbibed. However, I could handle it. Uh-huh.

Lightheaded from the celebrating, I staggered from the main lodge toward my room in an adjacent building. My eyes were like looking through a furball, and they hurt like hell when the late afternoon sun jabbed at them. Sweat beaded on my forehead, ran down my nose and dripped onto my already-saturated tan golf shirt. Although it was October, it was unusually hot and humid for this time of year in northern Alabama.

Sucking in deep breaths provided little relief: Instead of inhaling crisp autumn air as one might expect, I gulped down thick soggy swills of moisture. It was like breathing under water. Well, not quite, but you get the gist of it.

The can of beer I was toting helped some. I rubbed the cool container on my forehead and sipped on the precious liquid to keep my windpipe open until I could get to my air-conditioned room.

I had to climb four or five steps to the concrete walkway at the building where my room was located. Man, it was all I could do to hang onto the handrail and lift one foot above the other. That feat is difficult enough to do when one is sober, which I obviously was not.

Nevertheless, it was the only way to get to my floor. So I had to tough it out.

The stairs were directly in front of a room. Not my room, but someone else's. And the door was open. Wide open. And so were my eyes when I saw a gorgeous brunette of about twenty-eight sitting comfortably in an easy chair and reading a book. Her black skirt was pulled up some, revealing two very long, shapely legs. However, I—being a happily-married man—didn't look. Uh-huh; right.

I kid a lot—obviously. So, when her warm chocolate eyes peered over the book at the drunken fool stumbling up the steps and gawking at her, I had no choice but to say something—something stupid as usual.

"You with the group?" I asked before my booze-burdened brain reminded me that only men were in our party this time. My face turned from rosy pink to magenta while I struggled up the stairs and waited for her reply.

However, she didn't answer. Instead, she nonchalantly marked her place in the book, set it on a nearby table and got to her feet. She stretched her arms back behind her head. Her white blouse was tight. Real tight. Tight enough that the buttons would fly like popping corn if she took a deep enough breath.

I stopped on the steps as she glided toward the doorway. She leaned sideways against the doorframe, arched her back and folded her arms under her breasts— which didn't need any additional lifting. She glanced up and down the walkway as if expecting someone.

We were just a few feet apart. God, she was beautiful! Or maybe it was just the booze getting to me.

Her tongue wet her upper lip before she finally turned to me and replied, "What group would that be?"

I could feel my face redden even more because, as I said, none of our wives were here. Therefore, she obviously wouldn't be affiliated with us. She had to be a total stranger. A fine-looking stranger. Really fine. Yep, quite a package. A real bell-ringer. A genuine *ten*.

Enough already!

Anyway, I had started this…this…thing with her by opening my big mouth, so I had to think of something clever to wriggle my way out.

"The g-golfing group," I informed her as I cleared my throat.

Well, duh; this is a *golfing* resort!

Instead of her commenting about not being part of our crew, she smiled coyly and said, "Looks like you had a good day." Her voice was soft as a bluebird's whisper. It was difficult to tell if she was breathing in or out when she spoke. "Have a hole-in-one or something?" She tilted her head and gave me one of those "*you old fox, you*" looks, and then she glanced down the walkway again.

I stared at her until my lips managed to coordinate themselves. I shook my head sharply. "N-No," I stammered. "Nothing like that. I just had a pretty good round. A couple lucky shots and some long putts that dropped for birdies. Things like that, you know." I shrugged.

"Actually, I don't know," she replied, returning her melting chocolate eyes to mine. "Golf is not one of my hobbies. In fact, the only thing I've heard about the game is that the ball lands in the sand half the time, and you spend most of the day trying to dig it out." A hint of a smile creased her cherry-like lips, and she swept a hand in the direction of the small table where her book was resting. "I'd rather spend my time reading."

My eyes followed her gesture. I swallowed hard and nodded my understanding.

She glanced along the walkway again.

It was the third time she had done that. It made me nervous. Very nervous. Although my wife wasn't with me, I had the odd sensation she was somehow watching me. Not a very comforting feeling. And what if the guys saw me talking with this doll? Holy smokes! They'd have a ball with it. And it would probably get back to my less-than-understanding wife in the form of a joke; a joke I don't think she would find very amusing. You see, my wife has a narrow sense of humor, as you will later discover.

I found myself glancing around also. Now I was making myself a bit edgy—and paranoid.

"You look a little nervous," she said in a voice barely louder than a whisper.

Nervous? Why would I be nervous? I've never done anything with another woman except share a friendly handshake. Hey, I'm no angel, but I do draw the line at some things. So I wasn't going to worry that my wife might find out, divorce me, take my house, my kids, my car, my dog…and *my golf clubs*! Oh, the pain.

What? Don't raise your eyebrows at me. I love those clubs. A man's got to have his priorities, you know.

My eyes flashed back to hers. "N-No," I said, shaking my head vigorously. "I'm…I'm not nervous. I just —"

I didn't get to finish because my left knee buckled, and I started to fall. It wasn't because I was drunk—well, maybe a little. Actually, I have a bad knee from playing football, and it doesn't need much provoking to get my attention. My beer can went flying down the walkway when I attempted to grab the railing. However, the railing wasn't what I got: What I actually acquired was her—the doll. My eyes must have appeared the size of two compact discs when her hand flung out and caught my arm. I just stared for a moment as I grasped the softness of her skin.

"Thanks," I finally said. "I've got a bad knee, and it—"

She didn't let me finish. "Why don't you come in and sit for a minute?" she suggested, holding my arm and guiding me—no, actually pulling me—into her room. "Looks like you need to rest that leg of yours."

It was like I was being drawn into quicksand and had no control over what was happening. It all occurred so fast, the last thing I remembered was looking over my shoulder to see if any of my guys were around to help me out of this mess.

They weren't.

The door closed behind us. She had to have shut it, but I don't see how because she never let go of my arm. Maybe the door had one of those self-closing devices. No, that couldn't be; the door had been wide open when I walked up, remember? She must have closed it with a flick of her heel.

Anyway, it wasn't my *leg* that needed help—it was my *head*. It was spinning like a flying Frisbee. "Okay," I reluctantly agreed, "but just for a minute."

I caught my breath while swaying slightly. To keep from falling, I reached for the chair where she had been sitting when I walked up. However, I never made it. She yanked on my arm and sort of pushed me toward the bed. Did I say sort of? I was propelled toward that pile of pillows like Mark Spitz diving into a plunge pool. I tried to resist. Well, not really resist. It was more like I had no choice in the matter: There was nothing I could grab to stop my momentum before I landed face-first on the bed. Remember, this was a motel room: one main room, a

6

bathroom, two chairs, one table…and a *king-sized* bed. Anyway, after plopping down on that enormous bed, I quickly rolled over and sat up on my butt. I grabbed the edge of the mattress to steady myself.

I was still a little woozy, but this ordeal was sobering me up fast. You see, I've never cheated on my wife during the twelve years we've been married, and I wasn't about to—even though this little sweetie would be near the top of the list if I decided to start. She really was about the closest thing to a perfect ten as one could get.

The doll eased in front of me and slowly rubbed her inner thighs on my knee, which was now shaking like a dog in a cold rain. She must have felt the quivering, because she calmly said, "Relax. You're safe. No one knows you came in here."

Safe? With her? Not on your life!

I asked, "How do you know—?"

Cutting me short, she said, "I checked." She looked down at me with her soft brown eyes. "No one was around. No one saw us." Her voice had a bit of a raspy sing-songie rhythm to it. Cute, mellow, calming, reassuring and—sensual.

"That's…that's not it," I said. I leaned forward, trying to get to my feet. "I-I'm—"

"Really?" she said, shoving my shoulders backwards. "Then what's the problem, hon?"

Hon? What—we're close friends now?

I was about to tell her what the problem was—I was married! However, with her shoving me, I lost what little grip I had on the edge of the bed and fell onto my back. I don't know how she did it, but just that quick, her blouse was unbuttoned, her skirt pulled up, and she was on top of me. She wasn't wearing any underwear. Yikes!

My head was spinning, but my senses were quite in order. She leaned forward and her full lips met mine. I wanted to kiss her and make mad passionate love. Oh, how I wanted to. But that little voice inside my head wouldn't let me. I slid my mouth to the side and gasped for air.

She adjusted herself on my lap, and things that shouldn't happen to a married man began to happen. That wasn't good, because there's a point when a man's mind starts rationalizing and begins making excuses for times such as these. And my mind, with the help of the booze, was *rapidly* approaching that point.

Her luscious lips tasted like freshly-picked strawberries. And her perfumed hair spilled around my face like soft shadowy silk. But when her firm breasts molded against my chest, I had to take immediate and drastic measures—to escape, that is.

However, before either of us could accomplish our objectives, a hard knock rattled the door. Our heads snapped in that direction.

8

TWO

The silence-shattering bang on the door made my heart stop beating, and it choked off my windpipe. I was positive I had taken my last breath.

"Lynn!" a man's voice thundered through the front door. "Lynn, are you in there?"

She sat upright, returned her eyes to mine and placed a quieting finger on those hot, juicy lips of hers. I'm no genius, but I instantly got the message—and so did the rest of my body.

"Lynn?" the man hollered again.

She leaned toward me. "Quiet!" she whispered in my ear. "It's my husband!"

HUSBAND?

My eyes widened. My heart hammered, and breathing was impossible. My entire life flashed before me. I didn't want to die like this. I didn't want to die—period!

After a long moment, his footfalls could be heard pounding on the concrete as he tromped along the walkway away from the room.

"He doesn't have a key," she said, returning her sultry brown eyes to mine. "He'll check the pool, gift shop and other places he thinks I might be." A sly smile emerged on her large lips. "We have time."

Time? Time for what?

I inhaled deeply and rose to my elbows with her still sitting on me. Her white blouse sailed across the room and landed softly on the dark blue carpet. There she was. Just her. Sans bra. Unfettered.

I hoped she didn't notice me noticing her. Yeah, right.

When I attempted to push her off, she grabbed my hands. Man, she was fast—cat-like. Or, maybe it was my numbed reactions that slowed me. Or, maybe it was a little of both. Whatever—she had my hands pressed against her breasts before I knew what was happening. I simply froze.

Don't ask me if it was intentional, because I honestly don't know. It all happened so fast I can't remember. I simply held onto her and stared into her ravenous brown eyes.

Still clutching my hands, she pushed forward and again attempted to kiss me. Man, I really had my hands full. Maybe I should rephrase that: I had all I could do to keep her at arm's length. That's sounds a little better, right?

I locked my elbows so her lusting lips couldn't reach my mouth again. That took some strength—and some willpower. The thought of her irate husband barging through the door any second was paramount on my mind. It sobered me right up. Irate husbands have a tendency to do that to a person, you know.

Another pounding on the door.

Both of our heads swung in that direction again.

"Lynn!" the same gruff voice shouted. "Lynn, I know you're in there, damnit! Open the goddamn door!"

That didn't take long. Didn't she say he would check a dozen places before returning?

Lynn didn't answer the man, and she didn't shush me this time. She slid off the bed and dashed to her blouse. While she was slipping it on, she motioned for me to go to the door.

She didn't have to: I was already heading in that direction. When I got to the door, I cringed next to the hinges so the door would screen me when he opened it.

She grabbed the book off the table and tossed it onto the bed. She smoothed her hair and blouse with quick swipes of her hands, shot a quick glance at me, and once again, placed a quieting finger on her lips. She unlocked and opened the door, then faked a yawn while she stretched her arms above her head.

Nice touch.

I hid behind the door and tried not to make it rattle or shake—the same way my knees were behaving.

"Where the hell you been, girl?" a dark-haired, broad-shouldered guy about six-three and 240 pounds asked as he barged in. "I've been looking all over the goddamn place for you."

"Taking a nap," she said in a casual tone. "I guess the book wasn't interesting enough to keep me awake." She gestured toward the book on the bed and then took him into her arms, making sure his back was to me. With a flick of her hand, she motioned behind his back for me to leave.

That was not a problem, believe me. Hey, I'm no slouch at six feet tall and almost two hundred pounds, but this dude made me feel like the guy at the beach who gets sand kicked in his face.

I eased around the door, never taking my eyes off that damned linebacker. Man, he was huge. Muscular. Mean-looking—even from the back.

As I was about to leave, I noticed her attempting to say something to me. I paused, and like an idiot, I studied what she was trying to convey.

"The pool at ten. The pool at ten," she mouthed.

I'm pretty sure that's what she was saying.

11

Okay, sure. You betcha. I'll meet you there at ten, sweetie.

Right. Fat chance. No way. Not on your life.

I was out of that room in a flash, never to see either of them again. Ever.

You believe that, don't you?

THREE

When I awoke from my nap, my head was still spinning like a dish on a juggler's stick. It hurt like hell when I sat up, and shaking my head to clear it only made the sensation worse. Also, my mouth felt like it was stuffed with a carton of cotton balls. I needed a drink—water, that is. You see, I'm not really a drinking man; I just have a drink for fun with the guys now and then. Fun?

I rose from the bed and staggered into the bathroom. I gawked at the person in the mirror. I didn't recognize the guy. His eyes were more red than brown, and his dark hair looked like it had been teased with a vacuum cleaner. Not a pretty sight.

I leaned into the sink and splashed water on my face and slurped from the faucet. It helped a little, but the throbbing was still there. I wondered if I had anything in my shaving kit that would ease the pain. I trudged into the bedroom and spilled the items from the leather bag onto the dresser.

Bingo! Aspirin!

I returned to the bathroom and gulped down four of those little magic tablets with a glass of water. I set the glass on the sink and blinked a few times while I stared at myself in the mirror. What a mess: bloodshot eyes, dark bags that almost reached my cheeks, and hair that stood at attention.

My gaze slid to my watch. I still had time for a quick shave and shower before meeting the guys for dinner.

I didn't feel self-conscious because I was sure they would be in a similar condition. Men.

As I was stepping into the shower, I thought about the weird dream I'd had—being seduced by Lynn and all. However, the more I thought about it, the more I wondered if it actually were a dream. It was too vivid. Too real.

You don't usually remember every aspect of a dream. But this one was like reviewing a slow-motion replay. And the details were alarmingly clear. Crystal clear.

It had to be a dream. It was, wasn't it?

I shrugged off the nagging thought and wondered what the guys would say if I shared it with them. However, my common sense took control and advised me to keep my mouth shut. Good advice, Buddy.

I met the guys at the bar but declined the pre-dinner cocktail for obvious reasons. After a few teasing remarks about our golf match, we sauntered into the dining room. I can't tell you what I had to eat because my mind was focused elsewhere. The recurring image of the brunette mouthing *"The pool at ten"* hammered at my subconscious until my conscious mind finally accepted the fact that the dream may not have been a dream after all. Oh, really?

There was only one way to find out, right? Be at the pool at ten o'clock to see if she was there. But what if it wasn't a dream and she actually did show up?

Phew! Heavy stuff for this guy.

I lingered with the guys until about quarter till ten and then made some excuse to leave. I said goodnight and started toward my room, which had an outside entrance. However, about halfway down the walkway, the dream popped into my mind again. I glanced over my shoulder to see if anyone was following. I didn't spot anybody, so I headed toward the swimming pool.

14

The pool was located behind the motel, and beyond that was beautiful Gunter Lake. The lake was somewhere out there in the darkness, and it was a striking setting during the daytime. But it was now dark. Very dark. Not even a hint of a moon was visible. So you'll have to take my word about the wonderful lake vistas.

With it being so dark, I had to be careful where I stepped. I didn't want to trip over a chair and hurt my knee again, or worse yet—go ass-over-teakettle into the swimming pool.

There were no security lights, and even the pool lights were turned off. I waited a bit until I became accustomed to the dark, then I eased toward what appeared to be the pool.

It was quiet. Eerily quiet.

It was good that no one was around, because it validated that the earlier thing with Lynn had simply been a dream and nothing more. I turned to leave, but a noise near the pool caught my attention. I twisted around and strained both my ears and eyes to find what had made the odd sound.

The resort was located in the woods, so lots of raccoons had run of the place. *It must have been one of those little critters rummaging for food* was my thought.

Wrong.

A female voice whispered, "Wondered if you'd show."

Oh, hell.

The hairs on the back of my neck were never as stiff as they were at that instant. That low, sensual voice from my dream—which obviously had not been a dream— danced across the water. I blinked several times, and my eyes scanned from side to side, but I couldn't detect anyone in or near the pool.

15

A sudden *sploosh* and the emergence of someone in the pool at my feet startled the hell out of me. I jumped back a foot or two to keep from getting wet. When I regained my composure, I leaned over and had a closer look. I squinted at the sensuous brunette looking up at me.

"Didn't think you would," she said in that sultry voice of hers, "but I'm glad you did."

Damn!

I glanced around—as if I could see anything in that dark enclave. "Did what?" I asked, returning half of my attention to her.

She floated closer to the steps. "Show up," she said softly.

"Oh," I groaned.

She half whispered, "Just you and me. Together. Alone."

It was dark but not dark enough to conceal the fact she was wearing nothing but water. No top. No bottom. Nothing.

Ho-boy.

I gulped.

"Come in. The water's nice and warm," she said, twirling her finger in circles. "Maybe we can finish some… some unsettled business." She rolled over onto her back and floated near me.

Either the water wasn't as warm as she said, or the chill of the night air got to her and made her stick out of the water like two ripe grapes on top of a couple floating oranges. Wow! A fruit lover's delight.

Okay, doll, I'll be right in. You betcha. Can't wait. Let me get these darned clothes off.

I told her, "I don't think that's a good idea."

"Why not? Don't you think I'm pretty?"

Pretty wasn't even close to describing her.

16

"I don't even know you," I said. "Hell, I thought you were just a dream until a few minutes ago."

"Do I look like a dream?" she asked, batting her eyes. "Your dream girl, maybe?"

"Look," I said firmly, "I'm a happily mar—"

"Lynn."

"What?"

"You said you didn't know me. My name is Lynn."

Man, I didn't need that. Now we were buddies. Close chums even. Sheesh!

I glanced around once more. Her name cycled in the back of my mind until I recalled that huge husband of hers hammering on the door and shouting her name earlier. It definitely had not been a dream.

She rolled onto her stomach and glided over to the curved concrete steps. "Nervous again, I see," she said as she grabbed the stainless steel handrail. "There's no reason to be. My husband passed out over an hour ago. And I don't think anyone else would be brave enough to wander out here…do you?"

Nervous? I wasn't the least bit nervous. Why in the world would I be nervous? I hadn't done anything wrong—yet.

My eyes peered through the darkness and scanned every inch of the obscured lodge. "That's not the point," I said, returning my attention to her. "I shouldn't be here, period."

"What a shame," she cooed. "Looks like my handsome prince hasn't got what it takes after all."

I shook my head slowly. "I'm sorry…uh, Lynn." It took a moment for my frazzled brain to come up with her name. "You're absolutely beautiful, and if I wasn't mar—"

She cut me short again. "How about taking off your shoes and wading in the water? You don't have to get your clothes wet. Just roll up your pants a little."

My insides were trembling. I knew this was the time to book. Definitely time to leave. If I gave her a nickel, she'd want a dime. And if I…well, you get the picture.

"Please," she begged in that soft, captivating voice. "Don't make me stay here all by myself." She glanced around. "What if one of those wild animals decided to attack me or something? What would I do without you here to defend little ole me?"

I swallowed a deep breath. "How long you planning on staying out here?"

"Just a few more minutes. I don't want to go back to that rotten room with that drunken bum right now." She batted her long eyelashes. "I'd rather stay here and talk with you."

I shook my head no. "I-I don't—"

"Pleeeeeese?"

That was unfair. Definitely unfair. But how could I refuse someone in need of protection, right?

She said, "It's just your feet we're talking about here, you know."

"Oh, all right," I agreed, shaking my head in disgust at my lack of self-control. "But only my feet."

"You sweeeet thing, you."

I took off my shoes and socks, and rolled my pant legs up to my knees. I eased onto the top step, which was covered with about six inches of warm water. I grabbed the handrail to steady myself. Didn't want my knee buckling at a time like this. Also, I wanted to be prepared in case "sweeeet thing" had any ideas about pulling me into the pool with her.

18

She rolled onto her back once again and slowly bobbed away. I won't bother to describe the sight. I'm sure you can picture it quite clearly.

She asked in a louder voice, "Sure you won't change your mind about coming in?"

"Positive."

"Okay, handsome. But you have no idea what you're missing."

I think I do, my mind said. It also told me to put my shoes and socks back on and do a hasty retreat while it was still possible.

Her low, pleading voice asked, "What if I bumped my head and passed out and drowned?"

Well, sweetheart, you could always turn onto your stomach and watch where the hell you're going. That way you could see what was in front of you, and you wouldn't bump your head and pass out and drown. Of course, then I wouldn't be able to see you sunny-side up either.

Aw shucks. What's a fellow to do at a time like this?

LEAVE!

I stepped out of the pool. "Just be careful," I told her. I wiped my ankles with my socks and slipped my bare feet into my shoes. I stuffed my socks into my pocket. They were too damp to put on and then try to work my feet into my shoes. That sounds kind of complicated, but if you ever tried to slide wet socks into dry shoes, I think you know what I'm talking about.

Now that my eyes had pretty much grown accustomed to the dark, I could see that she had stopped swimming and was standing at the edge of the pool—close to me.

"Be careful?" she asked, responding to my comment. "Are you joking?" Her hands, palms up, shot toward me. "You can never be careful enough with a husband like mine!"

Husband?

I had temporarily forgotten about the guy. How in the world could I? He's as big as a gosh-darned billboard, for crying out loud!

My head snapped toward the walkway. He was nowhere in sight. But neither was the walkway, nor anything else beyond twenty feet; it was that dark. He could be lurking in the shadows, and we'd never know it. Heaven forbid!

Man, the last thing I needed right now was to tangle with a drunk and angry linebacker of a husband. How could I explain a black eye or broken nose to the guys—or my wife? Yikes!

I peered around once more. Chills I couldn't begin to describe coursed through me. Man, I didn't need this.

I'm outta here. Gone. History.

Adios, sweetheart!

FOUR

A loud knock on my door shattered the morning stillness. I rolled over in bed and rubbed the sand from my eyes. I couldn't make out what the clock read, and looking at my wristwatch was even worse. It was hard to believe I had overslept and the guys had to wake me for breakfast; I'm an early riser. However, anything—and I mean *anything*—was possible after yesterday.

The knocking continued. It sounded like someone pounding on a set of bongos. Something I really didn't need this morning.

I rolled out of bed and staggered to the door. "All right already!" I shouted, tugging at my undershorts. "I'm coming, for Pete's sake!"

I opened the door, and the sun shot in like a flash of lightning. My hand flew to my eyes, and my head lowered instinctively. My watch informed me it wasn't even seven o'clock yet. I swear I could kill those friends of mine sometimes.

"Mr. Bowers?" a strange voice asked.

Shielding my eyes from that sharp laser beam, I slowly raised my head. Two strange men wearing suits were standing at the door. I knew this wasn't good because it was too darned hot and humid for anybody with the least bit of common sense to be wearing anything except a golf shirt and shorts.

One of the guys was about as broad as he was tall, and the other was much taller and slender. The tall one was an Afro-American with a shaved head. I think he'd have to duck to enter the room.

Still screening my eyes, I nodded and said, "Yeah, I'm Bowers. Who wants to know?"

"Detective Small," the short, heavyset one replied. He flashed a silver badge and then jerked his balding head toward the other man. "He's Detective Biggs."

Small and Biggs. Of course.

The names were perfect for the two clowns. However, they didn't look like they were the least bit close to clowning around. They didn't even crack a smile.

Several clever things crossed my mind. However, I was now awake enough to realize it was not the time to get cute. I simply said, "What can I do for you, Detective?"

The short heavyset one—Small—is the one who spoke: "May we come in? We'd like to have a few words with you."

I glanced around to see if my friends were nearby and playing some sort of trick on me.

Nope. No such luck.

I returned my attention to Detective Small. "What's this all about?"

I suddenly realized I was standing in the open doorway wearing just my undershorts. I looked for something to slip on or drape in front of me.

"Mr. Bowers," the detective repeated, "may we come in, sir?"

"Uh...yeah," I mumbled, still looking for some clothes. "C-Come in." I grabbed my shirt that was draped over the chair and wiggled into it as I stepped aside.

The two men entered. I was right: The tall guy—Biggs—had to tilt his head to clear the doorframe. Detective Small eased past, but Biggs remained in front of the door—like I was going to run out or something.

I asked, "What is it you—?"

Small was quick to ask, "Where were you last evening?"

"Here," I said, my eyes darting from one detective to the other. "Why?"

"All night?" asked Small.

"Most of the night," I said, shrugging. "I mean, I had dinner with my friends and then came back here. You can ask them. They'll vouch for me." I riveted my eyes on Small. The other guy gave me the creeps. "I'm sure they're still in their rooms."

I tried to peak around Detective Biggs to see if my friends were anywhere in sight. Still nobody around.

The huge guy, Biggs, closed the door, but he never took his stalking tiger-like eyes off me. Creepy.

Small casually snooped around the room while he questioned me. "Anybody here with you last night?"

He didn't look at me. I wished he would look at me when asking me questions. It made me nervous when he didn't. It kind of made me feel like it wasn't me he was actually talking to—like I was watching one of those TV shows. You know: detective stuff...or crime scene investigations...or something.

I glanced at Detective Biggs. He was still staring at me. I wished he wouldn't look at me. It made me nervous.

That's the second time I said *nervous*. And for some reason, it made me think of Lynn asking me if I was nervous. That made me even more nervous.

"Mr. Bowers?" Small asked, finishing his perusal of the room and turning to me. "Anyone with you in your room?"

"I, uh...no," I replied. "No one was here with me. I came back by myself."

That was the truth, as best I could recall.

Small said, "So no one can verify you were here all evening; is that correct?"

My head swiveled between the two detectives. "What the heck's this all about?"

Small ignored my question. He simply said, "And you never left the room after you came back, right?"

My mind flashed to Lynn's naked body swimming in the pool. I wasn't about to admit to that. No siree. But what if something had happened to her and I was the last to see her? What if she was attacked or something? I should have stayed until she left, damnit!

Or, maybe her husband saw us together and was hiding in the shadows waiting for me to leave. And when I left, he...

Hell, I didn't even want to think about what could have happened. However, my mind wouldn't let go a gruesome vision of her naked body lying on the bottom of the pool. Beads of sweat rolled down my face, and I'm sure Detective Biggs was counting every one.

I didn't do it! I wanted to scream.

Detective Biggs, finally spoke: "I think the man's lyin'." He shook his head slowly back and forth. "Don't think he came back here after dinner like he said."

His words were sharp and to the point. And that point was piercing what little armor I had put up. It was obvious I couldn't continue the lie. You see, my problem— well, one of my problems—is that I don't lie very well. Something from my early childhood, I guess. *Thanks, Mom.*

Small asked, "Is that right, Bowers?"

I returned my attention to Detective Small. "Well, I may have gone out for some air or...or a short stroll. But I—"

24

Small asked, "Did that stroll take you to the swimming pool, perhaps?"

He was staring at me with prying eyes. I wish he wouldn't look at me like that when he's asking those intimidating questions. It gets on my nerves.

With my head swiveling between the two, I said, "What's going on here, guys? Did my golf group buddies put you up to this? That's it, isn't it? That's what this is all about. It's a joke, right?" Again I glanced through the window to see if my back-stabbing "friends" were anywhere in sight.

"It's no joke," jabbed Biggs.

Small asked, "When's the last time you saw Harry Thomas?"

My eyes flashed back to the short detective. "Harry who?"

"Weren't you in his room yesterday?" asked Small.

Oh-oh. Lynn's husband, I'll bet.

I said, "I don't know any Harry Thomas." True, because I only got to see the man's broad backside in the motel room.

"We've got a beer can from his room with fingerprints on it," said Small. "And I'll bet they're sure as hell gonna match yours. Whaddya think?"

"Well, sure," I said, shrugging. "They could possibly match mine. I had a beer in my hand and dropped it when I lost my balance climbing the darned stairs." My hands waved in that direction—as if they could see through the walls. "But the darned thing rolled down the walkway."

Small asked, "How do you explain the can ending up in Thomas' room?"

What? How could it? The thing must have rolled twenty feet down the sidewalk—away from Lynn's room.

I shook my head in disbelief. "Somebody must have picked it up and set it in the room." I thought of countless possibilities. "Maybe a cleaning lady did it before she had time to stuff it into a trash bag...or container..."

"Uh-huh," acknowledged Small, cocking an eyebrow. "And what about the swimming pool? You never did answer that. Did you go there...on your little stroll?"

My mind was spinning out of control trying to stay ahead of this guy's questions. "I may have," I said, shrugging. "I don't remember. I just walked around a little to let my dinner settle. I don't sleep well when I eat late."

"You know," interjected Biggs, "we found the same set of prints on the pool handrail. Yours...or just a coincidence?"

"Hell," I retorted, "everybody grabs that darned handrail when getting in or out of the pool."

Small pulled one of my socks from *his* pocket and held it in front of me. "How about this?" he asked, dangling the thing. "Look familiar?"

Okaaay. Got me there.

Damn! The thing must have dropped when I was stuffing them in my pocket. I knew I should have put them back on—wet or not. My eyes slid stealthily to my pants. My other sock was hanging from the pocket. I hoped they hadn't noticed.

Uh-huh.

Detective Small moseyed over and tweezed the sock flagging from the pocket. "Lookie here, Biggsie." He dangled the thing in front of us. "Whaddya know...a perfect match."

Biggs didn't bother to look at the sock. His eyes simply bored holes in me. He said, "Another coincidence, I reckon."

26

That scary guy, Biggs, was beginning to bug me. My shocked stare shifted from Biggs to the sock then to Detective Small. "Yeah," I replied to Small. "Come to think of it, I did wander out there. I took off my shoes and socks and soaked my feet in the water…on the top step, that is. I must have held onto the railing at that time. That's probably when my fingerprints—"

Biggs cut me short: "And you dropped your sock when you panicked and ran."

I glared at the tall black detective. "I didn't run," I snapped back. "And I certainly didn't pan—"

Small didn't let me finish: "Was Harry Thomas at the pool with you?"

My head swung between the two detectives. "I told you guys, I don't know any Harry Thomas."

That was the truth, more or less. I did see the furious linebacker's backside, but I didn't see his face. And, I really didn't get to *know* him, nor did I want to—if you know what I mean.

"So, you deny knowing Mr. Thomas?" said Small.

I nodded in agreement.

He picked up my pants and fished my wallet from the pocket. "And you deny being in his room—and being at the pool with him. Is that correct?" He was thumbing through my wallet the way a bad bookkeeper riffles through files.

That was making me nervous.

"That's right," I replied. My palms rose in defiance. "I swear I don't know the guy." The firmness of my voice showed that—I think.

"How'd you get the shiner?" asked Small.

My hand instinctively flew to my eye and felt the welt. Ouch! It was the size of a golf ball. "I-I must have whacked it on the railing when I tripped on the motel steps."

"Man," said Biggs, wagging his head slowly and methodically, "you're sure in one helluva fix."

My eyes flashed from Biggs to Detective Small. "Would one of you please tell me what the hell is going on?"

Small tossed my pants at me but held onto my wallet.

I grabbed my slacks and was about to ask about my wallet.

However, Detective Biggs didn't allow it. "Put them on!" he bellowed from across the room.

Small stared into my eyes. He was serious. *They* were serious.

I asked, "What the hell is going on? Is Lynn—?"

Small said, "Harry Thomas' body was found floating in the pool this morning."

Harry Thomas? Harry Thomas?

No!

FIVE

The detectives didn't believe a word I had to say, so they charged me with Harry Thomas' murder and threw me in jail. The one in Gunter. Yep, that crummy little jail in Gunter—not the big one in Huntsville. Can you believe that? Oy!

Anyway, Harry Thomas had been hit on the back of his head and was either tossed or fell into the pool, where they said he drowned. Well, he didn't actually drown. If he had drowned, his lungs and sinus cavities would have been full of water, and his body would have been lying on the bottom of the pool instead of floating on the surface. But who's going to enlighten those two rocket scientists who call themselves detectives? Not I.

Nevertheless, they had me: My fingerprints were on the beer can in Thomas' room and on the handrail leading into the pool. Remember when I took my shoes and socks off and waded on the top step and had to grab the railing for balance? Well, that's when my prints got on the darned handrail. They had me dead to rights.

I don't like that word *dead*; it makes me pucker a bit.

They read me my rights and took my mug shot and fingerprints, then they tossed me in a jail cell. I guess that's about as officially arrested as one can get. I felt like a felon who was an embarrassment to everyone. I guess that's because I was now officially an accused felon—who naturally would be an embarrassment to anyone, especially to a good family, his friends or his community. And that would definitely include my wife, Heather.

My golfing buddies must have gotten the word of my unfortunate situation, because there was no sign of them. Not a trace. Nothing. *Nada!*

They're not dumb. They scooted out before they could get involved. After all, they're the ones who got me into this situation in the first place, right? Or, maybe they simply left because I was such an embarrassment to them that they didn't want to associate further with me. Nonetheless, I'm sure they're now back in their beautiful homes, where they are safe and secure with their loving families—where I should be.

Damn, I hope the guys remembered to pick up my golf clubs.

What?

Don't look at me that way. As I said before, a man's got to have his priorities.

Anyway, back to the jail situation: The interrogation room had a small gray table and three metal chairs. A mirror comprised most of one wall, which I'm sure had people and recorders and highly technical stuff like that hidden behind it. It made me nervous.

Besides being nervous, I was very cold. I wished I had a jacket. They kept the temperature just above freezing in the place. I'd have blown into my hands, but I was afraid icicles would form between my fingers. It was that cold. No kidding.

Even though it's early autumn, it was almost ninety degrees outside. And quite humid. How's a body to adjust to such extremes? They have absolutely no consideration for their murderers. Sheesh!

I sat on one side of the gray metal table and Detective Small on the other. One chair remained empty because Detective Biggs was standing by the door.

Shocker. Where else?

We went over my story several times, and each time it seemed to change a little. What I'm trying to say is—the more I talked, the more truth came out. It wasn't that they were that good, or that I was intimidated (well, maybe a little), but as I said before—I have trouble lying. Or sticking to my lies, I should say.

A slew of thoughts galloped across my brain, but nothing seemed to surface that would add much to my story. I twisted and turned the thing until my mind was a soggy pretzel. Nothing helped.

I guess the final blow came when the detectives said they had an eyewitness who saw me leave Thomas' room. Ouch!

What could I say after that? They had me.

After adamantly denying that I knew Harry Thomas, I finally succumbed and admitted to being in his room. But I never actually saw Harry Thomas' face, so I couldn't be positive the body they had shown me at the pool was the same dude. However, the dead guy did have hair and massive shoulders like Harry's.

The detectives said they didn't need my corroboration, because others had already identified him. They also informed me that, apparently, I was the last one to see him alive.

Not good.

I guess that's when I told them the entire scenario—from the time Lynn grabbed my arm and yanked me into her room, until I slipped past her husband as I scrambled out the door. I even told them everything—well, almost everything—that transpired with Lynn at the pool.

31

They still didn't buy it.

Maybe they might have believed a good lie instead—that's if I had been capable of coming up with one. But I wasn't. And now that I think back on it all, I actually can't believe everything that happened myself.

So—the eyewitness, my fingerprints...and my dropped sock—confirmed that I was in Thomas' room and at the pool. There was no denying that. But here's the real kicker: They said Harry Thomas *wasn't married!*

There was no wife. No Lynn.

Huh?

Nobody had registered with the darned guy.

Oh-oh.

I told the detectives to check for Lynn's fingerprints and DNA in Thomas' room. They had a good laugh before reminding me it was a motel, and there would be hundreds of prints and DNA from previous guests. The same held true for the pool.

My fingerprints were the only ones they needed to verify. And that they did. I was in trouble—deep kimchi.

They asked if I wanted an attorney. I told them I didn't need any damned lawyer because I didn't do anything wrong. They strongly suggested I get one because of the evidence stacked against me.

Evidence? All purely circumstantial, right?

I finally relented and told them to let the state provide an attorney. I wasn't about to shell out hundreds of dollars an hour for some hotshot lawyer when I was totally innocent.

Big mistake.

The attorney assigned to me was a young man who had never defended anyone charged with more than a parking ticket, I'm guessing. He knew absolutely nothing about homicide. Nothing!

Okay. Thanks, Alabama.

I told him to get lost—I'd hire a private investigator.

Bail was set at $100,000. Now I don't have that kind of money. I'm a general contractor who builds things. Well, actually, *I* don't build them: I subcontract out to carpenters, painters, plumbers, electricians, roofers, et cetera; and they do the actual building. I just collect the money. Well, there's a little more to it than that, but I'm sure you get the picture.

The bottom line is that I didn't collect enough money to post bond for the hundred grand the judge had imposed. However, thanks to a *somewhat* understanding wife—whom you will meet later—and some very good affluent friends—whom you will *not* meet—I was able to accumulate enough cash to get my sorry ass out of the damned pokey.

The problem was—what in the world would I do next? Who would I go to?

SIX

One of the first things I did when I was released—other than having a *very* long talk with my wife—was to begin looking for a private investigator. One who was pretty sharp and with plenty of experience—but not too expensive. The money pot was just about empty after posting bond.

It was obvious the police weren't going to look for Lynn, or whatever the hell her name was. And the District Attorney felt there was enough compelling evidence to take my case all the way to court—and a jury. God forbid.

I began scanning the Huntsville phone book in search of an experienced but reasonable private investigator. However, when I telephoned and inquired, they all wanted healthy retainers, expenses and between $500 and $1000 a day. A thousand!

Maybe my case didn't require that much experience.

I continued down the list of agencies.

I finally made contact with a firm in Gunter that was more in line with what I had in mind: cheap. No retainer, $50 a day—plus expenses, of course.

I hurried over to their office figuring the sooner we got on Lynn's trail the easier it would be to find her. Well, it sounded good to me, but what the heck do I know? I'm not the expert in that area—homicide, that is.

I walked into the dank and dingy office of Diamond and Diamond, Private Investigators. It was like opening the door to a musty basement that hadn't been unlocked in years. I began sneezing and thought I would never stop.

I wiped my nose with my handkerchief as I approached the girl at the cluttered desk, who was cute as a button. I explained that I was the one who had telephoned earlier. Dusty, a petite redhead—22 at most—greeted me. I gawked at the kid for a moment. No less than six earrings—six, count 'em...*six!*—decorated her left ear. I tried not to look too dumbfounded. You see, I'm a little old-fashioned when it comes to things like that. Maybe I wouldn't have noticed three or four—but *six*?

Anyway, Dusty Diamond acknowledged that she was expecting me and asked me to have a seat in Mr. Diamond's office. I did just that—as soon as I moved the fat gray cat out of the *fur-lined* chair. What's a little cat hair on a guy's duff? I can't see it anyway, right?

Dusty followed me in and took a seat at Mr. Diamond's even more disorganized desk.

I asked Dusty if any of the investigators were in. She explained that her father was actually the investigator, and all she did was assist him with the paperwork. That eased my mind some. I nodded my understanding and asked to see Mr. Diamond.

"I'm 'fraid Daddy's not here," she said.

"When do you expect him?"

"Not for quite awhile," she explained. "He's in the dang hospital."

"Sorry to hear that. Hope it's not too serious."

She went on: "Broken arm. Broken leg. Concussion. Some internal bruises and—"

Enough, already!

I stopped her right there. I didn't want to hear any more. All kinds of thoughts went through my mind when I imagined myself being hunted down and hammered by some of his case-chasing thugs.

"How did it happen?" I asked, but I really didn't want to know. "Automobile accident?" I hoped.

She shook her head no. "One of his cases."

Oh-boy.

I could picture something like that happening to me, and I wondered if this was the appropriate time to leave. I swallowed hard and looked down and plucked a few of the gray cat hairs off my slacks. I thought I was going to sneeze again. I must be allergic to cats.

My gaze returned to her bright green eyes. "Are there any other investigators?" I asked with a silent prayer.

She forced a skewed smile and...and said *she* was it. Yep, Dusty Diamond, Private Investigator. Tons of experience, I'm sure.

Wrong.

It was definitely time to leave. I propped my hands on the arms of the chair and was about to get up. "Well, Miss Diamond...I don't think—"

"But he's still very alert," she interrupted with a quick, snappy voice. "And he'll share with me...with *us*, that is...his experience."

I could feel myself squirming in the nest of cat hair. I said, "I'm not sure, Dusty. Maybe I should just—"

"Sounds like an open and shut case to me," she said, raising her palms as well as arching her reddish eyebrows. "I've already found out where Harry Thomas lived and worked. And I'm pretty darn sure we'll be able to connect him to this Lynn friend of yers."

Lynn—my friend?

I sat up straight. "How did you hear about—?"

"I knew all about it," she said, cutting me off again. "Yer picture and the whole dang story was in the

36

newspaper, you know. Gunter ain't that big a place, and somethin' this big'll make the front page every time." She rummaged through the stack of junk on the desk and came up with the local newspaper. She waved it in front of me. "See?"

Great. So she had seen it too. Just what I needed: My face would soon be smeared across all the national newspapers for the whole country to see. God forbid.

Funny thing though, I didn't remember their taking my photograph. Must have been the damned mug shot. I buried my face in my hands and secretly apologized to my wife.

Dusty said, "If the fifty bucks a day is too much for you, we can like...negotiate, maybe?"

I raised my head and looked at her. Her eyes were sparkling like highly-polished emeralds. She was excited. Definitely all keyed up.

"The money's not the issue, Miss Diamond. I—"

She didn't let me finish. She slapped the newspaper down and pressed her fingers hard on the desk. She allowed her green eyes to glare at me. "You don't thank I can handle the dang thang, do you?"

She said *I*—not *we*—right? But didn't she just say she only helped her father with the paperwork? She did. Go back and check if you don't believe it. Heaven help me.

To be perfectly honest, Miss Diamond, I really don't think you can handle the case. But maybe in ten or fifteen years when you get a little older and a little wiser, and have a touch of experience—we'll be able to work something out.

I said, "Well, Dusty, I—"

"Heck, me and Daddy have had cases that make this one seem like child's play." She leaned back in Daddy's large, well-worn brown leather chair and folded her arms across her lime-green shirt. No bra—no need for one. However, the color of her shirt really brought out the green in her eyes. Fascinating. Captivating.

Man, it's hot in here!

I adjusted the collar of my shirt and asked, "How soon do you expect Mr. Diamond to be back at work?"

"Aw, shucks," she said, shrugging her slim shoulders, "he'll be on his feet in no time. Cain't keep a good man down, you know."

Didn't she say earlier that it would be quite a while before Daddy would be out of the hospital? I swear she did.

My mind cycled between Lynn possibly setting me up; Daddy Diamond getting mugged; my being back in jail with Detectives Small and Biggs bugging the hell out of me; and finally to this…this inexperienced kid who wanted to save my life. I didn't like my options.

She leaned forward, tapped her teeth with long red fingernails and stared at me. After a long moment, she asked, "Well?"

I wanted to answer her. I really did. However, all I could do was stare at those darned earrings. Those *six* earrings.

She got up and walked around the desk in her faded jeans. She wasn't very tall, but she now appeared much taller once she got out of Daddy's big chair. Or was it—*big Daddy's chair*? Does that make any sense?

Whatever.

Anyway, she plunked her tiny bottom onto the corner of the cluttered desk. The desk lamp, which had an inch of dust on its green glass, teetered to the point of almost falling over. However, several other things did slide off and fall onto the scratched and gouged wood-plank floor. The cat, now curled up on the floor, jumped a foot in the air. Dusty didn't seem to notice any of it. Totally focused. What a girl.

She folded her slim arms across her bony chest again. "Come on, Mr. Bowers. Give us a chance, man." She raised her palms once more. "There's no time to waste. I'll hafta get started on the case while the dang trail's still ripe." Those green eyes glared at me once again. "Whaddya say, huh?"

What the hell. I figured if she couldn't hack it, I wouldn't be out of pocket that much money; and I could always revert back to one of the more *experienced* firms. Ouch!

I finally nodded my okay.

She smiled and said, "You know, Mr. Bowers, you look a little like Harrison Ford—when he was a bit younger, of course."

Harrison Ford? Yeah, I could be Harrison Ford.

I said to her: "Call me Buddy."

SEVEN

The police and the crime lab had already been at Harry Thomas' house before Dusty Diamond—my private eye wannabe—and I got there. I don't know what the cops had been searching for, but if they were looking for some connection between Harry Thomas and me, they were flat out of luck. Nothing. Zilch.

Dusty parked across the street and down a few houses. Thomas' place was in an up-scale neighborhood where most of the homes were three-story brick with high-pitched roofs. Thomas' mini-mansion was similar to the others, but it was buried in lush landscaping—which I'm sure Harry Thomas didn't take care of himself—and it was surrounded by a forest of trees. Money didn't seem to be a problem for the guy.

We cautiously approached the place, making sure no one saw us and that nobody was inside. Dusty peeked through a window to the right of the small porch while I waited in some bushes near the front door. I felt like a burglar. I glanced around to see if we were being watched. When I didn't see anyone, I returned my attention to Dusty, who shook her head no—which I assumed meant no one was inside the place. A sigh of relief escaped me.

I stepped onto the porch, and my shaking finger pressed the doorbell. I stepped back and waited for someone to flick on the light or snatch open the door or something just as daunting.

Dusty slithered through the bushes and joined me on the porch. "Shouldna done that," she lectured, wagging her finger like a scolding school teacher. "Could attract attention."

I felt my face flush as I nodded my understanding. I felt like a real imbecile. We just got here, and already I've managed to screw up. What's new?

Dusty rummaged through her handbag, which resembled a tattered rucksack any Green Beret would have been proud to claim. She removed something and picked at the lock with it.

I glanced around again but didn't see anyone. I turned to her and leaned close. "You can't do that, Dusty," I said in a loud whisper. "It's Breaking and Entering!"

I'm quite aware of the fact that I'm no lawyer or cop, but I've seen enough movies to know a little about the law. And this definitely fit into the B & E category. I reached out to grab her hand and stop her, but I was too late. She had the door unlocked and was opening it.

Oh, hell. What else can they do to me? Throw my sorry ass in the slammer again. The way things were proceeding, it looked as though I was going to spend a few years behind bars anyway.

When the door was open wide enough, Dusty eased inside. I followed her in, and she shut the door behind me. For some reason I suddenly experienced a claustrophobic sensation. I felt as if I was now trapped inside, and the place was surrounded by a SWAT team—or something worse. Worse?

Anyway, I sensed that nothing but bad things—very bad things—were about to happen. The tiny hairs on the back of my neck prickled.

This snooping stuff was new to me, but it didn't seem to bother Dusty one iota: She zoomed through the

41

place like a Texas tornado, her head swiveling back and forth taking in every minute detail. She seemed to know what she was doing.

Maybe I was wrong about the kid.

I followed her lead and soon began to get the hang of it. I surveyed the place, looking for...I hadn't the slightest clue what. But it seemed to be the thing to do, since that was the reason we had broken into the place.

WHAT THE HELL AM I SAYING? I shouldn't be in here in the first damned place! I should be at home with my lovely wife. Heaven help me!

Dusty slipped on some surgical gloves. I wondered if Daddy had *procured* them from his suite in the hospital. You think? Nah, Daddy wouldn't do anything as devious as that, would he?

Anyway, Dusty began picking up things to study them closer. It was getting late, so there wasn't much natural light coming into the place. We had to hurry if we were to find anything of interest this evening. I moseyed over to the stone fireplace and glanced at some things on the thick wooden mantel. I was about to pick up a wood and brass plaque when Dusty grabbed my arm. Where the heck did she come from? She was just on the other side of the room.

"Don't touch a dang thang!" she warned, her green eyes narrowing. "They may come back and find yer prints and think they missed 'em the first time around."

She lost me. I gave her a dumb look.

She shook her head in disgust. "That could place you in here with Thomas *prior* to his murder!" she explained in a harsh whisper.

Oops! What was I thinking? I knew that.

I nodded my understanding. She didn't have to go into more detail. I'm pretty quick, you know. Yeah, *right*.

She picked up the plaque with her latex gloves and checked it. "Lookit," she said, turning it toward me.

"What's it say?"

"Very interestin'," she said, nodding slowly. "Salesman of the Year."

I studied the thing when the light—as little as it was—reflected off it. I noticed that in addition to what Dusty had read, it also gave the name of his workplace: Kantel Company. It was the same name that was in the newspaper—Kantel. Another good lead. We would have to check out the Kantel Company tomorrow.

Dusty placed the plaque exactly where it had been. A photo of three people rested next to the plaque: two men and a lady. I twisted my head this way and that, but it was now too dark inside the house to make out who they were.

"Not a problem," said Dusty, reaching into her bag. "I've got a flashlight."

Smart kid.

I was wrong. She did know her stuff.

Dusty pulled out the flashlight and grinned, letting me know she knew what the business required. She flicked on the light, and it glowed for almost five full seconds before going black. She glanced at me for an instant. It was a look of shock—I think.

She shook the light and slapped it a couple of times, but the thing remained dark. "Damnit!" she hissed.

I grinned, but she didn't see it. And it's probably a good thing. Who knows what the kid is capable of doing when she gets upset or angry?

Headlights flashed in the driveway and then went as dark as Dusty's flashlight. My grin quickly disappeared. I stared out the window—petrified. I knew my eyes had that *deer in the headlights* look. And my feet were locked in place. Frozen.

43

Dusty grabbed my arm and yanked me back to reality. "C'mon," she huffed. "Let's get goin'."

When I was finally able to take a step, she dragged me toward the rear of the house. I bumped into several things, but Dusty didn't let go of me until we were at the back entrance.

She opened the door and said, "We're outta here."

I turned and looked toward the front door. "Don't you think we should stay and see who it is, Dusty?"

"Not on yer life, Buddy Boy," she said, yanking at my arm again.

I resisted Dusty's tug. "Maybe it's Lynn," I retorted.

Dusty glared at me. Even in the failing light, I could see she was quite serious. She said, "Or, maybe it's some dang goon she hired."

Goon?

"Huh?"

EIGHT

I wanted to hang around Harry Thomas' house and find out who pulled into his driveway, but I'm sure Dusty knew what she was doing by getting us the hell out of there before somebody—like me—or her—got hurt...or dead.

We left Harry Thomas' place, but we didn't go back to Dusty's office like I thought we would. Instead, we drove Dusty's dusty Jeep to the Kantel Company. On the way, I thought of what Dusty had said about Lynn hiring a goon. And the more I thought about it, the more it bothered me. You see, a goon to me is like being one of Al Capone's heavyweights. And that's not somebody you want to get too close to. The thought of it drove deep into my troubled soul. Man, was I perplexed.

Talk about being confused: First there *was* a Lynn, then there *wasn't* a Lynn. But, now there's possibly a Lynn who's hired Al Capone Junior. Who the hell is this Lynn person anyway? She definitely wasn't Harry Thomas' wife like she had said—because he wasn't married. And she didn't seem nearly big or strong enough to get the best of Harry Thomas—the linebacker. Who the heck was she, darn it?

That thought bothered me big time all the way to the Kantel Company. When we arrived, I finally got my mind off that subject and onto the business at hand: Kantel—whomever or whatever that was. The Kantel building wasn't that big a place: a two-story brick structure about half a block long. It resembled a combination office and warehouse complex. There was a security light over the front entry, but no cameras or recording devices were visible, as far as we could determine when we drove by.

Dusty parked her blue Jeep about a hundred yards past the building so we wouldn't be spotted. *Good thinking, girl.*

I got out and checked the area. I kept an eye peeled for passersby: security personnel, cop cars and silly things like that—while Dusty inserted new batteries into her little flashlight. She had picked up the batteries at a convenience store on the way. The kid doesn't miss a thing, I tell you. Uh-huh.

Dusty checked the flashlight, then slid out of the Jeep. She reached back inside and hauled out her bag. It took a couple of strong tugs, but it finally popped out and into her hands. A fleeting smile once again appeared on her freckled face.

She joined me on the sidewalk, and after another quick look around, we headed down the street toward the Kantel Company. A chain-link fence surrounded the place, which made it resemble a prison—where I was probably going to end up. Ouch!

Nevertheless, it looked like the only way into the fortress was through the front door.

Dusty turned to me, smiled and whispered, "Good neighbors build good fences."

I think it's more like: "Good fences make good neighbors," Dusty.

What a gal.

Dusty led the way along the sidewalk toward the front of the building. I followed and made sure not to touch the darned fence. Never know if those things are electrically charged or not. And I definitely didn't want to get chewed out by Dusty again. Nope. Hands in my pocket, thank you.

When we got to the front door, Dusty withdrew a pistol from her bag.

I was terrified. It was the first time I had seen a gun in real life. I wanted to turn and run. But of course I couldn't. We had a job to do—find something that would lead us to the real killer and get my ass off the damned hook.

She aimed the pistol at the security light and pulled the trigger. I flinched. However, the gun made a muffled *whoosh* instead of the loud bang I was expecting. I glanced at the gun to see if it had a noise suppresser or something, but I couldn't see a thing because the light above the door was now shot out. Duh.

Dusty must have read my mind, because she whispered, "Pellet gun."

I nodded my understanding and approval, but she didn't see it. Her back was to me, and it was dark of course.

Dusty checked for an alarm. She must have found something on the door, because she fished into her bag and withdrew an object that she inserted between the door and the jamb.

"This'll short out the contacts and fool the security system into thankin' the door is still closed," she said in a quiet voice.

I nodded while she commenced picking the lock open. The hairs on the back of my neck began talking to me again while I waited for a bell or siren or something to scream at us.

However, the alarm didn't make a peep. It was quiet as a putting green at midnight. *Good job, kid.*

She slipped inside the building and motioned for me to join her.

47

I wanted to. I honestly did. But my feet refused to move.

She reached out and grabbed my windbreaker and yanked me inside the building. I thought my head was going to snap off my shoulders. She propped something between the door and the frame so the door wouldn't close all the way.

That was good. At least I wouldn't get that trapped feeling again. I'm not exactly claustrophobic, but something has made me want to be able to leave anytime I want. Maybe it has something to do with that little stint I pulled in jail.

Dusty switched on her miniature flashlight and began strolling through the place. Everything was posh and expensive. I wondered what kind of business permitted Kantel to make enough money to pay for all this finery.

The first office we encountered belonged to Harry Thomas. We stepped inside, being careful not to disturb anything. Jade statues and other exotic pieces adorned the shelves where books would normally be—if this were a lawyer's office, that is. Very nice.

Yep, Harry Thomas sure knew how to live—even if it wasn't for that long a time.

Dusty picked up a business card from the large mahogany desk. It read in part: Kantel Company, Importers.

Aha! That's where all the unique things originated. We were now on the right track. At least I though we were, because we seemed to be one step ahead of everyone else… and hadn't gotten caught. So far so good.

Dusty swung her flashlight around the office. A photograph of three people caught my eye. I was about to check it closer when flashing blue lights reflected off the walls.

Oh-oh.

The building must have had a silent alarm. Damn, I spoke too soon.

Dusty doused the light, and we both dashed to the window and peeked outside through the blinds. A police cruiser, with its blue lights flashing, was parked in front of the place—and so was Dusty's Jeep. The Jeep was now in the middle of the street, practically blocking traffic in both directions—not that it was exactly rush hour or anything. But still, it was like a neon sign telling the cops we were here—right inside this very building. Groan.

I gave Dusty a scornful look. *You're such a klutz, girl.*

Her shoulders raised. "Musta caught the straps of my handbag on the floorshift when I pulled out the dang thang," she sheepishly explained. "Probably yanked the Jeep outta gear, and the dadgum thang rolled down the street and stopped right out there." She pointed with her palms up at the street and shook her head in puzzlement.

No kidding. Good assumption, Ditsy. I mean, Dusty. Now what?

Two policemen were checking Dusty's jay-walking Jeep and peering around the area.

Dusty grabbed my arm. "You stay here in the buildin'," she said while leading us out of Harry Thomas' office. "I'll go out and tell 'em my Jeep stalled, and I couldn't get it started. I'll say I was lookin' fer a phone." She took her cell phone and pellet gun from her bag and pushed them at me. "Here…I don't want 'em findin' these on me."

I reluctantly took the gun and phone and asked, "What if they see you coming out of the building?"

"They won't."

"How can you be so sure, Dusty?"

49

"Because yer gonna watch 'em and let me know when it's clear."

Me? Great.

I pinched my eyebrows together and asked, "And how do I go about doing that?"

"Just wave yer hand," she said. "I'll be watchin' for yer signal."

Tough job, but I thought I could handle it. I nodded my understanding.

"I'll come back and get you after they've left," she said, pushing me toward a window. "Lemme know when it's safe."

I nodded again.

She gave me a hard stare. "And don't touch a damn thang till I get back."

I nodded a third time. Not only was I feeling like a child being scolded by his mother, but I was also beginning to feel like one of those bobble-head dolls from nodding so much.

She gave another hard look, turned and hurried toward the front door.

I twisted around and peered outside. One of the officers was looking directly at the building. I swear he could see me staring at him through the blinds. My face flushed, and marble-sized beads of sweat formed on my forehead. The violations of my bail agreement were steadily adding up for the judge: breaking and entering, jay-parking—and murder. Good grief.

"How's it?" Dusty asked in a loud whisper.

"Not good."

Right after I said that, the officer—who was looking at the building—stuck his face inside the Jeep where his partner's head was buried.

I waved my hand at Dusty. "Go!" I said in a sharp low voice. That was in case she didn't see me. I didn't want her wasting a second.

Dusty scooted out and closed the door behind her. She *closed* the damned door! I couldn't get out of the place now if I wanted. I would trigger the alarm. I wished Dusty had shown me what she had done to silence that darned thing. Oh, well, water over the dam. Or, was it under the bridge? Whatever. All I know is that I was definitely caught inside. Trapped again.

My eyes shifted to the street as I swiped at my dripping brow. Dusty ran around the back of her Jeep and approached it from the opposite side of the street.

Good thinking, kid.

The officers went to her and were obviously asking questions. She handed them her handbag and then opened the Jeep's hood. She fiddled with the wiring and other things I couldn't make out. She left the hood open while she tried the engine. And what do you know? It started. Can you believe that? A private eye who's also a mechanic. Yeah, right.

She looked so relieved I thought she was going to hug the officer nearest her. He took a step back. Apparently, he thought the same thing. She calmly closed the hood and got into the Jeep. They returned her handbag, and she waved to them as she drove off. *Some balls, Dusty.*

I watched the police cruiser pull away a few minutes later, and I waited patiently for Dusty to return. And that was no easy task since I had that claustrophobic sensation again. *Help me, Lord.*

After about ten minutes, lights flashed through the windows, and I was relieved that Dusty had returned. However, instead of Dusty's Jeep showing up, the same car that was at Harry Thomas' house pulled to a stop in front of the building. Now I was trapped for sure.

"Damnit!" I huffed into the quiet darkness.

Someone got out and approached the front door. A flashlight and key were already in hand.

With my heart thumping, I glanced around for a place to hide.

NINE

I couldn't feel my legs. Couldn't move a muscle. I had hidden in the men's room of the Kantel Company all night and had fallen asleep sitting on the toilet—of all places—while waiting for the interloper of the mysterious car to leave.

When I thought it was safe to leave my hiding place, I leaned forward, grabbed the door handle and pressed my other hand down against the toilet seat. I attempted to lift myself; however, nothing but rubbery legs stood between me and the floor tile. I went down like a sack of potatoes, hitting my head on the stall door. Man, did that ever hurt. I think part of the locking mechanism nicked my forehead. I wiped my hand across my face in the darkness. Sure enough, it was wet. Blood. Blood?

"Damnit!" I hissed.

Since I was already partially under the metal door, I dragged myself the rest of the way out of the stall. Some feeling was returning to my legs and feet. That was the good news. The bad news was that it stung like hell when the muscles and nerves came to life: Needles spiked every inch of skin.

I sat in the corner of the dark room and waited until things—my legs and senses, primarily—were pretty much back to normal. It took a few minutes, but I managed to get on my feet by pulling myself up with the help of the sink. After steadying myself for a moment, I felt my way along the wall until I came to the door, which I opened slightly.

No sign of anyone—not even Dusty. Where the hell was that kid anyway? Wasn't she supposed to come right back? That's pretty much the impression I had. Well, so much for *economical* help. I shut the restroom door and switched on the light. The glare was unbelievable. I shielded my eyes with my forearm.

I glanced down and noticed a trail of crimson on the gray tile. Great. Now they would have my DNA, even if I wiped it up. You know, it's impossible to get blood cleaned up without using chemicals. And, if you don't use the icky stuff to get it clean, those criminologist creeps will *always* find some trace of blood. In this case—*my* blood. And that would put me at the scene. Man, that's all I needed! Blood was also on my face and shirt. I washed my face but couldn't do much with the shirt. I heard that your own saliva is the best thing for getting off your blood. However, there was so much darned blood on my shirt that I would need a gallon of the slimy stuff to wet it. And that would probably mean spending the rest of the day spitting on myself. Yuck.

I said the heck with it. I'd toss the shirt away and get another one—that is, as soon as Dusty showed, I would do that.

I looked at myself in the mirror. The gash in my forehead was about an inch long and a foot wide—well, almost. Nevertheless, it was still bleeding. I grabbed a paper towel and pressed it against the cut. I was getting dizzy. Lightheaded.

Dusty?

I had to get out of that building fast, but there was something I had to do first. I switched off the restroom light and opened the door. I had the towel pressed against the cut and it covered one eye. I must have been a heck of a sight, but who was going to see me in the dark, right?

My unencumbered eye swept the place, but I didn't see anyone. I guess my little nap on the toilet seat gave him or her time to do whatever he or she had to do before he or she left.

I attempted to shake some sense into my brain while I was trying to locate Harry Thomas' office again. A trace of light from the breaking dawn was filtering through the blinds on the windows, so it was easier to find my way around than when it was pitch-black. What I'm trying to say is that locating Thomas' office wasn't that much trouble.

Trouble? Now there's a word I think I should avoid at this time, don't you? And, why does the word *trouble* bring to mind that private eye of mine? Think about it.

I eased into the late Harry Thomas' office and glimpsed at the things that had previously caught my interest. Sure enough, I was right. A picture of Harry wearing a football uniform rested on one of the shelves. Harry—the linebacker. I hate being right about things like that.

Another picture of him with no shirt—and muscles flexed until they were about to pop out of the frame—was next to the football shot. I was suddenly very glad Harry and I didn't have that little chat before I managed to get out of his motel room. Close call. Phew!

I scanned the room for the other photo: the one with Harry and another guy and girl. I knew exactly where it had been and went directly to that spot. However, the photo was no longer there.

Huh?

I gave a quick glance around the office to see if I might have been mistaken. Nope. That was the place all right. And I was now positive that was the same spot, because dust was where the picture frame easel had once been. Was that the reason the person came in? The photograph? Why?

I wonder.

Not seeing anything else in Harry's office that might help me, I slipped out and moved down the hallway. The sun was now igniting the morning sky with vibrant red and yellow clouds. The brilliant ball blasted laser-like arrows through the open blinds and painfully penetrated my good eye. My head snapped to the side to keep from going completely blind. With my head askew—as if my neck were broken—I continued along the hallway.

It was easy to spot Mr. Kantel's office: His name was painted in gold letters on the clear glass. From the rest of the stuff in the place, I would say it was *real* gold. I moved into the large office and looked around while slowly walking toward the large desk. A lot of things caught my interest, and I hoped there would be enough time to check them out before the employees came to work.

When I got to the handsome desk, I grabbed a business card and studied it in the morning light. Kantel's first name was Hans. I looked up from the card and glanced around the room. I had to hurry. It was getting light outside, and people would be coming in soon. The last thing I needed was to get caught in there, especially with my fluffy white and blood-red turban. If my private investigator were with me, she would come up with some plan, I'm sure. However, she…

Speaking of that girl, where the hell was she?

I got back to the business at hand. I continued to glean as much information as my uncovered eye could relay to my slightly comatose brain. Hey, what do you expect after what I'd been through? It's not every day you get smacked in the head by a toilet-stall door, is it? That's what I thought. Give a guy a break, huh?

56

Anyway, a large framed photograph caught my attention. It was on the credenza behind Hans Kantel's desk. I walked around the monster of a desk and over to the photo. I didn't touch a thing. Dusty would be proud.

Speaking of Dusty…ah, forget it.

The picture on the credenza was a striking blue-eyed blonde. Nice. Very nice.

Way to go, Hans.

The picture was signed: *Happy Birthday, Hans. With all my love, Marilyn.*

I went to grab it so I could study the girl more closely.

However, that's when everything went black.

TEN

"Breathe in deep, Mr. B," an obscured voice ordered. "Breathe deeply."

Mr. B?

I wondered who in the world was speaking to me. My eyes flickered open. A blurry Dusty Diamond was leaning over me and tending to the cut on my forehead. I blinked a few times and glanced around. I was no longer inside the Kantel building but sitting inside Dusty's trusty little Jeep. The passenger seat was reclined, so I was looking up at a canvas top—as well as into Dusty's fuzzy face.

She dabbed a tissue on my cut. "You musta tripped in the dark and hit yer head on somethin'."

I blinked a few more times until most of the stars were gone and Dusty had two green eyes instead of four. I attempted to sit up. Man, did my head ever hurt. That little hangover at the golf resort was nothing compared to this beaut. I shouldn't have thought of that little incident at the resort just now; that made my head hurt all the more.

Things were spinning around so fast I had to rest my head back against the seat. Yeow!

That's when I felt the knot on the *back* of my head. I didn't trip and hit my head like Dusty suggested. I didn't pass out. Somebody cold-cocked me from behind. The dirty bloodsucker.

However, I didn't pass that little bit of information on to Dusty. I figured I would tell her about it if-and-when the situation necessitated doing so. Also, as long as she thought I passed out from hitting my forehead, I wouldn't have to explain about the bathroom incident. That might get a little difficult...and embarrassing...to say the least. Good thinking, Buddy.

"You okay, Mr. B?" she asked, pinching her eyebrows together. "You look a little pale."

"I think I'll live." That's what I said, but I wasn't convinced. Some heavy-duty duct tape might help hold the two halves of my head together, however.

"Yeah, I guess," she agreed.

She leaned close enough that I could see the back of her head through her green-black pupils.

"However," she went on, "that's quite a slit in yer dang forehead."

"Is it still bleeding?" I asked, visualizing the Grand Canyon with the reddish Colorado River running over its banks.

"No," she replied. She backed off a little and dabbed at the cut with the tissue a few more times. "But I still thank you should have it looked at. Could use some stitches; that's fer sure."

I wasn't about to go to a doctor. He'd most likely find the lump on the back of my head while checking out the cut on my forehead. And, questions I didn't want to answer—or couldn't answer—might come up.

"Well, if it's stopped bleeding," I said, "why would I need to have it stitched up?"

"To keep the dang thang from openin' up again," she said. Her little nose scrunched up a little. "It's gunky-lookin': crusty and scabby and yucky and—"

Stop!

"I get the picture, Dusty," I said.

"Okay, but—"

59

I cut her off. "You got a Band-Aid?"

"Lemme check the first-aid kit." She reached into the glove box and withdrew a small container. She opened it and tweezed out a medium-sized bandage. "Let's try this one," she said, stripping off the paper backing. She applied it to my forehead.

Funny thing, it didn't hurt. Maybe it was because she was so gentle. Or, because I was so numb. Or, maybe it was because the lump on the back of my head was pounding so hard it offset the pain in the front.

"There," she said, putting things away. "That should do it…unless you whack it again."

I didn't whack it, Dusty. Well, actually I did. But not the way she thought.

My eyes focused on hers again. "By the way, Dusty, what the hell took you so long? I thought I was—"

"Couldn't go into the building until that darn car left," she said, cutting me off. "So, to kill some time, I went back to Thomas' house and finished lookin' 'round."

"All night?"

"Well, not actually," she explained with a shrug. "When I got back here, the same car was still parked out front. So I drove on past and parked up the street. Guess I sorta fell asleep."

"Sorta?"

She pursed her lips. "Sorry."

I nodded, accepting her apology. What else could I do?

I asked her, "What did you glean there?"

Her eyebrows pinched together. "Huh?"

"Find anything new?"

She studied my face.

"Where?"

Duh.

"At Thomas' house!" I practically yelled. "Find anything we didn't see before we had to scram out of the damned place?"

Easy, Buddy. Be patient with the kid.

She waggled her head from side to side. "Yes, and no."

My eyes rolled again. "Now what the hell does that mean, Dusty—yes and no?"

She shrugged her tiny shoulders. "Well, I didn't find anythang new," she explained. "But what I did find, you know, is that the photograph that was next to the plaque…well, it wasn't there. It was gone. Missin'. Swiped. Disappeared."

Small world.

I asked her, "The photo with the girl and two guys?"

"Yep, the very one."

"I'll be damned!"

"Why?"

Because, dear girl, that's what was missing from Thomas' office in the Kantel building also. However, that's something else I decided to keep under wraps a while longer.

I quickly changed subjects. "How did I get out of the building?" I asked, swiveling my head around to see where we were parked. My head weighed a ton and hurt as if an elephant were stepping on it.

"I dragged you out," she said. She shook her head. "Man, you've gotta watch yer diet. Too much red meat and pasta, I'll bet."

Too much beer.

I continued, "And you lifted me into the Jeep too?"

"Yep. I may not look like much, but what little of me there be is all muscle."

61

She made a fist and showed me her biceps. Man, was she ever proud of it. It was about the size of Harry Thomas' thumb. But I didn't share that thought with her. There are some things you just don't tell a lady. Am I right or what?

I nodded and said, "Very impressive."

She looked at her muscle for a moment, nodded her approval, and lowered her arm.

"Thanks, Dusty," I said with a hint of a smile. "You probably saved my life."

"Shucks, Mr. B, that's what yer payin' me for."

"Well, thanks, anyway."

She twisted the key and cranked the engine. "Let's go get you cleaned up and then grab some grub."

"Good. Then we'll pay Mr. Kantel a little visit."

ELEVEN

Kantel's secretary, a buxom blue-eyed blonde with a tight yellow sweater and a dark blue skirt that exposed most of her thighs, led Dusty and me to Mr. Kantel's office. The secretary looked quite similar to Marilyn in the picture that was on Kantel's credenza as far as I could recall. But I guess all beautiful blue-eyed blondes look pretty much alike—except my wife—who is quite special. Anyway, I was anxious to check out that photo a little more closely to see if it was or wasn't the same buxom secretary.

Kantel's office was posh and much larger than Harry Thomas'. And Kantel had a lot more expensive artsy-fartsy things than did Thomas. For starters, the Persian carpet we were standing on looked like it was made of silk. And, the light fixtures were definitely made from imported crystal. My eyes did a quick scan of the place before Kantel had a chance to eyeball me and get cautious or suspicious.

That didn't take very long.

Kantel wasn't much heavier than Dusty, but he was a little taller than she was. He jumped up from his chair and hustled around the large desk. His hand flew out toward me. "Hans Kantel," he said with a thick accent. European, I think.

"Buddy…Buddy…J-Jones," I lied, accepting his handshake.

Where in the world did that come from? I guess I had a last-minute thought about giving him my real name, even though he might recognize me from the photo in the newspaper—the photo of me next to one deceased Harry Thomas. The one the whole darned country, including my wife and her family, most likely saw. However, on second thought, he probably wouldn't identify me from the stupid photo—especially with me now sporting a swollen nose, blackening eye, and a patch about the size of Shea Stadium on my forehead.

I turned and motioned with my hand toward Dusty. "This is—"

"His wife…Irene," Dusty interjected with a smile. She extended her hand to him.

Wife? Irene?

My eyes widened, and my jaw dropped.

Kantel didn't seem to notice my startled reaction; he was too infatuated with Dusty. He smiled back at her. His teeth were perfect—as were his manicured nails, Italian shoes, tailored black suit and slicked-back black hair.

Sickening.

He took her hand but didn't shake it. That would be crass, I suppose. Instead, he bent over and kissed it. Well, he didn't actually kiss it but came very close. I guess that's what Europeans do: pretend to kiss the hand.

Hey, where I come from, if you're going to kiss a girl's hand, then kiss the damned thing. Don't pussyfoot around. You with me on this?

He straightened and gazed at Dusty for a long moment. "What lovely eyes," he said, cocking his head to get a more favorable look at them. "Emerald green, correct?"

"How wonderfully observant of you," she said, fluttering her eyelashes. "Yes, they are very close to that particular shade of green." She nodded and smiled sheepishly. "Thank you. Thank you so very much."

Really sickening.

Kantel asked Dusty, "What can I do for you?" He obviously remembered his manners. "Oh, excuse me if you will," he said, shaking his head at his rudeness. "Please have a seat." He swung an arm toward two black leather-and-mahogany chairs. "How inconsiderate of me."

Oh, yes; how uncouth, Hans.

We sat ourselves down, while Kantel returned to the large black leather wingback chair behind his massive mahogany desk.

I was trying to think of something clever to say. I seem to be stuck for words quite often, and this was one of those times. Anyway, Dusty bailed me out—again.

"First of all," she said, crossing her legs and smoothing her skirt, "we'd like to offer our condolences for the most unfortunate and untimely death of your salesman, Mr. Thomas."

"Thank you," said Kantel. His glassy-black eyes narrowed, and the smile was gone. "He was a partner, however...not a salesman." His words were sharp.

Uh-huh. Maybe a connection there.

I glanced at Dusty, but she didn't seem to pick up on it.

She said, "We'd like to procure something special... but maybe you won't be able to obtain it for us."

Procure? Something special? Where the hell's Dusty going with this little charade of hers?

"Anything," retorted Kantel. "And I mean *anything* you want, we'll be able to get." He cocked a full, dark eyebrow. "It could add to the price, however."

"Price is not an issue," she said. "We just don't want to cause any...any unnecessary inconvenience."

"Not an inconvenience, my dear. That's what we do here at the Kantel Company. We travel all around the world

65

obtaining rare and unique items for *special* people...such as yourself."

Kantel's shark-like smile was back. He was probably anticipating he was about to make a killing. Oops, poor choice of words, maybe?

While Dusty and Kantel chatted about precious gems and the like, I surveyed the office. There were several fascinating items: marble statues, bronze busts, jade figurines—to name a few. However, the one thing I was most interested in—Marilyn's photograph—was no longer there. Gone. Disappeared. Vanished.

Huh?

I returned my attention to Dusty and Kantel and eventually pried my way into their conversation. "I imagine your wife accompanies you on your business trips, Mr. Kantel," I said.

He shook his head no and once again arched a thick black eyebrow. "I have no wife," he retorted quickly and sharply in his strong European accent.

I didn't like the way he responded. It made me wonder if he was telling the truth. Maybe he had a wife in Europe but didn't have one here. Or, maybe he had one, or more, in both places. Or, maybe he had a mistress whom his wife didn't know about. Or, maybe he was simply a gigolo playing the field—starting with that buxom, blue-eyed secretary of his. Man, I could go on forever with this *maybe* stuff.

I forced a smile. "Oh," I said, hoping he hadn't noticed the astonished expression on my face. "I'm sorry; I guess I made a wrong assumption."

Another stern stare from Kantel. "Indeed you did."

Dusty was at it again: She cocked her head and said with a demure smile, "I don't see how such a handsome man such as yourself could go unattached for very long."

What a buncha bull.

Dusty lowered her head and pretended to pull her skirt down over her bony knees.

Kantel's smile got bigger and wider than ever—if that's possible. He said, "Maybe that's because I just met...you."

Oh, baloney.

"You're so very kind," she said, flicking her hand at him, "and such a gentleman—a real gentleman. And that's something so difficult to find these days."

Oh, come on. Give me a break.

I looked for a wastebasket. This was making me sick.

"That's very grand of you, dear," he said, smoothing back his hair with the palm of his hand. "Thank you ever so much."

Dusty smiled again and got to her feet. "Well, we thank you for your valuable time, Mr. Kantel. We'll—"

"Hans," he said, cutting her short. He also stood. "Please call me Hans."

She continued: "As I was about to say—Hans—we'll surely get back with you."

He practically ran around the desk to take Dusty's hand. "I certainly hope it won't be too long."

Get me outta here. I'm gonna gag.

Dusty released her hand and extended it to me, which I accepted. "Come on, dear," she said with her chin raised slightly. "We don't want to overstay our welcome."

Well, thank God. It's about time.

Her free hand dotted her forehead with her hanky. "We have many things to do today," she said. "Mustn't tarry now, dear."

Man, did she pick up on his bull crap in one hell of a hurry or what? What happened to *thang* and *yer* and the rest of that slang of hers?

I got to my feet and said good-bye to Hans Kantel—the rogue. He took my hand and shook it gently, but his dirty, devouring eyes never left Dusty. I wanted to smack the guy. It was as if he were trying to hit on my daughter or something. That really got my dander up.

Cool it, Buddy.

Anyway, I couldn't wait to get away from that sleazebag. He sorta made my ass pucker.

TWELVE

Never return to the scene of the crime—so the experts say. But since I didn't commit the crime, I didn't see where it would do any harm. If anything, it might prove beneficial in providing some information my conscious mind couldn't recall. Therefore, Dusty and I drove her Jeep back to the golfing resort outside of Gunter where I was framed by Lynn or whoever.

The resort was a huge place: Several buildings made up the complex; but the biggest was the main building where the lodge, restaurant, offices, gift shop, party rooms, guest suites and registration desk were located. Other buildings comprised of motel-like units and individual cottages that were within walking distance of the main building. And that walk was quite pleasant. Squirrels were burying nuts for the upcoming winter—even though it doesn't get extremely cold in northern Alabama. A multitude of trees clustered the seemingly endless grounds. And those trees—most of them oaks, with some hickory, poplar, dogwood and maple—were now showing their brilliant reds and golds. Simply beautiful.

As we walked toward the resort's registration office, I gathered in all the surrounding beauty—including Dusty. She was wearing a green shirt that made her eyes appear all the greener. Very striking. Maybe Hans Kantel was on to something there.

Easy, Buddy. Something similar to this is what got your butt into hot water in the first place.

However, Dusty didn't seem to appreciate the natural splendor as much as I did. Her mind appeared to be elsewhere. For some strange reason—and very uncharacteristically from what I'd seen so far—she was immersed in profound thought. Deep stuff for Dusty.

After a few minutes of silent walking, she turned to me and remarked, "Daddy thanks Mr. Kantel set up Harry Thomas and had him killed." Her empty gaze was full of thoughts. "Or, maybe he, Kantel himself, was the one who killed Thomas."

"Kantel?" I asked, a little surprised at her train of thought. "Why would he kill his friend and partner?"

"Oh...I don't know," she replied, shrugging her frail shoulders. "He probably has lotsa reasons."

"Like what?" I asked as we continued walking toward the main lodge.

"Like what?" she repeated my question, cocking an eyebrow. "Well, the most obvious is that Harry Thomas was his partner...and Kantel may have gotten greedy and wanted the operation to hisself. Wanted Harry outta the picture."

"But why?" I asked, reaching for the handle on the massive wooden door.

"That's what we hafta find out."

I nodded in agreement as I opened the door and stepped back so Dusty could enter.

"Maybe," she continued as she went inside, "there was a thang goin' on between the secretary and the two men. And Hans wanted Blondie all to hisself."

I nodded again. Handsome Hans.

However, this time I wasn't so convinced with Dusty's second theory. My hypothesis was that Harry Thomas may have known something that happened in the business and was trying to blackmail Kantel. And, therefore, Thomas had to be dealt with; and someone—like me—was set up to take the fall and make it look like Kantel had nothing to do with it. Either way, it wasn't a very good situation for Thomas. Obviously—someone killed the poor guy. Duh.

The lodge was quite rustic: high, wooden ceiling; minimal lighting; dark, hardwood floor; and stuffed animals mounted on the natural wood walls. Your typical hunting lodge, right? However, it was a golfing resort. Go figure.

Dusty spoke loud enough for the whole place to hear. "Yep, Hans Kantel definitely wanted his partner, Harry Thomas, out of the way," she said, nodding in agreement with herself. "Out—gone—offed—wasted—"

The desk clerk was watching, so I cut Dusty short. "Okay, I get the picture," I said in a sharp whisper. However, I wondered if she had done that intentionally to see if there would be a reaction from one or more of the employees. My eyes covertly scanned the three people near us. Nothing.

We walked to the counter, and I explained (lied) to the clerk that we wanted to see a particular room: one where I had stayed on a previous golf trip with the guys—partly true—to see if my "wife, *Irene*" liked the room and the view.

The clerk, a plump woman in her fifties, showed us the one I requested—Lynn's room. I would like to say Harry Thomas' room, but that gives me bad vibes for some reason—like the guy got killed there, right? So we'll just stick with calling it Lynn's room for now.

The other two people, a man in a green and tan ranger-looking uniform and an elderly Afro-American maid, were no longer in sight. I wondered if they had overheard "Irene's" comments and disappeared for some reason.

The clerk led us to Lynn's room, let us in; and asked if we would be all right by ourselves, since she was alone at the front desk and had to get back. That was just fine and dandy with us—of course.

We waited until she was out of sight, closed the door, then scoured the room from top to bottom. However, we couldn't find anything new that might help us. Dusty asked me to describe exactly what had transpired the day I met Lynn. And so I did. Well, maybe not *exactly*. But Dusty got enough to get the gist of it. Too much information for a young girl like Dusty might corrupt the poor thing, right?

Satisfied there was nothing in the room that was of any use, we locked the door and strolled to the pool area. It was a warm sunny day, and the sun was reflecting off the pool. I wished I had worn sunglasses. It was so bright I had to squint and visor my eyes with a cupped hand to see where I was walking. I didn't want to fall into the darned pool, which was much larger than I remembered. My eyes caught sight of the steps and railing where my fingerprints had been. I had to turn away. Bad vibes.

We strolled around the pool area once again, and Dusty required a play-by-play description of what went on the night Lynn and I were at the pool. Again, I gave Dusty *most* of the details of what had happened the night when Lynn and I were alone together.

Darn; I really don't like the sound of that. It kinda makes me feel guilty. Not of murder, but of something worse—cheating on my wife. Worse—did I say? Hey, you don't know my wife!

Dusty walked around the pool and glanced at the cloudless autumn sky. She scratched her head through her red hair—which was now glowing brilliantly in the sunshine. She stared into space for a moment. I figured she was attempting to find some holes in my story.

After a few minutes, she sat on a bench overlooking beautiful Gunter Lake. It had gorgeous vistas: a wide, expansive body of water with islands dotting most of the shoreline. Several boats, with their gleaming sails ballooning in the morning breeze, gently glided across the tranquil surface.

Dusty nodded her approval. "Nice," she said. "Very nice."

I agreed and sat beside her.

Looking straight ahead, she said, "But I guess you couldn't see any of it on that particular night, huh?"

Why did I get the feeling she was now working for Detective Small? At least, that's how her questioning made it feel. I glanced around before answering. An attorney once advised me not to answer a question until it had a few seconds to sink in. I thought I'd give it a try. What the heck, it was only Dusty, for crying out loud.

I finally explained in a sharp voice, "As I said before, it was a moonless night, Dusty. I could *barely*—probably not a good word—see the pool, much less the damned lake, for criminy sakes!"

Dusty must have sensed my irritation because she changed the subject. "That was the golf course we passed on the way here, right?"

"Uh-huh."

"Pretty hilly."

I shrugged. "A little, I guess."

A little cat-and-mouse going on, I thought.

She asked, "What's with all the dang dirt?"

"Dirt?"

73

"Yeah," she said, giving me a dumb look, "the large holes in the middle of the darn course. They diggin' it up for some reason?"

I had to rack my brain as to what we saw on the way up the hill that she might be referring to. All I could picture were the lush green fairways that were lined with those beautiful trees flourishing their gold and red bouquets. No construction or anything like that was going on as far as I could recall.

Dusty must have sensed my lack of understanding, because she attempted to explain again. "The round holes," she said, making circles with her hands. "Fer godsake, they're big enough to hide a dang locomotive. How could you miss 'em, fer cryin' out loud?"

A grin swept across my lips. "Oh, those," I said when the light finally turned on in my head. "They're sand traps."

"Kinda messes up the place, don't it?"

"Messes up your golf game...and your mind."

She twirled her hair around a finger and stared at me. "Explain."

"Well, let's say you hit what you think is a good shot. However, the ball goes a little off line and ends up in one of those traps." My hands were flashing left and right trying to demonstrate the flight of an errant shot. "It might get buried or end up under the lip, or—"

She cut me short. "Why do they call it a *trap*? Makes it sound like yer bein'...uh...set up...or framed...or somethin' nasty like that."

"No," I said, chuckling. "It's not that kind of a trap. They're just hazards."

"They're hazards all right. I don't thank my Jeep— or even a darn tank—could negotiate some of those blasted canyons."

I tried to suppress a grin. "The best way to think of them, Dusty, is…bunkers."

"Bunkers?"

"Don't ask."

She shook her head. "Dumb game."

"You're probably right."

I wanted to explain how easy it is to get hooked on the game. All it takes is one good shot, or a good putt, or a halfway decent round. And then you're required by the golf gods to return for more fun. Fun? Frustration and punishment would be more like it. But with Dusty not being a golfer, there's no way she would understand.

However, her comment about being trapped—or framed—made my stomach churn.

THIRTEEN

Dusty and I were sitting next to the resort's swimming pool and quietly staring at the mesmerizing ripples on the clear blue water. I turned to her and said, "You're not from around here, are you?"

She kept staring at the pool. "Why you ask that?"

"Your accent is...um...it's a little different," I said, shrugging. "Some words are the same...but others are... well, they're—"

"Texas," she said abruptly. "We're originally from Texas."

Uh-huh.

I nodded and smiled at being correct. As I said, I like being right. I'm pretty quick—sometimes.

"Yep," she continued, her eyes still fixed on the pool. "Daddy and Mom didn't get 'long all that well, you know."

Big surprise.

Dusty went on, "So, one day Mom just ups and leaves. Just like that. No note. No nothin'."

"So you decided to stay with your dad, huh?"

"Not a helluva lotta choice," she said, shrugging. "As I said, we didn't know where Mom took off to. Maybe she had another man. Who knows?"

I could sense I had hit a nerve.

She continued, "But I was always a chip off the old block, if you know what I mean."

"Oh?"

She nodded. "Yep. Daddy was an ex-cop, and I figured I could learn some thangs from him to keep me outta trouble."

Bingo!

"A cop, huh?"

"Uh-huh."

That piqued my interest, and I really did want to know the history behind it. "What happened? He retire?"

"Nope, they ran 'im off the force after he ratted on a coupla guys who were on the take." She gave me a stern look. "They don't like that kinda stuff, you know... even if yer right."

I nodded my understanding and said, "And your dad didn't bother look for your mom. Seems to me, with all his connections and experience, he'd be able to track her down."

She shook her head no. "'Good riddance' was all Daddy had to say 'bout the whole damn thang."

Some cop, huh?

I asked, "You ever miss your mother?"

Dusty shook her head. "Nah." There was a slight hesitation while her mind spun thoughts. "But I do miss those beautiful Texas bluebonnets in the spring." Her head twisted toward me. "Ever see 'em?"

"Bluebonnets? Can't say I have, Dusty. Why?"

"They grow wild, you know...simply gorgeous," she explained with a wistful sigh. "It's as if God sprinkled beautiful blue powder all over the fields." A warm, contented smile crept across her lips. "They come up every year, you know. Don't hafta plant 'em or nothin'." She searched her mind for a second. "Whaddya call that?"

"Perennial."

She nodded sharply. "Yep. That's it."

"I'll have to make a trip to Texas sometime, I guess."

She slapped her thighs and smiled. "Damn straight, Mr. B."

A warm smile touched my lips. "That's if I'm not behind bars," I quipped.

Apparently Dusty didn't see any humor in my attempt to make light of the situation: Her smile vanished as quickly as had Lynn Thomas. Dusty simply got to her feet and strolled around the stark-white pool deck.

I remained sitting and silent as my eyes followed her. She had a meditative stare as she gazed at the pool for quite a while.

I thought, *Oh-oh, here comes Detective Diamond again with more of her dumb questions.*

However, she fooled me. She turned to me and said, "Me and Daddy thank you should go to the police with what we've discovered."

What? The police? THE POLICE??? Are you crazy, girl—plumb out of your cotton-pickin' mind?

"That would be the last place I would turn for help. They'd find some reason to toss me back in jail—especially that Detective Small. That little guy really has it in for me."

She continued: "They might start lookin' for the real killer and leave you alone. That would give us more freedom to do our investigatin' without being messed with."

"Really?" I asked, as if it might be a good idea.

"Yep," she said, still pacing. "Evidence disappearin', someone snoopin' around—"

Someone whacking me on the head, I thought—but didn't say it to her.

I said, "Besides us, you mean."

She ignored my comment. "Kantel's the greedy sort. He wants everythin'. Didn't want to share nothin' with his partner, Harry Thomas." She nodded in agreement with herself. "It all makes sense to me."

Maybe Hans didn't want to share the buxom secretary and decided to end that triangle also. However, we'll never know for certain now that the photograph is missing. But Dusty doesn't know about that photograph, remember?

I said, "Nothing concrete, kid. All circumstantial."

"Who knows?" she said, shrugging. "The cops mighta come up with some other evidence that, when added to what we've got—"

I cut her off. "I hate to pop your balloon, Dusty, but we've really got nothing. Absolutely nothing." I folded my arms and crossed my outstretched legs. "I suggest we do more research on Hans Kantel before we show our hand to the cops."

She stopped pacing and stared at me. "Yo, Buddy!" she said, attempting to get my undivided attention. "We don't have a helluva lotta time before your damn trial, you know."

I lowered my head. "I know."

"Well, whaddaya suggest?" she asked, standing at a brace in front of me with her arms folded. "You know—it's not my tush that's on the choppin' block, Mr. Buddy Bowers."

I looked up at her. I figured it was time I opened Pandora's box a little. "I suggest we find out who Marilyn is."

Her eyebrow cocked. "Who?"

"The blue-eyed blonde in the photograph."

She gave me another one of her lost looks—dumb, but cute.

79

I figured I'd better let her in on Marilyn, so I told her about the photograph in Kantel's office. And when she said there was no such thing in his office, I had to explain how I had seen the thing before it disappeared. You know, the night I got—whomped? Blind-sided?

She was upset. No, *upset* is too mild a term. It was more like…irate. Yeah, that comes very close.

She jammed her hands into what little hips she had and asked why I hadn't gotten it and shown it to her. That's what I was paying her for—she reminded me again.

Of course, that led to me explaining about getting hit in the head and losing consciousness…and the toilet thing… and all that.

Man, I just knew some smelly stuff was about to hit the fan.

Ho-boy.

FOURTEEN

After I explained *practically* everything that had happened at Kantel's to Dusty, she had to go to the hospital and talk with Daddy again. She dropped me off at my motel where I was staying. Unfortunately, my wife was not waiting for me. Heather was at our home in Nashville. She decided it was best if she stayed out of the picture until things got cleared up. In other words—until I could prove to her I wasn't lying; that my story was true, that I had nothing (well, not *exactly* nothing) to do with Lynn, and that I was totally innocent of all charges.

Lots of luck, Buddy.

It had been quite a day, and I was really bushed. I was looking forward to hitting the sack, even if it was alone. I missed my wife though. I needed a hug. You know that feeling, I'm sure.

I unlocked the door to my room and flipped on the light. My eyes must have been the size of two small pizzas when I glanced around the small room. It was a total mess: The bedspread was on the floor, the dresser drawers were on the floor, everything that had been hanging in the closet was on the floor, and my suitcase was on the floor. The suitcase was wide open, looking like a gigantic brown butterfly that had bit the dust. Nothing was in the case. The culprits scattered everything about the room. I could have saved the guy—or gal—or both—some trouble by telling him or her or them that it was already empty. Who? Why?

Don't you hate it when that happens?

I tiptoed through the room as if it were a minefield. I peeked into the corner of the closet and released a deep sigh of relief. My golf clubs were still there! Thank God, there's still some justice in this world.

I called Dusty to see what I should do. I wasn't accustomed to this kind of thing. I mean, it didn't exactly happen to my kind of guy every day. It most likely never happened to Dusty either. And she probably never knew of anyone who had it happen to him or her before. But who else was I going to call for advice? My wife? Detective Small? That weasel was just itching to find something else to charge me with so he could slap me back in the slammer. No, thank you.

Dusty, it would be.

I telephoned her office and let it ring about a thousand times. She obviously wasn't there—probably still with Daddy—and she must have shut off her answering machine for some stupid reason. I hung up and stared at the phone—disbelieving. How could she not be waiting for my call? After all, fifty bucks a day should get you a little attention and respect, wouldn't you think? Jeez.

My eyes scanned the debris in the room looking for clues or something. I wondered what the perpetrator was after. I had nothing of interest. Nothing that I knew of anyway.

Dusty's cell phone and pellet gun had been lifted when I was knocked unconscious at Kantel's, so there was nothing left of any value, except my sticks—golf clubs, that is. And they, as I said, hadn't been touched. They were worth about a thousand bucks, which might bring five hundred or so on the street. Maybe the perp was checking to make sure I hadn't taken anything from Thomas' house or office. I wondered what I could have overlooked there— or here. What? WHAT?

My mind doesn't function very well when I'm tired, and right now I was totally exhausted. I needed some sleep, so I decided to go out and get something to eat.

I know. Don't tell me. Eating hasn't anything to do with my getting some sleep. But sleeping would have to wait, because I was too upset and was not about to crawl into that upturned bed in that ransacked room right now.

I locked the door but don't know why; it didn't seem to inhibit the bad guys much. Anyway, I did it so no one would go in and straighten up the mess. Fat chance.

Well, I needed a reason, so pick one. Habit, I suppose. Nevertheless, after the door was made secure as possible, I checked the hallway. No one was around—that I could see anyway.

I went to my car. When I got there, I couldn't believe what I saw.

No! All four tires were flat! All four! What a coincidence. Huh!

I wondered if the same person or persons who broke into my room also did this to my car. How did they know it was *my* car? After all, it's not actually my car. As I said, it's a rental. Either someone has contacts downtown...or I'm being followed. God forbid.

I glanced around but saw nobody suspicious. I even checked all the parked cars for glowing cigarettes and men pretending to be reading newspapers—that kind of detective stuff.

Nothing.

You think someone was trying to leave me a message?

Dusty, where the hell are you?

I unlocked the car door and stuck my head inside. I checked under the front seat and then the rear seats. I didn't know what I was looking for, but nothing seemed to be out of place. Then again, I'm not the cops...or the investigator—she's with Daddy. I even checked inside the trunk. Nope, no dead bodies there. So, I've got that much going for me—which is nice.

Maybe some of the local kids were messing around and slit the tires just to have some fun. You think?

No, not likely—not after what happened to my dog-goned room.

So much for the trip to the restaurant. I relocked the car door and headed back to my room to make a call. I wasn't quite to the motel's front door when— BLAMMMM!!!

My survival instincts immediately took over. In other words, I ducked and covered my head. Parts of my car went flying all around me like shrapnel from an exploding hand grenade. I checked my body for extra holes but didn't see any. Thank God for small favors.

It was suddenly very quiet. I turned and looked at what remained of my car. There wasn't enough to fill a bucket. A small bucket.

The motel clerk ran up to me and said something. I knew he was talking to me because I could see his lips moving. I screwed my fingers into my ears, trying to clear them.

No luck.

I studied the clerk's mouth carefully. I'm no lip reader, but I clearly got the message.

"What happened?" he mouthed.

"I can't hear a thing!" I hollered at the young man. "Ears are plugged from the blast."

He nodded his understanding and tried to help me to my feet. I hadn't realized that I was sitting on the sidewalk. I pushed him away and shook my head no. I had to wait for the world to stop spinning before I could attempt to stand. Otherwise, I'd be back on my duff on the littered sidewalk.

I dug into my pocket and pulled out Detective Small's card. Despite my gut-wrenched intuition, I handed it to the kid and told him to give the cop a call.

Now why in the world would I do a stupid thing like that? I dreaded being around the guy, and he would surely find some way to blame me for turning my room upside down and blowing up my own car. Imagine that. Do you get the feeling the man has his mind made up about my being guilty?

The kid snatched the card from my hand and flew toward the office. I guess he didn't want to remain next to me for very long in case "Vinnie" and the boys returned. Or, maybe he just didn't want to be around if and when the next car decided to turn into another Fourth of July display.

What a coward.

Right now, it wouldn't bother me if Vinnie did come around the corner with guns-ablazing. That would put an end to my current situation—and misery. Then again, he would probably just wound me so that I couldn't walk or play golf the rest of my life. Hey, that's the way my luck's been going lately.

Again, I needed a big hug. I thought about calling my wife, but right now my ears were ringing so loudly I wouldn't know if she answered the phone or not. Anyway, you think my wife would believe any of this happened the way it did—especially coming from an accused murderer? Not on your life.

I don't think I had ever been this low. And I don't mean from sitting on the sidewalk either. I just couldn't imagine how things could get any worse.

Nevertheless, I was left sitting there—alone, deaf, burglarized, carless, wifeless…and Dustyless.

Anybody have the slightest idea where that doggoned girl could be? Man, you pay good money—well, not that much, I guess. But what I am paying for her *expertise* is still hard-earned dough, for heaven's sake.

Lordy, Lordy.

FIFTEEN

By the time Detective Small arrived, my ears had cleared up a little, and I was able to hear a few things. I could even understand people when they spoke to me; that's if they talked slowly and loudly while facing directly toward me.

I was seated in the motel's nondescript lobby: small and dark with minimal furnishings. It wasn't exactly a pimp's hangout—but not far from it, if you can picture the place.

What am I doing here?

This place is about the best I could afford, so *"ya get whacha pay fer,"* as Dusty would say.

The desk clerk gave me a towel packed with ice. I pressed it against my head as I lay back in a chair upholstered with worn tan fabric. The ice helped some but not enough to say I felt well or anything close to it. The worst part about it all was that I was still suffering from those earlier blows to the head in the Kantel building. Man, I didn't need this—either.

A short time later, Detective Small arrived and sauntered over to where I was sitting. They should have named the guy *Wide* instead of Small, because he blocked out most of the light from the windows when he stood in front of me.

He let out a belch that a hippopotamus would be proud of, then he took out a pen and his little notebook. He flipped it open and asked me what happened. I told him about the room and the car. I thought it would be best if I held back the other things that had happened until I spoke with Dusty. Maybe Daddy had some better ideas. Sure.

The bomb squad showed up and went to work scraping my car off the walls and sidewalk. Lots of luck.

Detective Biggs eased around his partner and gawked at me. I hadn't seen him up to that point. Maybe he was also blocked out by Detective *Wide*—I mean, Detective Small. Or, maybe he had been outside with the bomb squad. I dunno.

Whatever.

Detective Small helped me to my feet, and he and Biggs escorted me to my room. My ears were still ringing, and I had trouble keeping my balance. I kept my mouth shut on the way so I could concentrate on keeping my feet under me. Not an easy task.

When we got to my room, I inserted the key into the lock. I suddenly had the odd feeling the room would be in perfect order. That none of it had even happened. Or, that it had happened, but someone had returned while I was outside and straightened it up.

Wrong.

It looked even worse the second time around.

Detective Small asked if I had touched anything. I glanced around and thought for a second. I don't think I did. Did I?

Anyway, I shook my head no.

While we were wading through the things littered on the floor, the telephone rang. Detective Biggs, the tall black man with the shaved head, answered it. He grunted and pointed the phone at my head like it was a gun. He said it was for me.

The desk clerk with a pizza? I don't think so. My wife? Heather, I love you, sweetheart. May I come home now?

I took the phone and pressed it to my good ear—well, my better ear. My hearing still wasn't the best, so I hoped I could hear and understand whomever was on the line.

It wasn't my wife as I had hoped. Darn it, I really needed a hug.

Dusty shouted into the phone, "Who was that?"

I shouted right back at her: "Where have you been, girl? I—"

She cut me short. "Who answered the dang phone?"

"You won't believe what happened," I said, trying to avoid eye contact with the detectives. "My—"

"Who answered the goldarn phone?" she persisted.

"Einstein," I whispered.

"Who?"

"Detective Biggs."

"Detective Biggs? DETECTIVE BIGGS?" she yelled. "What the heck's he doin' there?"

"I had to call them. My—"

"Why in the world did you do a dumb thang like that?" she practically screamed. "You know they're lookin' for any reason to toss yer butt back in the damn kapokey, don't you?"

Kapokey?

I pulled the phone away from my ear and stared at it. *If I remember correctly, Dusty, you're the one who suggested I go to the police in the first place.*

I pressed the phone against my good ear again—the one with the least amount of ringing. I said, "Dusty, I'm trying to tell you what happened, but you keep—"

Damn! She did it again.

89

"You haven't come clean so far," she said in a huff. "So why the heck should I believe what yer sayin's true now?"

"Dusty, I—"

Damnit! There she goes again! Man, that's frustrating when she interrupts me. She gets me so darned tongue-tied, I swear my words are about to squirt out my ringing ears.

She said, "Don't tell 'em a dang thang till I get there." There was a slight pause. "Understand?"

"What—you my attorney now?"

"Very funny, Buddy. Just don't tell 'em anymore than you hafta. Okay?"

"All right. But you better hurry, girl, because they're looking at me like two starving lions eyeing a tasty T-bone." I turned my head away so I wouldn't have to look at the twitchy detectives. "I'm sure they're gonna start grilling me *real* soon." My voice was as low as I could make it and still be talking. Remember, my ears were suffering from the bomb blast...and Dusty's blasting barrages.

"Dusty? Hello, Dusty?"

She hung up. She actually hung up on me. Can you imagine that—hanging up on a high-paying client? The nerve.

She must be in her Jeep and on her way by now, because she hadn't uttered another word since I said, "... you better hurry, girl..."

I stared at the phone. I felt kind of hurt not getting any respect...and not being interrupted again. You know the feeling, I'm sure.

Detective Small asked, "Who was that?"

My mind cycled rapidly. I could tell him it was my attorney, but he probably knew Dusty and would recognize

the kid when she arrived. Or, I could say it was my wife—
but he also knew her, and that would be even more difficult
to explain when Dusty showed up. I was lost again.

As I said, I'm not very good at lying.

However, thanks to Dusty—I'm learning.

SIXTEEN

I hung up the telephone and stared at the thing for a moment. I really didn't want to tell Detective Small who had called, but I honestly had no choice.

He repeated his question: "Who was that on the phone, Bowers?"

Firmness filled his voice, and I knew I had to answer the impatient detective's question sooner rather than later. I was running out of delaying tactics, so I turned to him and flatly said, "Dusty Diamond."

Small shook his head no, which I think meant he didn't recognize the name.

"From 'Diamond and Diamond,'" I explained.

No help.

The detectives stared blankly at each other.

Still not a connection for the highly perceptive detectives.

Again, I thought about stalling until Dusty arrived, but that could be a while, and I didn't have my tap-dancing shoes on at the moment. And besides, Dusty wasn't really my lawyer; so there was no attorney-client privilege I could hide behind, as far as I knew.

Once again I attempted to enlighten the detectives: "'Diamond and Diamond'…Private Investigators."

Biggs disgustedly rolled his eyes. "Gum shoes?"

Small cocked an eyebrow. "Why in the world would you hire snoops…especially unknowns?" he asked, shaking his head in disgust. "What the hell you trying to pull here, Bowers?"

"I'm not trying to pull anything." I sat down and folded my arms and crossed my legs. "You guys are so damned convinced I killed Harry Thomas that you're not willing to look beyond me to find the real murderer."

The detectives stared at each other. *Who us?*

I couldn't determine if they were dumbfounded or if they'd been doing something about the case behind my back and had some information they didn't want to share.

Man, I really wanted to tell them about that odious person sneaking around Kantel's office and scarfing up those photos—and bonking me on the head. However, I had promised Dusty I wouldn't. And when I make a promise, I always keep it. Well, almost always. I mean, I usually keep it. I do my best to keep it. However, there are times when extenuating circumstances cause a person to…well, to have to deviate slightly. Nevertheless, I was going to do my damnedest to keep this promise to Dusty.

Where the hell was that girl, anyway? I thought she'd be here by now. Probably chasing her wandering Jeep down the street again. Great. Just great.

Detective Small's eyes locked on mine. "What did you come up with, Bowers?"

Photos.

"Photos?" Small would probably ask.

Yep, photos of a blonde gal with two guys on either side of her. Too bad you guys missed them—that's if you bothered to look. And, too bad they disappeared before I was able to get my hands on them so I could identify who the hell they were and let you know who might be involved in Harry Thomas' killing.

I shrugged and finally said, "Nothing."

"C'mon," said Biggs, raising his chin a little. "You must have come up with something...or we wouldn't be looking at this damn mess here." His long arm swung around the room.

Hurry, Dusty!

Small scratched his head. He does that a lot. Either he has bad dandruff, psoriasis, eczema...or lice. Yuck!

"'Fess up, Bowers!" Small practically yelled. "We know you been up to something, damnit! So, come clean while it still has a chance to look good on your lousy record."

Record? Oh, the agony.

I sure would like to, Detective; but my trustworthy confidant told me not to say diddly-squat about it until she got here.

I shook my head slowly, as if I truly wanted to come up with something for them. "Sure wish I could, Detectives."

Small seemed to calm down some. He asked, "Any idea who did this?"

Yeah. It was that suave womanizer, Hans Kantel. You know, the one who was trying to schmooze Dusty. Well, Detectives, he set me up, and now that I won't go away nice and quiet-like, he's taking more drastic measures. And if you two dummies would open your eyes, you'd see that what the hell I'm talking about is true, and you'd put Kantel behind bars before he succeeds in offing me too.

I said, "I honestly don't—"

Guess who interrupted me?

The door burst open and Dusty popped into the room. "Dusty Diamond," she blurted, fishing in her handbag for her business cards. She had to step around the things on the floor to get to the detectives, especially

94

Biggs—who was farthest away and leaning against the bathroom door. After giving them her cards, she returned to me and—acting as if she were my attorney—folded her arms across her chest and sat next to me on the arm of my chair.

They didn't buy it. Nice try, kid.

Biggs looked at her card and slipped it into his pocket. Small took a different approach: He glanced at her card and let it drop to the floor. It quickly got lost in the clutter.

Dusty fidgeted. Her confidence was waning. A rare sight. A rare sight indeed.

Small shook his head in what appeared to be disgust or disappointment or something. He glared at Dusty. "Whacha got?" he finally asked her.

"We knew all along who done it."

What? She going to let the cat out of the bag to these two clowns? No way. They sure as hell will find some way to botch it.

Small cocked an eyebrow and said, "Oh?"

"Yep. Hans Kantel's yer man. He's the one who killed Harry Thomas and…and set up my client here, Mr. Bowers." Her hand flew so close to my face I had to duck to avoid getting whacked.

Biggs looked at me, then at Dusty.

Her statement caught me by surprise too. Especially after she told me to keep my mouth shut and not to let them in on anything we knew or suspected. I guess the girl knows what she's doing. *Uh-huh.*

You get what you pay for, I suppose. Sound familiar?

Small folded his heavy arms and rocked back. "Is that a fact?" he asked Dusty. "And how do you know this?"

"Evidence," was all she said.

95

"What kind of evidence?"

Dusty told Small, "We went to Kantel's office, and—"

Small stopped her in mid-sentence. "You did? When was that?"

"Yesterday."

"Well, you better have a mighty good alibi," Small said, shaking his head as if we were in trouble—again.

Dusty asked, "Why's that?"

"Because your so-called-killer...Mr. Hans Kantel," replied Small, shifting his icy stare from Dusty to me, "well, ...he was murdered earlier today."

Huh?

My jaw dropped.

So much for that theory.

I gawked at Dusty.

Dusty stared at me.

SEVENTEEN

Sooooo, thanks to that untimely outburst by my brilliant private investigator, Dusty Diamond, here I am back in the Gunter City Jail. However, this time there will be no bail according to the judge. Not with two counts of murder, she said. Imagine that, innocent little-old-me being charged with murder—two of them, no less. Two! Heaven help me.

And I'm not sure how Hans Kantel died. Not a clue. They wouldn't tell me. It's as if they were sure I already knew. Cops do things like that, you know.

And why the hell Dusty's skinny little ass didn't land in jail along with mine is another mystery. Didn't she tell the detectives that *we* were at Kantel's office? She did. I know she did.

But nooooo, she's not in here with me. Dusty's free as a damned dove. She must have done some fast talking again. Big surprise.

So, *I'm* the one—*I*, not *we*—who is behind bars again. Is there no justice?

Nevertheless, I figure Dusty must have pulled the same stunt she did when she was with Hans Kantel. You know: fluttering her eyebrows, the fancy talk and all that other stuff that made my stomach turn. That's the only thing I can think of that could have kept her out of jail. I honestly don't know. Maybe her experience, as limited as it is, was enough for her to skate on this one. Go figure.

However, when you think about it, I'm sure it's in our best interest that she isn't locked up too. This way, she's free to snoop around. Maybe she'll get lucky and talk to someone else prior to him or her getting killed.

Lucky?

What am I saying?

The bottom line is that I'm here in jail alone, once again. Well, I'm not exactly alone. My lovely wife, Heather, is sitting across the table and looking at me like I was Hannibal Lecter (or, should I say "Cannibal Lecter?"). And, to me, despite that piercing stare from her azure-blue eyes, she still is the most beautiful thing in the world. If she would just stop that darned staring so I wouldn't have to look into those condemning eyes of hers, I'd feel a lot better—I think. I'm certainly glad she's not the judge, because if she were, I think they'd be getting the gallows ready. Whew!

"Heather, sweetie," I said with the most sugar-coated voice I could come up with, "you know how much I love you." It's impossible to be too mushy at a time like this. "And I would never lie to you...or do anything to embarrass you."

Yeah, like getting trapped inside a beautiful girl's room and two charges of murder aren't embarrassing! Get real, Buddy.

She folded her arms across her chest, which tended to embellish her breasts. Her dress was dark blue with little white flowers. A gold pendant and chain bounced in her cleavage when she moved. Nice.

She turned her head to the side to avoid looking at me. "Uh-huh," she said with a voice that wasn't the least bit convincing.

I wish she wouldn't look away. She has such pretty blue eyes. I love to look at them.

When her head snapped to the side, her blonde ponytail flipped onto her shoulder. Man, do I ever love it when she wears her hair like that: ponytail popping up from the top of her head and flowing over her shoulder. She's a real *killer*—when she wants to be.

Maybe another choice of words would be better here, eh?

I asked her, "Do you actually think I'm capable of murdering people, Heather?"

Maybe I honestly didn't want to know her answer. Sometimes you think you really know someone, but at times of stress—like this—true feelings surface.

She spun her hair into a bun with two fingers and pinned it on top of her head. I didn't see where she got the pin. It was almost as if she grabbed the thing out of thin air. I don't like it when she does that—the bun thing, that is. Now she looks like a teacher who is about to lecture a student on his manners—or lack thereof. Not a good sign. I am never amenable when it comes to being chastised.

She turned to me. "You said you were drunk when the first one happened, correct?"

I nodded yes.

"So, who really knows what someone is capable of doing when totally inebriated?" she continued as she stared at me. "The analytical mind is shut down—unable to rationalize."

Where the hell's she going with this damned psycho-babble stuff?

She glowered at me with such a fierce glare it made me feel like melted margarine. I wish she wouldn't do that—the staring thing.

I tried to explain. "I wasn't really *that* inebri—"

She cut me short: "However…the second one occurred when your head was perfectly clear."

99

Oh-oh.

"Heather," I asked in a pleading voice, "do you honestly think I killed those people?"

She placed her elbows on the gray-topped table and steepled her fingers under her perfect chin. After a minute, her cold stare softened a bit, and she said, "No, I don't think you killed anyone."

A wistful sigh of relief escaped from my lips.

"However," she said with her eyes narrowing again, "I'd like to know just what the hell you were doing in that guy's room with that damn gal."

So would I. Not a clue. Maybe I *was* totally inebriated, huh?

"I-I—"

She cut me short...again. She wasn't exactly in a listening mood, I don't think. "And if you think for one minute your being in jail isn't embarrassing to your friends and family...then you've got..."

"*...another think coming,*" I knew she was going to say.

But she didn't.

Instead, she finished with, "...to get your stupid head out of your dumb ass."

Don't you hate it when that happens? Just when you think you know exactly what someone is going to say, she trips you up and says just the opposite. Darn.

My eyes must have widened twice their normal size. I hoped she didn't notice the startled look on my face. You see, my quiet and reticent wife has problems saying things like: darn and gosh and crap and...well, you get the picture. So, this was a pretty good indication of just how upset my little cupcake really was. I guess there would be a better word than *upset* to describe her. But I'd rather not think about it right now.

She got to her feet, crossed her arms over her chest again and paced the small room. I looked up at her. She is tall and slender and quite shapely. Nice. Very nice.

I told you I missed her. And now you can see why. Sleeping alone in a jail cell makes one appreciate the simpler things in life. Simpler?

She stopped pacing and glared at me again. However, this stare wasn't quite as penetrating as the other. She asked, "What's your idiot attorney doing to get you out of this dump?" She looked around like she was standing in the middle of a trash bin loaded with last week's yucky garbage. Her pert nose rose a bit.

"I'm not counting on that guy for very much." I watched my fingers drumming on the table. I had difficulty looking into her prying eyes since I was stretching the truth a bit.

She asked, "Why is that?"

I clasped my hands together and looked up at her. "He's got zilch for experience."

She exhaled a long deep breath and stared at the ceiling. "Great! Just freaking great!"

Freaking? This was my shy, calm, collected wife talking. Mercy me.

She leaned on the table and stared into my eyes. I hate it when she does that. Makes me feel like I've done something wrong and have to go to a corner and have a time-out.

I wanted to tell her that I told the young attorney to buzz off because I didn't need another clown tightening the noose around my neck. But her relentless stare somehow made me conveniently forget I told him not to come back.

What?

Hey, there are some things a guy just doesn't share: I think it's called attorney-client privilege.

101

"Well?" she asked, her eyes returning to mine and narrowing again.

"Well, what?" was the best I could come up with. I honestly had no idea where she was going with that question.

"Well, what the hell are we going to do about it?"

I had to do some rapid tap-dancing here. However, I liked the way she said *we* instead of you. Also, it sounded like she wanted me out of this place and didn't want me spending the rest of my life sleeping next to Vinnie, Moose, and the rest of the boys down at the state penitentiary. Isn't that what it sounded like? It sure sounded that way to me. And that was good. Very good.

A hint of a grin crept across my lips. However, due to the mental state she was in, I didn't know if I wanted her to see my relief. Anyway, I couldn't help it, and I didn't care a rat's patooty if she noticed. Her concern for getting me out of jail told me she still loved me—I think.

I finally replied to her question: "I've got someone else working on it."

"Thank God," she said, sitting again. "You had me worried for a minute."

Had *you* worried?

I could feel my face flush, because I knew what the next question was going to be—W*ho?*

"And who might that be?"

See, I told you.

"It's…it's a…smallish firm," I mumbled.

"What's the name?"

"'Diamond and Diamond.'"

"Who's the lead person?"

Her questions were sounding like she worked for Detective Small. Damn, does everyone around here work for that mental midget?

102

I didn't want to say Dusty because that would… well, you know where that would lead, and I wasn't about to go there. And I didn't want to say *Daddy* either. But I never thought to ask Dusty her father's name.

Dumb.

Hey, I'm new at this. Whom did you expect… Columbo?

My reply was, "Mr. Diamond himself."

"When do I get to meet this Mr. Diamond?"

More tap-dancing. "He could be here at any time," I said, turning toward the door, as if I actually expected him to enter the room. My eyes returned to hers. "He's so darned busy working on the case, you never know when he'll show up. He just pops in every now and then. In and out like a flash."

Did I say I had trouble lying? I used to. But I guess that's what jail does to a person—makes him a better liar.

She stood up again. "Well, I can't wait." She gathered up her things, then glared at me. "I've got to get back and do some…no, not *some*…a *lot*…of explaining."

I nodded my understanding and also got to my feet. The best thing about it was that I was wise enough to keep my mouth shut.

She said, "Set up a meeting for me."

I faked a smile. "I'll do my best, sweetheart."

She gave me an odd look that seemed to say, *"You damned sure will, mister!"* She spun around and headed for the door. "The sooner, the better," she called over her shoulder as she departed.

Yikes!

Where the hell's Dusty?

103

EIGHTEEN

Dusty found out where the late Hans Kantel's residence was located and drove her beloved Jeep there to see if she could find any clues. She wisely parked it down the road and hiked back to the main gate. Notice I said road and not street. His place was located far from town—and other homes. Kantel must have liked his privacy.

Kantel's house was a castle compared to Harry Thomas' place—and Harry's wasn't too shabby. The two-story house was ivy-covered stone and was about the size of a football field. A brick wall—hidden behind thick bushes—was taller than Dusty. It isolated the place from everything and everybody.

Dusty perused the details of the enormous grounds. Kantel's security system was top-of-the-line: cameras, sensors, motion detectors...dogs; you name it. The place seemed impenetrable, but Dusty had to get in somehow.

She checked to see if the new pellet gun, with a fully-charged air cartridge, was in her bag. It was. She was ready for those dogs if they showed. She noticed the front gate resembled a fortress, so there was no sense wasting time there. Plus, the security cameras would surely get her picture. Even though it was dark, the place was lighted better than the Jefferson Memorial. Therefore, she opted for the wall some distance away from the main entrance. She pushed her way between the bushes until her fingers touched the brick. She looked up and could hardly see the top of the wall. No way she could get over it. She glanced around for something to stand on, but nothing was handy. Someone had seen to that.

Something flashed in Dusty's mind, and she ran back to her Jeep. She plopped her shoulder bag on the ground and began removing the spare tire from the back of the Jeep. As she was doing that, her eyes scanned the area for roving patrols.

Nothing.

By the time she had the large wheel off and had rolled it back to the wall, she was exhausted. She took a deep breath and leaned the wheel and herself against the wall. After a brief rest, she placed a foot through the center of the rim and another on top of the wheel. With her bag slung over her shoulder, she pinched the bricks between her fingers and hoisted herself on top of the wall. She balanced there while she scanned the grounds. No dogs.

The ornate wall was rough, but she could manage it: She was wearing jeans, so the bricks didn't scratch her legs when she hurtled over. After she dropped to the ground, she thought about the wheel being on the other side of the wall. Not much could be done about that now. She would have to find another way out when the time came.

Dusty navigated her way across the large yard and through the trees to the house. She located a window that was at ground level. A light was on inside. She glanced around to make sure no one had spotted her, then returned her attention to the room. Two people inside were talking—a man and a woman. Dusty grabbed the sill and stood on her toes to peek in.

Aha.

A blue-eyed blonde, with a cleavage Dusty would kill for, was puffing on a cigarette and pacing back and forth. Kantel's secretary? Wife? During their visit to his office, Kantel said he had no wife. Did he lie about that? Or, did he mean he was no longer married?

Dusty cursed herself for not getting a good look at Kantel's secretary when she and Buddy visited with him. All Dusty could recall was a buxom blonde with a tight yellow sweater and short blue skirt. No distinguishing facial features.

Some PI, huh?

The blonde at Kantel's house was now arguing with a muscular guy wearing all black: black tee shirt, black slacks and black boots. Even his slicked-back hair was black.

Dusty pressed her ear to the window to hear what they were arguing about. However, the window was thermopane, double glass. Impossible to hear anything clearly. Only muffled sounds emerged—especially the blonde's irate shrieks.

Although Dusty couldn't hear what they were saying, she could sense by the couple's body language that something had gone awry. She thought, by their yelling and less-than-affectionate gestures, one of them would surely kill the other right then and there—right before her eyes!

Dusty wondered what it was that made them so upset. She thought about the information she previously gleaned from Detective Small: Kantel had been shot in the head while driving away from his office. He died immediately. And there were no witnesses to give the cops a lead.

However, these two probably didn't know there were no witnesses. So, maybe they were arguing because they thought things hadn't gone according to plan. Or, maybe things had gone well, and now the two vultures were quarreling over their shares of the booty. Whatever,

Hans Kantel's death was definitely not being mourned. Not by these two scoundrels anyway.

Kantel had told Buddy he wasn't married; however, the busty blonde inside seemed to have free access to the place. Did Hans Kantel lie? Was the blonde Mrs. Kantel? And, if she was Mrs. Kantel, did she give the order—and Blackie do the shooting? Dusty wondered. She would have to check on that marriage situation the first thing in the morning.

After burning a picture of their faces in her mind, Dusty circled the huge house. She was looking for an open window, unlocked door—anything. However, before she got halfway around the place, lights flashed on, and a siren howled.

"Damnit!" she hissed in a low voice. "Musta tripped a dang sensor."

She searched for an opening in the wall where she could get through or climb over; however, nothing was visible. And there weren't any ladders or things of that sort to assist her. Of course.

Dusty let out another curse when she heard dogs barking. None were in sight, but she knew it was simply a matter of time before some devouring doggies would be at her heels. She spun around and began running toward the gate. She hadn't taken five steps when the strap of her bag caught on a tree branch. It spun her around and lifted her off the ground. She momentarily resembled a karate kicker with both feet off the ground. However, Dusty didn't quite have the same agility as a karate kicker; she hit the lawn with a solid *whoomp*!

The lawn was plush and soft; so it didn't hurt her; just knocked the wind from her lungs. She sat for a second while she gasped for breath and regained her composure. After a moment, she got to her feet, adjusted her bag and glanced around. She heard the dogs barking in the distance but didn't see anyone approaching, so she sprinted toward the estate's main entrance as fast as her skinny legs would take her. She resembled the *Caped Crusader* as she sped across the massive yard: her red hair flagging out and the long-strapped bag flapping against her back.

While she was running, she eyed the gate area and hoped like hell it had a sensor to let people out without requiring a key or code number or something dumb like that. She also saw the dogs approaching from her right. They were heading for the gate also. How did they know where to go? Maybe that's what they were trained to do in situations like this. Ratsofats!

The two Dobermans raced toward the gate like greyhounds chasing a railed rabbit. And it was quite obvious they were going to get there before Dusty. She slowed so she could swing her bag around to her front. She reached inside and withdrew the pellet gun. The pellets were good: She wouldn't have to kill the dogs to make them stop. The only problem was hitting them while they, as well as she, were running. If she stopped to shoot at them, the guards from the house might appear and get to her before she got to the gate. Oh, yes, the problem of negotiating that darn gate also had to be dealt with. One problem at a time, she told herself.

One of the dogs stopped running and took a defensive stance when it saw Dusty running toward it. Dusty fired a pellet. However, the dog didn't move.

Missed.

"Damnit!"

The only thing the noise did was get the attention of the other dog. Now she had two to contend with. She wasn't that far from the gate, however. The best thing to do—she figured—was to slow to a walk, catch her breath and remember what Daddy had taught her at the shooting range: Take a deep breath and squeeze—don't jerk—the trigger.

That's exactly what she did. The dog nearest her let out a yelp and went galloping off. The other dog also began galloping—but this one was heading right toward her.

Be calm, Dusty said to herself. *Be calm, girl.*

She took careful aim at the charging black dog, which was now only twenty feet away. If she missed, there wouldn't be time for another shot before the dog had her by the throat. And then...?

How would she ever explain that to Buddy? Obviously not by talking to him, that's for sure. Maybe a note would work. Except the dog would probably eat it after it finished with her.

However, she didn't miss, and the dog fled off, yelping, in the same direction as the first one.

Dusty ran toward the gate while looking for a sensor. She located one about three feet off the ground. She hoped it was for motion and not detection.

Motion it was.

As she approached the large, prison-like gates, they groaned and creaked and slowly opened. She slipped through before they were a foot apart, and after a quick glance over her shoulder, she ran as fast as she could in the direction of her Jeep.

She couldn't believe her luck. Nobody was following—not even the dogs. Thank God for small favors.

Slowing as she neared her Jeep, Dusty noticed that the area was much brighter than when she had parked it earlier. Maybe a streetlight had been slow in turning on.

Wrong.

"No!" she gasped when noticing flames licking at the canvas top and spreading to the rest of the vehicle. "Not my Jeep!"

The guy from the house with the black tee shirt, black slacks, etc. was walking away from the Jeep. He took a pistol—a real pistol—from a holster at his back.

How did he get there so damn fast? A twin? Not likely.

Maybe he got the jump on her when she fell. Or, maybe there was another service gate she hadn't seen.

Dusty froze in her tracks.

"Oh, sheeit!" was all she could say.

NINETEEN

I, Buddy Bowers, had a visitor. No, it wasn't my wife, Heather, like I had hoped. And it wasn't Dusty Diamond. It was my *genius friend*, Detective Small. He was alone—no Detective Biggs at his side. That was good because Biggs' tiger-like stare tended to make me nervous. I think I told you that. Detective Small I could handle one-on-one, I think.

A guard let Small into my tiny cell, and the detective sat on the bunk beside me—real buddy-buddy like. He raked his hand through what little light brown hair remained on his head and wiped his forehead with his same old faded blue tie. And when the tie didn't soak up enough perspiration, he used the back of his shirtsleeve. Gross.

I figured from his appearance it must be pretty hot outside. Fortunately, the jail is air-conditioned. Maybe he just came in to cool off some. Fat chance.

"We should have a little chat," he said, looking at the floor. His voice was soft and kind...instead of the sharp, gruff rhetoric he'd been using.

I knew something was up. Maybe he was going to offer me some sort of plea where I would only get 50 years instead of life. Let's see, I'd be about 90 when I got out. I'm sure my beautiful wife would be waiting for me. Yeah, sure.

Small continued: "I guess we should have been paying a little closer attention to what you were saying."

My ears perked up.

I told you guys I wasn't your murderer, you idiot. But no, you wouldn't listen. You had your stupid minds made up and weren't about to give an innocent guy a break. My left eyebrow cocked instinctively. It does that when someone tosses me a red herring, or when I think they're blowing smoke up my duff.

I asked him, "What are you getting at, Detective?"

"I'd like you to go over everything once more." He paused briefly while his gaze shifted about my cell. "That's in case we overlooked something important."

What you and your dumb partner overlooked that was real important is the fact that I was telling the truth... and that I'm not guilty of either murder.

Idiots.

I said, "Really? What brought this about, Detective?" *Someone waste your congenial partner while I was in here sleeping?*

Small's brown eyes locked on mine. "Kantel's office building burned to the ground last night."

You could have knocked me over with a withered walnut leaf, I was so shocked. I couldn't believe it. Dusty and I were just inside the place. I hope the detective doesn't put that connection together and charge us with arson. Yikes!

"No kidding?" I asked.

He shook his head. "Nope. And his warehouse with millions of dollars in rare artifacts was also consumed."

The warehouse too? Both buildings were now gone. Somebody really didn't want to leave any clues, did he—or she? Or, maybe he or she wanted everything gone to collect the insurance money. I wondered if any of the valuable stuff was covertly removed prior to the blaze.

I said, "It's pretty obvious I didn't do it from inside this damned jail."

He fidgeted on the bunk. "I realize that, Bowers. That's why I'm here."

"So, you're finally willing to listen, huh?"

He got up and began pacing. "Maybe you picked up on something we haven't. Something that would connect the arson with the two murders."

My fingers raked through my thick hair while my brain spun like a roulette wheel. I hoped it would stop on some clue that Dusty and I had overlooked.

"It would look good in your file if you cooperated," he continued; "maybe even get your sentence reduced."

Reduced? Get with it, Detective. Give me a break. 'Thrown out' would be a little better, don't you think?

I frowned and said, "Or maybe get my ass outta this place when you find the *real* killers."

His voice became firm. "If you're not guilty, Bowers, we'll find that out."

Detective, you and your inept partner couldn't find water if you both fell out of a boat and had to swim.

He continued: "And we'll make a proper determination about all of it...if and when that time comes."

Uh-huh.

"Well, Detective Small, you and your partner haven't exactly been doing a very good job at it so far, have you?"

That was dumb.

He crossed his arms and glared at me. "Look, Bowers, I didn't have to come here." His voice was harsh. Sharp. "There's enough evidence to let you rot in jail the rest of your goddamn useless life."

Good grief!

I needed him to get back on the other track—the one about making a deal. "All right," I said, waving my hands in an I-give-up motion. "I'll tell you everything I know."

He nodded once. "That's more like it, Bowers." He sat next to me again and pulled out his little notebook.

I went over every single detail, sometimes twice, just to make sure this *intellectual* got all the facts. The missing photos seemed to attract most of his attention.

They—the photos, that is—had my interest also. What was the connection with the three people in the photos? Did somebody not want to be associated with Kantel and Thomas? Who? Why?

I told Small it was hard to believe that both Harry Thomas and Hans Kantel weren't married. After all, both men seemed to have it all: money, good looks…money. Some women go for that kind of stuff, you know.

However, Small did inform me that Thomas had been married but had divorced at least twice. He wasn't sure about Kantel, but he jotted down a note.

I also suggested he find the beautiful brunette—Lynn. She was probably Thomas' most recent "significant other," and she could be the detective's missing link.

Another note.

I wondered what Dusty was doing about that situation. Not about taking notes—but about finding Lynn. I think that little gal—Dusty, that is—could find anybody anywhere. In fact, she's probably at Lynn's place right now, snooping around and finding enough evidence to have me set free. Wishful thinking?

Anyway, I also suggested to the detective that in light of this new information, he might see what he could do about getting me released on bail so I could help. I assured him I wasn't about to go anywhere until my name was cleared. Besides, my wife wouldn't let me into the house until that was done. However, I didn't share that last part with the detective.

He said he would see what he could do. But he didn't jot it down.

Do you think he would remember to check into releasing me once he left my cell?

I doubt it.

I had to find a way to get out of that jail.

TWENTY

Dusty dragged herself into the jail's visiting room and spilled herself into the metal chair across the table from where I was sitting. She looked like she had just gone ten rounds with Mike Tyson, the heavy-weight boxer, only both her ears were still intact. She reminded me of the way I looked the morning after partying with the guys. Good grief!

Now why the heck did I have to bring up that terrible thought at a time like this? I definitely did not need that reminder hanging—not a good word—over my head. Dumb.

Dusty's bag plopped to the floor. She leaned forward and rested her bony elbows on the table. They were covered with dirt—as was her face, hair and clothes. What a mess.

I asked her, "What in the world have you been up to, girl?"

"You wouldn't believe me if I told you, Mr. B."

"Try me, kid. I've got nothing but time."

She sucked in a deep breath and tapped the table with her dirty fingernails a couple times. Finally she asked in a depressed voice, "Does the loss of my Jeep come under the 'expenses' category?"

I leaned back and folded my arms. "I think that may be stretching it a bit, Dusty."

Her blank stare dropped to the table where her hands were now folded—as if in prayer. "Dang," she said hardly louder than a whisper.

I thought she was kidding at first. However, my attention piqued when I realized she probably wasn't. I sat up and leaned toward her. "What happened, Dusty?"

Those pitiful green eyes rose from the table and looked into mine. "You wouldn't believe it if I told you, Mr. B," she said in a weak, shallow voice. "Cain't hardly believe it m'self."

"Sounds serious," I said. I placed my hands gently on hers. "Tell old Buddy all about it."

She explained about visiting Kantel's house, seeing the buxom blonde arguing with the guy dressed in black, having the dogs chase her—and having her Jeep set on fire. She said she was positive the guy in black was going to shoot her before she got away.

He obviously didn't.

She figured the guy couldn't see her with his eyes blinded by the fire's blaze and with her hiding in the shadows. He had disappeared into the bushes—to another hidden gate, she assumed.

Dusty continued by saying she walked for a mile or so before getting a lift by a patrolling policeman. She told the cop her Jeep had caught on fire while she was driving, so the cop had it towed to the junkyard. She had spent the night in the police station.

She sniffed.

I swear she looked like she had lost a close member of the family and was about to break into tears.

"It was only a Jeep, Dusty." *And a dirty one at that.*

"But it was the first and only car I ever had," she said in a whining voice. "And, it wasn't insured!"

117

My heart felt her pain. But for some reason, a grin magically appeared on my lips. "I tell you what, Dusty," I said in an upbeat tone. "If you get proof that I didn't do the killings...and you get me out of this place...I'll buy you a brand new Jeep. How's that?"

Her chin rose, and her eyes lit up like wet emeralds. "Really, Mr. B?"

"Really," I replied, nodding. "And that's a promise...even if I have to take up a collection from my golfing buddies." *Fat chance.*

"Oh, that's cool, Mr. B." She was grinning from ear to ear. "I mean...like...like totally cool."

I returned her smile. I felt like I had just given my daughter the best gift she had ever received.

"If they'd let me get to you," she said, bouncing in her chair, "I'd give you a great big kiss...and anythin' else you wanted."

Did I say daughter?

I rolled my eyes.

It was a good thing the table was between us, or she'd have had me in a giant bear hug, I'm sure. I glanced at the guard. He simply grinned.

I returned my attention to Dusty. "Get hold of yourself, kid. We still have to get me out of here, remember?"

"Oh," she said, smacking her forehead with an open palm, "I almost forgot, Mr. B; Daddy has some contacts in Vegas...Las Veg—"

I cut her short. "I'm familiar with the place."

"Right. Anyway, Daddy found out that Kantel had gotten married in Vegas to—"

"Don't tell me," I said, cutting her off again; "a blonde by the name of Marilyn."

She pulled back, and her green eyes widened. "How'd you know that, Mr. B?"

"Lucky guess."

I probably should have told Dusty about the photo of Hans and Marilyn, but this way she would think she discovered it all on her own.

"So," Dusty said, nodding, "that bugger, Kantel, lied to us, huh?"

That bugger?

"Looks that way," I said, leaning back and folding my arms. I wondered if Detective Small uncovered that little detail. Nah. That's a little too much to ask for.

"And one more thang, Mr. B."

"What's that, Dusty?"

"You won't believe this, but Daddy says Mrs. Kantel is the beneficiary on the insurance policies."

Big surprise.

"For him…and the business?" I asked. However, I had already guessed the answer.

"Yep," she replied, nodding slowly and methodically. "Sure's I'm sittin' here in front of you."

My lips pursed while the wheels in my head spun. I had to think of what to tell Small—and what not to. One little mistake with that yo-yo, and I could be kissing my beautiful wife good-bye from between bars.

Dusty reached for her bag. "I'll go question Mrs. Kantel," she said, getting to her feet. "No way that bitch is gonna let you take the fall fer her, Mr. B."

That bitch?

I shook my head no. "Don't do that, Dusty. Tell Detective Small about the situation and let him do the questioning. And try to do it in a way that'll make it appear it's his idea."

She shrugged her skinny shoulders. "Gee, Mr. B, I dunno." She placed two fingers on her chin. "How'm I gonna do that?"

I'm sure you'll find a way, kid. You're about the most imaginative and manipulative person I've ever met. If you can't do it...nobody can.

I grinned and said, "Ask Daddy."

TWENTY-ONE

A couple hours after Dusty left, Detectives Small and Biggs approached my jail cell. They didn't bother entering, just stood outside the bars: Small scratching his crotch and Biggs standing slightly behind him. Biggs had his arms folded and was staring at me with those scary tiger-like eyes again. I hate it when he does that. I think you already know that.

I rose from my bunk and sauntered toward them. "To what do I owe this honor, Detectives?"

Small scratched his head this time—more out of habit than an itch. I hope he washes his hands. He said, "Spoke with your gal Diamond."

"And?"

"We already knew everything she had to tell us," he announced, sliding his hands into his pockets. He glanced at his partner.

Biggs nodded in agreement.

You guys are so damned sharp—always one step ahead of us. Yeah, right.

I said, "Really?"

Small explained, "Yeah, she came to us just before we were fixin' to check out Mr. Kantel's place."

Uh-huh. Liar, liar, pants on fire.

Now, where the hell did that come from? I must be reverting to my childhood. This jail cell—and these two dingbats—will do that to a person.

I wondered why Hans Kantel had told me and Dusty he wasn't married. Was it for Dusty's sake so he could hit on the kid? Or, was there another hidden agenda that he had with his wife?

Clinging to the bars with both hands, I asked Detective Small, "So, did you get to question Marilyn Kantel? What did she have to say? Denied everything, I'll bet—even being married to Kantel, right?"

That was quite a mouthful, especially for Detective Small, who was scratching his head again—with the same hand that had scratched—well, you know.

Maybe I should start over and give him one question at a time.

Small glanced at his partner. "Didn't get to ask Mrs. Kantel the first damn question, did we, Biggsie?"

Biggs wagged his head slowly from side to side. "Nope."

What a couple of clowns. With them working my case, my goose was as good as cooked—like a turkey on Thanksgiving Day.

Small said, "Looks like the broad booked." He shook his head out of disgust.

Or, maybe he shook his head out of frustration. Nah, I'm the one who's frustrated here. They're not. They've already got a fall guy even if they don't find the real killer or killers. Me!

"You're kidding," I said. My jaw dropped, and my hands slid slowly down the cold steel bars.

"Nope," Small answered. "And it looks like she's gone for good."

"Why's that?"

"Because everything of value has been cleaned outta her place." Small glanced at his partner, who gave another slow, agreeing nod.

122

"Probably on a flight to Paris or Tahiti by now," Small went on. "We'll never find out where she went—ever."

Biggs said, "Too bad for your sorry ass, Bowers."

I didn't hear that.

I asked Small, "What about the insurance money?"

They looked at each other like a couple of stooges.

I rolled my eyes. "Well, did she get it yet?"

Another couple of dumb stares.

Man, I was steaming. It was my ass on the line, and these dimwits just stood there like a couple of bobble-head dolls. Imbeciles!

I continued: "Could I suggest you have someone contact the insurance companies and put a hold on their money before Mrs. Kantel leaves the country…that's if it's not too much trouble, Detectives?"

Small jerked his head toward Biggs, who did an about face and left the holding area.

Again, I shook my head in total disgust at the two narrow-minded numbnuts.

Small must have noticed, because he said, "We were just about to do that."

Yeah, sure.

I returned to my bunk, sat down, and buried my head in my hands. I had all I could do to keep my cool. I didn't want to say anything that would tick off the detective. Who knows how the guy would react to an insult—that's if he were capable of recognizing one.

Small remarked, "Maybe she already has the dough from the insurance company."

I raised my head and glared at him. *Don't say anything dumb, Buddy.* "I'm sure it would have been in the form of a cashier's check, Detective Small. There'd be a trail when she cashed it, wouldn't there?"

He nodded in agreement.

"Flash her photograph at the airports and on TV," I suggested. "Someone is sure to spot that blonde bombshell."

"We're already doing that," he said, his eyes shifting to the side.

Another lie. Why can't the guy just say, *"Good idea. Thanks, Buddy."*?

I can see I'm in the wrong line of work. I pick up on the obvious quicker than I thought. Or, maybe it's because they're a little slow. A *little*?

You think Small would take me as a partner?

No, thanks.

It was time to shift gears. I asked Small, "Did Miss Diamond happen to mention anything about her Jeep?"

Another dumb stare from the detective. "Her Jeep? No. What about it?"

"Oh, it's nothing," I said, shrugging. "I think she was having problems getting it started."

Getting it started? Finding all the pieces is more like it.

He asked, "What else don't you think we're doing?"

Man, that's slick. He could have asked what else I thought he *should* be doing. But that's not the man's style—obviously.

"Hey," I said, "**why** don't you get me out of here so I can grab this gal and her pal before they—?"

"Her pal?" he asked, cutting me short.

Uh-oh. Dusty didn't tell him *everything*. I wish she had briefed me on exactly what she told these guys before they got here. Chances of my getting out of jail now were slim and none. None, being more realistic.

I shrugged. "I imagine she had some help. I don't think Mrs. Kantel's strong enough to have handled those two brutes—Hans and Harry—do you?"

He scratched his balding head again. "She probably had some help," he said, nodding at his astute observation. "Couldn't do it alone, I'm sure."

"Boy, you're correct about that, Detective. You're right on top of things, aren't you?"

Man, my nose was so far up this guy's butt right now I couldn't stand myself. But, hey, I'll do just about anything to get out of this place—even if it means kissing his hairy duff. Yuck!

But think about it: The detectives really haven't done a darned thing except follow our leads. And, unless Dusty and I come up with something, these two dumbbells will be there at the end of the day with their palms raised in total bewilderment. Like—*well, we did the best we could.*

Right. And I'll be swinging in a rope necktie.

Man, I hope Small doesn't hide behind that badge of his again. I really have to get out of here—fast.

"You know," Small said, nodding slowly, "I think we've got enough for me to go to the DA and see if we can get you released under my recognizance."

About friggin' time, Detective. I thought that's what you were going to do days ago.

"Great idea," I said with a fake smile. "Wish I had thought of it."

He stared at me for a moment, then turned away.

I returned to my position at the bars. "Maybe I can be of some help," I hollered.

"Uh-huh," he mumbled as he waddled away.

As I watched Detective Small leaving, I glanced at the tiny window that was about eight feet off the floor and covered with iron bars. I was glad I had a window and was

125

able to look outside and see the sky and white billowy clouds and the birds and things. It made me feel kind of free. Not really emancipated but not totally cooped up either. Does that make sense?

Anyway, I couldn't see any birds today. It was raining outside. It hadn't rained in quite a while. Been a hot and dry autumn, so the rain was really needed. Indian Summer, I think they call it. Whatever. The rain made me feel kind of gloomy and depressed. You know how dark, rainy days can do that to you. I hate to get depressed. I wished I didn't have a window to look out.

I turned my attention to the disappearing detective. I wondered what he was going to do. I couldn't count on him for anything. I had to think of what to do either way: if I got out...or if I remained in jail.

Remained?

Ouch!

TWENTY-TWO

Detective Small finally did something smart for a change: He got me out of the slammer. I should thank him, but I think when it's all said and done, he's the one who will be doing the thanking.

Dusty picked me up in front of the vine-choked brick jailhouse. She was driving Daddy's car: an old rusted, yellow Ford station wagon. It made Dusty's dusty Jeep look showroom clean. Boxes of papers cluttered the entire rear storage area, which was probably a blessing. God only knows what lurked beneath all that stuff.

However, the wagon ran okay, and it sure as hell beat walking. But it wasn't a pretty sight. Don't see many of those old wagons around anymore, especially in our group. Most of us drive minivans—better for golf trips. Oops! There I go again with another lousy golf outing reminder. I have to stop doing that.

Anyway, I told Dusty to head straight to the Huntsville airport. I figured that would be the quickest way Kantel's wife could get out of the state—and the country, for that matter. The airport at Gunter had only a few small private planes, so I took a chance she wouldn't bother with them. She had clear sailing now, and chartering a private plane might attract unnecessary attention. So the larger airport at Huntsville with flights scheduled out every day would be her easiest and safest way to leave. That's a chance Dusty and I had to take.

We still hadn't heard whether the insurance companies determined if Mrs. Kantel was married to Hans when he was killed and whether she had gotten any of the settlement money. I think the insurance folks were stalling the detectives. Waiting for a warrant, maybe. However, that was a problem for the detectives, not for us to get involved in. Our job was to make sure Mrs. Kantel didn't leave the area without a few questions being answered.

Daddy had found out Marilyn Kantel drove a silver Jaguar, Alabama license MK V12. Daddy sure gets a lot done from a hospital bed, doesn't he?

Dusty and I floated Daddy's *boat* into the airport parking lot. The Jag would be easy to spot at an airport the size of Huntsville's. I mean, Huntsville's airport is pretty big, but it's nothing compared to those in Chicago or New York or Los Angeles. Anyway, the point is—there aren't too many shiny new silver Jags in the Huntsville area, period.

We drove around the lot but didn't see Kantel's car. I told Dusty to swing around again.

Nothing.

"Damnit!" I said more to myself than to Dusty. "I was so darned positive she would come to this airport." I slapped the leather dash, and dust—more like sand from a desert windstorm—billowed from beneath my palm.

Dusty raised a calming hand. "Easy, Mr. B. She may have taken a taxi…or gotten a ride with a friend."

Dusty was right. I took a deep relaxing breath—of dust.

"Sorry for the dang dust," she said. "You'd think it'd be gone with all the rain we've had. I mean, it rained cats and rats, for gosh sakes."

I think it's cats and dogs, sweetheart.

She continued: "Or, maybe they came in his car."

My head snapped toward her. "They? His?"

"Yep." She nodded once. "The guy dressed in black I told you about—Blackie."

"Oh, yeah," I managed, trying to clear the dust from my throat. "I'll bet he drives a black SUV or van." I scanned the lot for something big and black.

Dusty shook her head no. "Nah…a big black pickup would be more his style."

It didn't matter: no black SUV or black pickup or black van. Nothing like that was parked in the lot.

Dusty asked, "What do you want me to do?"

"Anchor this boat, and we'll check inside the terminal."

Dusty swung the Ford wagon into a space. Well, actually, *two* spaces. And we hurried into the terminal. I figured if we got to the planes before the passengers boarded, we might get lucky and spot the conspicuous blonde beauty. Not a problem: It would be like hiding a vanilla wafer in a box of Oreos.

However, in our haste, there's one thing we forgot about: the security check. I just about panicked when I saw the line of people waiting to be searched. "Damnit!" I said, not so quietly this time.

Dusty raised a cautioning hand. "Don't attract attention," she whispered.

I nodded my concurrence, but it sure irked me that I hadn't thought about it sooner. Darn it! How could I have forgotten something as important as that? I'm losing it, I guess.

We got in line and impatiently waited our turn. I was anxious—no, fearful—Mrs. Kantel would get away before we got through the gate. However, I didn't want to make a scene and have them strip-search me. Now I would have been a little more patient if they were in the process of strip-searching Mrs. Kantel, the buxom blonde. Uh-huh.

No such luck, so I remained cool and calm like Dusty suggested.

When we got to the guard, an Afro-American (the size of an NFL tight end) asked for our boarding passes. Dusty explained that we were not boarding but were looking for someone.

He raised a halting hand. "Gotta have a boarding pass to get through," he said in a low voice. "No exceptions."

No exceptions. Great.

Dusty pulled the guy aside and said something to him. I figured she was telling him she was some kind of police official who was investigating a murder case, and she suspected the killer was attempting to escape via airplanes. Or something like that.

He asked to see some sort of identification. She withdrew her PI license, or whatever the heck it was, from her shoulder bag and showed it to him. He nodded his okay, and she tossed her bag onto the conveyor belt that led to the X-ray machine. Thank God.

I stepped behind Dusty and was about to follow her through the metal-detecting doughnut ring when the huge guard grabbed my arm.

"Just her," he growled.

"But I'm with her and—"

"No exceptions," he repeated. His tenacious glare said he wasn't kidding.

No exceptions? No exceptions? Didn't he just make a damned exception for Dusty? Man!

I was about to yell instructions to Dusty, but she was already down the concourse and out of sight. It didn't matter. She knew what to do. Plus, she saw the two of them at Kantel's house, so she would have no trouble identifying Mrs. Kantel and the guy dressed in black.

I doubled back to the gift shop, bought a magazine and found an empty seat. I made sure my line of sight was clear in case Dusty and her entourage came running down the long corridor.

Her *entourage*?

Yikes!

TWENTY-THREE

I finished the magazine, stood up, stretched my legs and arms, and yawned about as wide as humanly possible. It had been more than half an hour since Dusty went into the boarding area. What was keeping that girl? All sorts of thoughts rambled through my mind: Maybe she spotted Marilyn Kantel and Blackie, and airport security was detaining all three. Or, maybe Dusty had to board a plane to check the passengers who had already gotten on. Or, maybe she spotted them and was chasing them all around the place. Who knows?

Hell, the security guards may have Dusty locked up by now. Heaven forbid.

I approached the black security guard. You know— *Mr. No Exceptions.*

He raised his hand to stop me.

"I'm *not* trying to get through," I explained. "I just want to know what happened to my…my partner."

He glanced down the long hallway then back at me. "Maybe she took a flight somewhere."

Well, when do you expect her back, smartass?

I said, "I don't think so." I really fought the urge to roll my eyes. "Is there any way possible you could radio the terminal to see if she's in need of assistance?"

He nodded yes but didn't leave his post. Didn't do a thing as a matter of fact.

I said, "Well?"

"Don't have no radio."

Now I rolled my eyes. "Anyone around here have one?"

"Why don't you use the white courtesy phone over there?" he suggested, pointing over my shoulder.

Good thinking, wiseass. He must have gotten his training from Detective Small. I hurried to the telephone and had Dusty paged.

It wasn't ten seconds before she was on the line. "Yeah?" was all she said.

"Dusty, what's keeping you? What the hell are you doing in there? Any sign of them?"

I knew that was a lot of questions to throw at her, but I was a bit excited and frustrated and anxious. Besides, I knew she wasn't like Detective Small: Her brain could cipher through all that and more if it had to.

"Nope. No sign of 'em," she said. "No buxom blonde. No guy in black. In fact, nothin' close to their description."

"Well, what the hell's taking you so—?"

She cut me short: "I'm at the computer with the desk clerk. We're checkin' manifests for today's flights and those for the past several days. We're even checkin' reservations for the next week or so."

I never thought of doing that. I felt like a heel for getting on her case like I had just done.

"Any luck with the manifests?" I asked in as pleasant a voice as I could manage.

"Not yet. No Mrs. Kantel...or Marilyn Kantel."

"Damnit!" I huffed.

"No sense gettin' tight-assed about it Mr. B. We're still checkin' it out, you know."

"I'm not getting tight-assed about it," I yelled into the phone.

"Sounds like yer gettin' tight-assed to me."

133

I wasn't getting tight-assed—just concerned. Did I sound like I was getting tight-assed?

"Hold on a minute," said Dusty. "I see someone who looks kinda suspicious."

"Why's that?" I asked. I found myself glancing around as if I might also see someone suspicious. Paranoid?

"She looks nervous," said Dusty in a soft voice. "Keeps lookin' around…like she thinks somebody may be followin' her or somethin'."

"Anything else?"

"She smells of money—fine clothes, a lot of expensive-looking jewelry, and tons of fancy carry-on stuff—a real highfalutin hussy, I'd say."

"Anyone with her?"

"Nope. All by her lonesome. Whoops! She's gettin' in line to board—first class. I told you she smelled of money."

"She blonde?"

"Nope."

"No? Then why are you wasting your time following her?"

"Because she's—"

I cut her off: "Well, at least see if you can get her name and where she's heading, Dusty. Dusty? Hello?"

I slammed the receiver into the holder. Damn that girl anyway. Maybe I should have spent the extra grand a day and gotten someone who knew what the hell he or she was doing, for Pete's sake!

Now I sounded tight-assed.

I started back to the chairs again when I glanced down the corridor and glimpsed Dusty running toward me. Nobody was chasing her, so I had no idea what it was all about.

134

When she got close, Dusty slowed to a fast walk and took several deep breaths. She adjusted the bag on her shoulder and flicked some strands of red hair from her green eyes. "What did yer girl look like?" she gasped, groping at my arm.

"What girl is that?"

"The one at the motel," she said with an impatient huff, "and at the pool!"

"I told you, Dusty...a shapely brunette with chocolate brown eyes."

Dusty sucked in a deep breath. "Pretty...with long legs, nice butt and full-figured?"

I shrugged my shoulders. "I guess," I said with little conviction. "I was half-bagged, if you remember."

"Silicone?"

"What?" I asked, pinching my eyebrows together.

"Boob-job, damnit?"

"Damn, Dusty. How would I know something like that? I'm really not the kind of guy who—"

"You said you had to shove her off of you, right?"

I had told her that, but I didn't share anything about Lynn not having her blouse on, nor did I tell her about having my hands full of Lynn's chest. How does this girl pick up on these things anyway? Women.

I nodded while my brain sorted things out. "Yeah," I said slowly.

"Was she extra firm...or normal?"

I could feel my face reddening. "Gee, Dusty. I was too much out of it to notice if—"

She raised a halting palm. "Okay. Okay," she said rapidly. "Didn't you say she was floatin' on her backside in the pool?"

"Well...yeah."

"Did she look like she was wearin'...like...an orange vest?"

"She wasn't wearing a vest...or anything, for that matter."

"That's not what I meant," she said, rolling her eyes in frustration. "Did she look like her chest had...had two floatin' oranges?"

Floating oranges? That was a tough one. Really.

All I remember was being nervous as a cat on a pancake griddle and glancing around for someone...anyone ...except the naked girl swimming around the pool. It was hard to keep my eyes off her, but I do recall doing my best not to look. Well, at least not to stare or to take mental notes.

I said, "I really don't know, Dusty. It was very dark that night. No moon; and the lights were—"

"Thank, damnit!" she snapped, grabbing the front of my shirt. "Thank, man!"

I cracked a grin. "Now who's getting tight-assed?"

She released my shirt but didn't return the grin. "Will you quit jerkin' around and answer my damn question, fer godsake?" She straightened my shirt and glanced toward the planes. "We're runnin' outta time here."

I finally answered about the oranges: "I guess she did, Dusty." I raked my fingers through my hair. "Yeah, now that I think back, a helluva lot of her was sticking out of the water."

"Bingo!" she said, smacking her hands together. "That's her, damnit!" She nodded sharply while looking down the concourse. "Yep, we've got her fancy ass!"

"Who?" I asked, also looking in the direction of the planes. "You said there was no blonde, or Mrs. Kantel, at the boarding area."

She faced me. "I'm not talkin' about no blonde, damnit!" She grabbed my arm and dragged me toward the ticket counter. "It's yer brown-eyed brunette friend—Lynn!"

LYNN???

"Lynn?" I asked, my eyes about as large as they could possibly get. "How can you be sure it's Lynn?"

"Gut feelin'."

"Gut feeling?"

"Yep," replied Dusty, nodding. "That...plus the fact the dumb bitch is usin' the name Lynn Smith."

My face crinkled into a perplexed expression. "Lynn Thomas is Lynn Smith?"

"No, Lynn Smith is Lynn Thomas."

Oh?

TWENTY-FOUR

As Dusty and I rushed toward the ticket counter, I wondered what the connection was between my mysterious lovable Lynn "Thomas" and Mrs. Kantel. Friends? Lovers? Associates? Partners in crime?

I was stumped. All sorts of scenarios buzzed through my brain. Some I didn't even want to think about. But once I got past those thoughts, things seemed a little easier to puzzle out: Lynn could have been a friend of the guy in black whom Dusty had seen. And Mrs. Kantel could have hired him and Lynn to kill her husband and make it look like I did it. But what really bugged me was why they also killed Hans Kantel. That gave me a rock-solid alibi, for crying out loud.

That just didn't add up—unless the killers suspected Hans of telling me something about them and their operation. The blonde secretary did see us talking to Hans; and if she were, in fact, Mrs. Kantel...well, it would then all add up—I think. The three of them—Lynn, Blackie and Mrs. Kantel—knew we had been in Hans' office; and they most likely guessed it was Dusty *and* me prowling around his house. So when Hans bought the farm, they would naturally expect the cops to come to me... especially if the threesome figured I had no alibi, for crying out loud. I **was** out on bail at the time, if you recall.

And that sorta made sense, because it had all happened so damned fast: *Mutt and Jeff* had my ass back behind bars before anyone, including the media, knew what had happened.

Yeah, I'll bet the treacherous trio had it all planned out, and they knew Hans' murder would also be pinned on me. But Dusty and I now have the upper hand: We know what they're up to and have them in **our** sights.

Gotcha, Blondie.

"Get us two tickets to Atlanta," said Dusty, breaking my chain of thought. "I gotta call Daddy."

My eyes widened with her startling outburst. I turned to her. "Atlanta?"

Dusty nodded. "That's where she's headin', for starters. Could fly anywhere from there: New York, Europe…anywhere."

I stopped in my tracks.

Dusty also stopped walking. "What?" she asked, raising her palms.

I shook my head in frustration. "I can't leave the Huntsville area," I said. "Detective Small will—"

"Screw him. Get the damn tickets."

I threw up my hands. "If we were absolutely positive it was the same Lynn…or even Kantel's wife, I might take a chance, Dusty. But if it's just a wild goose chase, that damned Detective Small will think I've jumped bail and—"

She cut me short and rolled those gorgeous green eyes again. I didn't know if it was out of frustration or revulsion. Whatever it was, she definitely didn't look very happy.

"Just get one for me then," she said, shaking her head again. "That's what the hell yer payin' me for."

Seems like I've heard that before.

"Okay," I finally relented. "Don't get your undies all knotted up over it."

139

"My undies ain't gettin' knotted up, damnit!" she said, pinching her eyebrows together. "And besides, what my undies are doin' ain't none of yer goldarn business."

I wish you could see those once-beautiful green eyes of hers right now. They're like lacerating laser beams piercing deep into my soul. If looks could kill, I'd be in the morgue—or well on my way.

"All right," I said, "I'll get you a ticket."

"And hurry, damnit!" she yelled over her shoulder as she hurried back to the boarding area to keep an eye on Lynn.

"Yes, ma'am," I said, saluting with two fingers.

However, she didn't see or hear me. She was practically out of sight before I could lower my hand.

I rushed to the ticket counter and told the clerk I needed a ticket on the same flight Lynn Smith had boarded. The clerk informed me the flight was full and that it was about to leave the gate. There was no way to stop the plane, even when I told the clerk at the ticket counter it was a police emergency. Of course, that only works if you've got a badge—which I didn't.

Therefore, I got a ticket for Dusty on the *next* flight to Atlanta, which left in two hours. That's right, two long wasted hours. I couldn't wait to hear Dusty's reaction when I gave her the news. Heaven help me.

Dusty came charging back with her bag flopping on her back. It looked like she was in a hurry—like maybe she actually expected to get on the same flight as Lynn. Sorry, Dusty.

She sucked in a deep breath. "Get the ticket?"

"Want the good news or the bad news?"

She didn't answer. Just cocked an eyebrow.

I skipped the bad news. I figured that was the wisest thing to do under the present circumstances. Hey, I'm no wimp, but why bring on more of the kid's wrath, when there was nothing either of us could do to get her on that same flight, right?

Isn't it funny how such a pip-squeak of a kid—like Dusty—can make a grown man—like me—cringe and cower? And, not ha-ha funny either.

I waved the ticket in front of her.

"First class, right?" she asked, reaching for the envelope.

Now that was ha-ha funny—to me, that is.

It was my turn to cock an eyebrow.

"Never mind, damnit!" she said, shaking her head in disgust. "Give me the damn thang." She snatched the ticket from my hand. "Tight ass."

She said that under her breath, but I still managed to read her lips. If she was disgusted now, wait until she finds out the ticket's for a later flight. God help me.

"Here take these," she said, handing me her cell phone and the keys to Daddy's station wagon.

I studied the buttons on the tiny instrument.

She asked, "Ever use one of those before?"

"Of course," I said, pretending to be insulted. "What kind of dummy do you think I am, anyway?"

"Do you honestly want me to answer that?"

I just stared at her.

"Didn't thank so," she said.

I was thinking of something smart to say, but she didn't give me the chance.

"I gotta run," she said, shoving the bag around to her back. "Keep that damn phone handy so I can contact you whenever I need to."

"Where's your pistol?" I shouted as she got absorbed into the crowd. I immediately looked around to see if anyone had heard.

141

Oh-oh. That little outburst got all kinds of weird looks. Wouldn't you be a little concerned if you heard something like that just before you boarded an airplane? I certainly would.

I glanced around, half-expecting to see that huge security guard approaching. He'd have me on the floor within seconds if he had heard.

"Left it in the car," Dusty hollered, jumping up and down so we could see each other. "Knew I couldn't get it through security."

Great! More piercing stares.

Screw 'em, as Dusty would say.

"Good luck," I shouted to her.

I don't know if I meant good luck to her or to myself. You see, I would need all the luck I could muster—and then some—when Dusty found out she wasn't on Lynn's flight, and that her flight—Dusty's—didn't leave for two more hours. The decision now was for me to wait for Dusty to come charging back and take it like a man...or leave while the leaving was good. I thought hard about it until she was out of sight—then I booked.

Hey, she's a big girl. Well, she's not big physically, but she sure as hell has a sharp tongue. That's an understatement. Wonder where she gets that?

Anyway, for a little shaver, she seems to know her way around, right? And who knows, Lynn's flight might be delayed; and Dusty might still get a seat on it.

And, it could rain lollipops too.

But really, if anyone could stop that plane and find a way to get aboard, it would be Dusty Diamond.

142

TWENTY-FIVE

I started the boat—Daddy's station wagon, that is. Blue smoke curled from under the engine. It smelled like an orange grove's smoldering smudge-pot. The blue-gray cloud didn't last long; it quickly dissipated into the hazy humid Alabama air. And another good thing—the wagon didn't blow up. So I had that going for me. Which is nice. Especially after what Dusty and I had been through with our cars lately.

I had the sudden urge to call Detective Small and tell him what Dusty was doing. However, that brainless impulse quickly passed. I can't begin to imagine how I let that thought cross my mind. God only knows what that dimwit would do at this point. And, one thing for certain, I definitely didn't want him to toss my ass in jail again. Nosiree.

A visit to Daddy Diamond might prove valuable, since I hadn't the slightest clue as to what to do next. Maybe that wouldn't be a good idea either: Once I told him I had put his darling daughter in harm's way and at the mercy of a killer…or two…or three…who knows what the guy would do? But what in the world could I have done about stopping her? Once that gal got her mind made up about doing something, get the hell out of her way because she would run over, around or through you if you tried to stop her. I'll tell you one thing—which you may have already noticed by now—for a smallish girl, she sure has a huge set of *cojones*.

Anyway, Daddy would be the one I would go to for advice. Somehow or other, I'd think of something to smooth things over. After all, the guy's laid up in the hospital; and he's probably short, fat and balding. I could handle someone like that—I think.

Daddy had his back to me and was staring out the window when I entered his room.

OOPS!

I had to back out of the room and look at the number on the door to make sure I had the right guy. Daddy was not at all like I had pictured. From my angle, all I could see was the back of his head, which was covered with reddish-brown hair—thicker than Grandma's floor-mop. And that fuzz-covered head was resting on shoulders as wide as Harry Thomas' had been.

He must have heard me shuffling around, because he turned to face me. Wow! What a surprise. He was handsome, about forty-five, a full mustache, dark suntan, and his blue-green eyes sparkled from the glint of the afternoon sun.

I had second thoughts about being there, especially when I had to tell him about Dusty's latest adventure. I had to think of something quick. But that could be a problem. As I said, I have trouble lying.

"Not another goddamn doctor!" was how he greeted me.

I forced a smile. "Nope. I'm Buddy Bowers, your daughter's—"

He cut me off: "Our damn client," he said, struggling to sit up higher. "It's about goddamn time I got to meet cha, dadgumit!" He thrust out a massive hand, which was attached to an even nastier-looking forearm with bulging biceps.

144

I took his hand and tried not to show how much pain I was suffering when he squeezed—no, crushed—my fingers. "Good to meet you too," I said, easing my swollen hand from the vice. "Dusty's had nothing but great things to say about you. And you've been quite a help solving the case from what she tells me."

He stared at me for a moment before saying. "Let's cut through the bullshit and get down to the nut-cuttin', okay?"

I nodded. What else could I do?

"Okaaay," I said.

"Pull up a damn chair," he ordered, waving an arm…the one without the IV tube hanging from it.

I did just that.

"Fill me in," he said, his eyes narrowing. "Have you caught the bastards yet?"

"Not yet. But we're close."

"Close in our business means no, so I guess yer fulla horseshit and jist blowin' smoke up my—"

"Not exactly, sir," I said, cutting him off. "We're pretty sure we know who did it, and we're following one of them right now."

He cocked an eyebrow. "What the hell's with this *we* crap?" he barked. "Half of *we* is sittin' here in front of me, goddamnit!" He glanced toward the door. "Why the hell ain't Dusty here with you? She's supposed to be keepin' me posted, damnit!" His glaring blue-green lasers returned to me. "Where the hell is she, anyway?"

Think, Buddy. Think.

"As I said, we…I mean she…is following one of them as we speak."

"Sumbitch!" he bellowed. "Which one, fer Crissake?"

"You familiar with the—?"

145

He interrupted me by saying, "Of course I am." He disgustedly rolled his blue-green eyes and shook his head with disdain. "Who the hell you thank's been steerin' this goddamn ship, anyway?"

He was obviously a no-nonsense type of guy. It's easy to see where Dusty gets her tenacity and persistence. Like she said: *a chip off the old block.*

I said, "I know Dusty's been briefing you, but I didn't know exactly how much—"

"Briefin' me?"

It doesn't look like I'm going to finish a sentence with this guy either, does it?

He pulled the covers off his legs. He was obviously heating up. "Hell, I'm the one who's been tellin' her what to do all along. Cain't rely on a senseless half-wit like you…kin we now?"

I pulled back slightly and said, "Excuse me, but—"

"And I say that with deepest respect 'cause yer our damn client. But it's quite obvious that's what you are…or you wouldn't be in the damn fix yer in fer doin' all those dumb things. Am I right or what, numbnuts?"

His stare melted my contacts.

Did he say "with deepest respect"?

Huh.

I started to say, "Well, I wouldn't—"

"Which one, damnit?"

I gave him a dumb look.

"Which one she followin', damnit?"

"The brunette, Lynn," I retorted. "She's going by the name of Lynn Smith."

He smiled wide. "Hope you weren't gullible enough to buy inta that crap."

I shook my head no. "We don't know what her actual name is. Don't even know if Lynn is her—"

"It ain't."

Man that caught me by surprise. I'm the one who's been looking at that Lynn person face-to-face, and I hadn't come up with that quick of an evaluation. Is this guy psychic or something?

He fidgeted in the bed. "Where the hell's Dusty? I told that gal to keep checkin' in with me, damnit!"

"I'm sure she'll be doing so shortly," I said, getting to my feet. "She's quite reliable."

"Humph!" he snorted.

My feet inched toward the door. "I hate to run, but I've got to brief the detective on what we've got so far."

"Which detective?"

"Detective Small."

"From Gunter?"

"Yeah," I replied, nodding. "One and the same."

His eyes rolled again. "Sheeeit!"

TWENTY-SIX

I couldn't get out of that hospital room fast enough. I wanted to ask Daddy Diamond how he knew *Lynn* wasn't Lynn's real name, but to be perfectly honest; I just didn't have the nerve...or backbone...or whatever. The guy was simply too much for me—too overwhelming, or too overbearing, or too damned something. You know the type.

I tell you, being in that hospital room with Mr. Diamond was worse than being in jail and being interrogated by Detective Small. Well, maybe not quite—but close. Very close.

While I was driving to my motel, the cell phone rang. It was Dusty, of course. I had to spend five minutes listening to her scream at me for not letting her know she wouldn't be on the same flight as Lynn Smith. There was no sense trying to explain, so I didn't bother try. I simply let her ramble on until she ran out of steam. When she finished, I said, "I'm sorry."

"**Sorry?**" she screamed. "That's the best you can come up with—**sorry?** Do you have any idea what I've had to go through here in Atlanta, Bowers? Of course you don't. How the heck could you? Yer there, and I'm here. And I'm the one runnin' around like a chicken with no neck, damnit!"

"Calm down, Dusty."

"I'm not ready to calm down. I'll let you know when I'm ready to calm down. I'm real mad, and yer gonna hear me out, damnit!"

"Go ahead, kid. It's your phone."

"Yeah," she huffed and puffed, "and yer the one who's gonna pay the dang bill too."

Can't you just picture her green eyes glaring and her red hair spiraling out of sight? Funny. Well, that's easy for me to say because I'm here, and she's there. If she were here with me, it wouldn't be so humorous. Well, it might be, but I wouldn't let on to it, because she would whack me with that shoulder bag of hers.

There was a long pause, so I guess she had let off enough steam to start talking coherently. "Any luck?" I asked in a calm voice.

"More than you can believe."

She sounded a little more rational now. I might go as far as to say…friendly?

I asked, "How's that, Dusty?"

"You were probably too dang busy scrammin' outta the airport to notice; but mine was a direct flight, while hers had to make a stop."

I smiled and could sense her doing the same. "So I guess you both got there about the same time, huh?"

"Pretty close," she said in a civil tone. "Lynn's flight got in about twenty minutes before mine. However, she was still waitin' for her luggage when I arrived."

"Guess we finally had some good luck, huh?"

"Luck had little to do with it," she said, sounding a little aggravated. "I about broke my ankle runnin' down those damn moving stairs to the baggage claim area. Didn't want the bitch leavin' the airport before I got to her."

They're called escalators, Dusty.

I said, "I'm surprised she had luggage, especially with all the carry-on stuff you said she had."

"Oh, she's got a ton of stuff all right. I thank the carry-on thangs were the high-value items—jewelry, jade, junk."

Junk?

I asked Dusty, "Is she booked on a flight overseas?"

"I didn't have time to check at the airport. Had to hurry to get a taxi to stay with her. But I can do that by phone from the hotel."

"You staying at the same place?"

"Yep. I'm in the lobby keepin' an eye on thangs. Don't want that Lynn gal goin' anywhere without my nose two steps from her dancin' duff."

"Good thinking, kid."

"Hold on a sec."

"What's going on, Dusty?"

"Omigod!" she blurted into the phone. "Damn! You won't believe this, Mr. B."

"What?"

"They're *both* here."

"Who?"

"Lynn Smith and Mrs. Kantel!"

"What? How do you know that, Dusty? They together?"

"Not really. But I followed Lynn into the place. Boy, is this place ever fancy. It's like—"

I hated to cut her short, but she really had my interest piqued, and I needed to know more about what the hell was happening. The description of the plush hotel could wait.

"Dusty!" I said in a harried voice. "Dusty, what the hell's going on there?"

I felt blind as a bat. I kept looking at the cell phone, thinking—like an idiot—that I might be able to see what

150

Dusty was looking at. I wished she had one of those photo-phones, then she could have shown me what she saw.

"What do you see, Dusty?"

"I see Mrs. Kantel. That's what I see."

"The blue-eyed buxom blonde?"

"None other, Mr. B."

"You're kidding?"

"Nope."

"What the heck is Mrs. Kantel doing there?"

"Beats me," Dusty replied. "Musta entered the dang hotel when I was dialin' you. Guess this is where they planned to meet up."

"Well, what's Mrs. Kantel doing now...at this moment?"

"She's at another phone in the lobby," replied Dusty. "Probably makin' airline reservations to Europe...or she could be talkin' to that Lynn gal upstairs...and makin' plans for their next move."

"So, they're in it together, huh?"

"Yep."

"They probably had your guy in black do in Harry Thomas at the pool," I speculated. "And, Blackie most likely killed Hans Kantel and set the fires to create a diversion."

"More likely fer the insurance money," Dusty suggested.

"That's right, kid. Might as well collect on the business as well as on the guys."

"Yer lucky you didn't end up in the dang pool also, Mr. B."

"Nah. They needed a fall guy. Someone to take the rap for them. And I was that guy. Actually, they had to see that nothing happened to me. Nothing fatal, that is."

151

"You just happened to be the poor schmuck who came along at the wrong time...and they set a trap fer yer dumb ass."

Schmuck? Dumb ass? Sounds a bit like Daddy, doesn't it? I thought I was the client here. Sheesh!

I said, "Looks that way, I'm ashamed to say."

"Yep, and you fell fer it hook, line and anchor."

"I think it's *sinker*, Dusty."

"Whatever."

"Well, don't let them leave the country," I ordered. "If they do, we'll never see them again. And once they're gone, Detective Small won't bother to look any further...and I'll be hanging from the highest hickory in Huntsville."

"Hey, Blondie's on the move," Dusty said in a panic. "Gotta go. Gotta get some help. This is too dang much fer one person to cover."

"Dusty, I can't afford another investigative firm... especially one from Atlanta. They're way too expensive, Dusty. Dusty? Hello, Dusty?"

Damn her!

TWENTY-SEVEN

Dusty slapped the phone into its cradle and zipped through the hotel lobby toward the revolving doors at the main entrance. She was in one hell of a hurry in the pursuit of Mrs. Kantel, and heaven help anyone who got in her way. However, there was a matter of some revolving doors to negotiate. Dusty detested them because they gave her the feeling she was whirling around in a washing machine that was stuck on the spin cycle. The doors not only made her nervous and nauseous, but she also became quite claustrophobic when trapped inside the circular monsters.

When she got to the revolving doors, Dusty stepped to the side and attempted to exit through the swinging glass door. However, a tall and lanky bellhop was pulling a clothes rack/luggage carrier into the hotel and had the door blocked. She went this way and that, but he seemed to dance right along with her. Somehow, in the middle of all this wriggling about, the bellhop managed to get the wheels twisted sideways; and the cart wedged itself in the middle of the opening.

"Damnit!" Dusty snapped in a low huff.

The bellhop gave her a stupid grin and shrugged his shoulders like this was the biggest undertaking he'd ever been tasked with.

She gave him a disgusted look and turned her attention to the other swinging door on the opposite side of the revolving doors. A stream of people had that door completely jammed. From their hats, banners and other souvenirs, they appeared to be coming from a Braves baseball game. And they didn't look very happy. *The Braves must have lost a crucial game*, Dusty figured.

She wasn't about to buck that mob. No, thank you.

So, it was back to the revolving doors.

Dusty got in line, but when her turn came, she couldn't take that daunting first step. One opening arrived, then another. But her feet remained frozen. People behind her yelled and hollered things that weren't exactly for children's ears.

Suddenly, with the aid of a strong hand from behind, Dusty found herself inside the doors. She turned to see who had done it, but the revolving door slapped against her side and almost knocked her off her feet. She pushed against the curved glass to keep from falling. However, the same partition smacked her again, but this time it propelled her outside. She stumbled and would have fallen onto the sidewalk if it hadn't been for the doorman grabbing her at the last second.

"You all right, Miss?" the doorman asked, lifting her at the waist as if she were a limp rag-doll. She was bent in half, her arms dangling and her red hair dragging on the sidewalk.

Dusty straightened up, got her balance and pushed his hand away. She had no need for his unwanted attention. She attempted to look unfazed and dignified.

Anyway, once Dusty composed herself, she glanced around for Mrs. Kantel. She looked in one direction then the other. Nothing.

Dusty turned to the doorman, who was now signaling a taxi. She knew she had to eat crow, but he was her only hope. "Sir?" she said in a calm tone.

He turned to her but immediately jerked his head away as if she wasn't there. Now just because she snubbed the guy doesn't give him the right to do the same to her, does it?

"Bastard!" she said under her breath.

He opened the door to a taxi and helped a couple get into it.

Dusty approached the doorman. "Excuse me, sir," she said in a firmer voice.

This time when he turned to her, all he noticed was the ten-dollar-bill she had folded in her extended hand.

"Yes?" he said, accepting the money. A wide smile spread across his lips. "What can I do for you, Miss?"

Yep, money talks.

Dusty asked, "Did you happen to see a buxom blonde come outta the hotel a few minutes ago?" Dusty's head was turning back and forth, as she scanned the crowd.

"Excuse me?"

Dusty turned back to him. "Did you...?"

That's when she noticed what he meant.

Hello.

At least ten buxom blondes were standing in front of the hotel at that very moment.

Atlanta.

"Damnit!" she uttered, a bit louder this time.

She jammed her hands into her hips and glared at the dispassionate doorman, who simply shrugged and turned away.

That's all you get for ten bucks, I guess.

When she finished letting the doorman have a nonverbal piece of her mind, Dusty stomped back into the hotel—through the *swinging* door this time. She scurried to the front desk, flashed her identification and asked if she could see the register. "Official business," she informed the clerk, tucking away her PI license.

A "You've-got-to-be-kidding-me grin" was what she got instead of the hotel register.

Another smartass. Is this town full of these or what?

"Look, I really need to reach a Mrs. Kantel," Dusty said in a pleading tone. "It's a bit of an emergency, you see."

The clerk—a handsome dark-haired, blue-eyed lad of about 25—folded his arms at his chest and slowly shook his head from side to side.

"How about Lynn Smith?" asked Dusty, whisking away a few red strands from her face as she batted her eyelashes. "Did she register here?"

The clerk did nothing. Said nothing. Nothing.

"Up yours!" breathed Dusty as she turned away. She wondered what to do next. A call to Daddy might be prudent.

She headed toward the telephones; however, before she got twenty paces, the same bellhop who had the cart wedged in the lobby doors stepped in front of her. He flashed a grin similar to what he had shown her earlier.

Dusty shook her head in disgust. *Not again.*

She was about to tell him she didn't have time for any more of his fun and games, when he said, "I happened to overhear what you were saying to the desk clerk."

Dusty perked up like a baby bird waiting to be fed. Her eyes widened and fluttered. "Oh, is that so?"

"Yeah," he said, jerking his head in the direction of the front desk. "Kurt there, well he's a real stickler when it comes to rules and regulations."

Dusty looked over her shoulder at Kurt, who was occupied with a guest. "He sure the hell is," agreed Dusty, turning back to the bellhop.

"I'm Ronnie," he said, taking off his red bellhop cap and holding out his hand.

156

She accepted his handshake. "Dusty."

"Maybe I can be of some help, Dusty," he said, leading her around the corner and out of Kurt's line of sight.

Sorry, Ronnie, I'm running low on tens.

She flashed him her best smile. "You might, Ronnie." She started to open her handbag.

He held up a halting hand. "No. That won't be necessary."

What's it gonna cost me? What you see...ain't what yer gonna get, Ronnie Boy.

She smiled and said, "Now, that's refreshing, Ronnie. Everyone 'round here seems to have his damn hand out."

"Well, that's how we make our living, you know."

She nodded her understanding. "Uh-huh."

He continued: "But you look like you're in a bit of a dilemma...and maybe I had something to do with it when I got that cart jammed in the doorway earlier. Besides, I owe that idiot Kurt."

Really? Well, whacha gonna do about it, Ronnie?

He went on: "Tell me the name of the person you're after, and maybe I can get the room number."

"You'd do that for me, Ronnie?"

"Sure," he said, nodding. "Maybe we could have dinner and go to a movie...or something."

Dusty flashed him a coy grin. "Maybe."

Dusty gave him both names: Lynn Smith and Mrs. Hans Kantel.

Ronnie told her where to wait, put his cap back on and disappeared.

While she waited, Dusty wondered what that *or something* might be after their dinner and a movie.

Lots of luck, Ron.

157

TWENTY-EIGHT

It couldn't have been two minutes before Ronnie—the bellhop—returned from the office. He told Dusty there was no Lynn Smith registered; however, he did have the key to Mrs. Kantel's room. Dusty didn't need a key, but she didn't tell him that. There are some things a private investigator should keep to herself, if you follow.

They rode the shiny brass and rich-walnut elevator to the ninth floor; and after allowing Dusty to get out, Ronnie led the way on the blue-and-gold carpet to Mrs. Kantel's room. He knocked on the door and waited.

A slurry of thoughts sloshed through Dusty's mind: What if she had missed Mrs. Kantel returning to the room? Or, what if Lynn was in there? Or worse yet—Blackie? Omigod!

When no one answered after the third series of knocks, Ronnie unlocked and opened the door slightly. He yelled in, "Room service."

No reply.

That didn't mean Blackie wasn't in there. It simply meant nobody answered the door.

Ronnie turned to her and sheepishly whispered, "Doesn't look like anyone's here." He opened the door all the way and eased into the room on his tiptoes.

Dusty followed, her eyes scanning the room like radar piercing the darkness on a foggy night. Nothing appeared out of the ordinary, so she opened the closet door and gave a cursory glance inside.

Ronnie must have gotten cold feet, because he did a quick about-face and headed toward the door. "I've…I've got to get back to work before I'm missed."

Dusty nodded her understanding and shut the closet door after grabbing a small leather bag off the shelf. She hid it behind her as she turned to Ronnie..

"You can wait here for your friend," he said as he was leaving the room. "But don't tell anyone who let you in. Okay?"

Dusty gave him a sexy smile, then zipped her fingers across her lips. She waited until the door was closed before snooping around further. Nothing seemed to be out of place in the posh room. The paintings hung straight on the walls, and the padded maroon chairs were organized perfectly. Even the large, fluffy white bed was undisturbed. No reading or whatever had occurred on it, so she ambled into the bathroom. The sink was unlike the rest of the place: Things were cluttered all over the white marble top. She picked up some of the items, not sure what to look for.

Suddenly a noise came from the bedroom. She swung around, and the strap on her handbag caught on the bathroom door handle. The heavy wood door slammed shut with a loud *klunk*.

"Damnit!" she hissed after making the attention-getting racket. No doubt, whoever had entered the room must have heard it. Her head swiveled around as she looked for a place to hide. The shower had to be it.

However, before she could lock the door and duck behind the curtain, the doorknob twisted. Was it Mrs. Kantel? Lynn? Or, was it Blackie? Damn; he would do some really bad things if he got to her.

Dusty eased away from the door, reeling back against the marble sink. Her eyes were wide with fright. And fear coursed through her shaking body. Her eyes were

159

attracted to the turning doorknob like moths drawn to a campsite lantern. She reached into her bag for her gun. In her moment of panic, she forgot she had left the thing in her father's car at the Huntsville airport. *Dang!*

No gun. No cell phone. No mace. No nothing.

Her heart thumped like it was about to leap out of her chest. The blood drained from her head. Her face was colorless. Ashen.

The door swung open slowly, and Dusty's hand involuntarily flew to her lips. The fingers of her other hand clawed at the marble sink behind her.

Ronnie poked his head into the bathroom. "I get off at six," he said with a mischievous grin.

Damn you, Ronnie!

Dusty stealthily sucked in a deep calming breath. She didn't want him to see her in an overwrought state and get suspicious as to why she was in Mrs. Kantel's room. After taking another reassuring breath, she forced a smile and calmly said, "Um…six it is."

He nodded, returned her smile and departed—again.

She waited a moment, then swung around to check herself in the huge wall-to-wall mirror. As she did, her bag swept the things off the marble sink top. They hit the white floor tiles like marbles dropping in a tin can. *Damnit!* she said under her breath.

Her eyes slowly rose from the items on the floor, and she peered at the handle to make sure no one had heard. The handle didn't turn. All safe—she hoped.

A dull *click* caught Dusty's attention. She grabbed the handle, opened the bathroom door slightly, and peeked out. Nobody was there. Nothing moved. No other sounds. She drew in a deep composing breath. *It must have been Ronnie closing the door on his way out*, was her thought.

She returned her attention to the items scattered on the floor.

Dusty was hurriedly picking up things when she noticed one side of the contact lens case had opened and one of the lenses had fallen out. She scoured the gleaming white tile floor, looking and feeling with her fingers for the transparent thing. Impossible, she told herself. She opened the other side of the case to see if both lenses were in that compartment. Only one was in there, but it wasn't transparent like she had thought: It was tinted. Therefore, the renegade lens should be easy to find on the white floor tiles. All she had to do was look more closely. She commenced searching again.

Voila! There it was.

The lens had rolled or slid under the vanity. She tweezed it up with two peachy-red fingernails and placed it in the container. As she was closing the lid, a voice in the back of her brain asked why Mrs. Kantel wasn't wearing her contacts. Two pair perhaps?

Dusty placed the things on the marble counter as close to the way they had been prior to her fiasco. After a quick scan of the place to make sure everything was in order, she scurried out of the bathroom.

She entered the bedroom and glanced around again. As she stared at the closet, a premonition told her something was in there, and that she should search it again. As she grasped the knob, something deep inside her said she shouldn't open it. However, the compelling force of her profession, and the possibility that she might find something to clear Buddy's name, gave her no choice. She had to do it.

After inhaling deeply, she snatched open the closet door. Her eyes scanned the small room, and then...

You won't believe what she saw: two black boots.

161

And in those boots was a guy.
And the guy was dressed in black.

Two massive hands exploded from between the hanging clothes, and they grabbed Dusty by the throat. She attempted to scream, but it was useless: She couldn't breathe, much less scream for help. Her arms flailed at the clinging hands as the big man stepped out of the closet. She dangled in his grasp like a cat being carried by the nape of its neck. Her feet barely touched the carpet. Her bulging eyes somehow managed to recognize him—BLACKIE!

Marilyn Kantel's hired thug was the last thing Dusty saw. She may have fainted or passed out from lack of oxygen to her brain, but either way, she was unconscious—hanging like a lifeless rag doll in his massive hands.

TWENTY-NINE

I was awakened the next morning by Detectives Small and Biggs. They were standing next to my bed in my hotel room. Well, Small was next to the bed. But Biggs was in his usual position at the door with his arms crossed and a toothpick sticking between his teeth.

"C'mon, Bowers," said Small, prodding me with a finger. "Get your good-for-nothing ass outta bed."

I rubbed the sleep from my eyes and glanced at the clock. It wasn't even eight o'clock yet. Southern hospitality?

"What's this about now?" I asked, yawning and stretching. "Haven't you guys ever learned how to knock? I'm not a criminal, you know!"

Small crossed his arms similar to his partner. "We got a phone call from Mr. Diamond. Seems his daughter…you know, the one you've been…whatever the hell the two of you've been doing—well, his daughter's missing."

I shrugged. "And?"

Biggs's voice boomed from across the room. "And Mr. Diamond thinks something might have happened to his precious little girl."

Precious little girl? Are we talking about the same person here—Dusty Diamond? Precious? I could think of a lot of words to describe Dusty, but I don't think *precious* would be on the list.

My eyes cut from Biggs to Small. I said to the short, heavy detective, "She's in a dangerous profession, you know."

Small glanced at his partner. "Very dangerous, wouldn't you say, Biggsie?"

"Extremely," replied Biggs with a slow, exaggerated nod.

"What's this got to do with me?" I asked, my bewildered gaze shifting from one detective to the other.

Small replied, "Her father's car is parked outside."

My eyes locked on Small. "Yeah. So?" I said, shrugging. "She let me borrow the thing."

"Uh-huh," mumbled Small.

"She let you borrow her pistol too?" asked Biggs. "It's still in the old man's car."

"It's not really a pistol," I said, a hint of a smile emerging on my dry lips. "It's a—"

Small cut me off: "A person in her profession...a *dangerous* profession, I think you said." He turned to his partner. "Ain't that what he said, Biggsie?"

Biggs nodded in agreement again.

Small continued: "Well, she wouldn't go anywhere without her pistol, now would she, Bowers?"

"I can explain," I said, sitting up. "That's not actually a—"

"Can you also explain this?" asked Small, holding Dusty's cell phone in front of me. "You told her father she'd be calling him. But how the hell can she do that if you've got her phone?" He glanced at Biggs, then back at me.

I had the feeling something real clever was about to be expounded by the less-than-brainy detective.

Small said, "She got one of them built-in microdish whachamacallits hidden up her ass?"

164

He glanced at Biggs, who chuckled loudly.

See, I told you something witty was coming.

I said, "She told me to hang onto it while she—"

Small raised his palms to stop my explanation. "While she what? Went for a swim in another pool or...or disappeared in another fire?"

Here I am in another tight spot. Should I tell the detectives where Dusty is and what she's doing? Or, should I keep procrastinating until...until when? Hell, I don't know.

However, what if something did actually happen to Dusty in Atlanta? Those two gals she was following weren't exactly amateurs. They knew precisely what they were doing. And what if Blackie also showed up there? Dusty could have fallen into one of their dirty traps the same way they hoodwinked me. Well, not exactly the *same* way. But you know what I mean.

It would be easy for those two gaming gals to have someone waste Dusty. Hell, Atlanta is a huge city, and Dusty could end up in a dumpster or someplace equally unpleasant. I don't think they would hire another guy though—too risky if too many got involved. Dusty hadn't mentioned Blackie. Nevertheless, Huntsville is only a half-day's drive from Atlanta, and Blackie could have easily joined the two gals there. Or, he could have flown on ahead and already be in Atlanta watching their backs—right where Dusty was snooping. Heaven help her.

I let out a deep sigh.

"And another one bites the dust," Detective Biggs sang in his baritone voice.

Very funny.

I pretended to ignore the guy. The last thing I needed right now was a singing comedian—and a bad one at that.

165

I turned my attention to Detective Small. I sure wanted to tell him about Dusty being in Atlanta because she was following Lynn and Mrs. Kantel. However, I'm sure if I did, he'd get involved and somehow manage to screw up the whole damned thing. So I decided not to.

I knew where Detective Small's line of questioning was going, but I decided to take my chances that Dusty would come through and bail me out. She always had in the past.

Small threw some clothes at me. "Get dressed," he demanded. "I think you're smart enough to know where we're going."

"I wouldn't be too sure about that," added Biggs. "The guy's about as dumb as any two-bit crook we've ever dealt with."

I gave him a glare that said, *Look at who the hell's talking.*

I got dressed but never took my eyes off Dusty's cell phone. I knew it was going to ring any second. She could tell the detectives she was alive and well. And, she could fill me in on what the hell was going on in Atlanta.

However, the phone didn't ring.

And the detectives didn't believe a word I had to say.

And I was in world of hurt—again.

Dusty?

THIRTY

When Dusty awoke, she realized she was gagged, her feet were bound, and her hands were tied behind her back. And, she was locked in the trunk of a car—a moving car. She strained at her bindings, but they wouldn't give; all they did was cut into her skin, which was now chafed nearly to the point of bleeding. It was dark in the trunk, but a small amount of light could be seen when the car's brakes were applied. She recalled reading that the best thing to do in this situation was to break the taillight and wave a hand out through the hole. It was possible someone would see it and report it to the police. That sounded all well and good; however, her hands were secured behind her back. Nevertheless, she thought it was worth a try. She inched around until her feet were in a position to kick at the light. With her face crunched into the trunk's carpet, she attempted to kick out the taillight.

However, she never got the chance. The car suddenly came to a stop, and Dusty was launched forward and came to rest crumpled against the rear seat partition. The car rocked back and forth, then stopped moving all together. Dusty didn't know how long she had been in the trunk. It could have been an hour or all night, therefore, she had no idea how long the car had been traveling. All she knew for sure was that Blackie had her by the throat before she passed out.

The trunk lid popped open, and the glare of the bright morning sunlight shot into the tiny compartment and into Dusty's face. Her eyes snapped shut, then slowly opened, squinting to see who had opened the lid, She had a hunch who it would be, but she hoped it was not him—Marilyn Kantel's goon—who had abducted her. Wrong.

Blackie leaned into the trunk and grasped Dusty by the ankles. He yanked her toward him and then lifted her from the trunk as if she were a bag of groceries. He tossed her on his massive shoulder and began walking. Dusty looked around from her upside-down position. All she saw were trees. Lots of trees.

They were in a thick wooded area, and Dusty feared that was where he was going to kill her. She struggled to get free, but he was too big and strong; and he had a grip on her that would have kept her from falling out of an airplane; her efforts were futile.

He trudged thirty or forty yards into the woods, then dropped Dusty in the leaves and underbrush like a canvas sack. She hit the ground with a dull *thud*. An involuntary moan came from deep within.

"You think that hurts," he snarled, leaning over her; "wait till I start working you over."

She couldn't stop looking at his evil, glaring stare.

He spun around and disappeared. Dusty wondered if he was going to leave her there for the black bears to feast upon. She shuddered at the thought. She tugged at her restraints, but they held firm. "Damnit!" she whimpered to herself.

"What do you know about all this?" asked a female voice, snatching the gag from Dusty's mouth.

Dusty rolled over and, to her surprise, saw Marilyn Kantel hovering over her. "Nothing," said Dusty.

Marilyn had changed clothes: jeans, dark-blue sweater, windbreaker and western boots. One of those boots kicked Dusty in the stomach.

"Ow!" gasped Dusty, doubling up and wincing in pain.

"I'll ask you once more," snarled Marilyn. "What do you know? And why the hell were you snooping around in my hotel room?"

"Screw you!" snapped Dusty from her pretzel position.

"Why you little bitch," growled Marilyn, grabbing Dusty by the hair. "I'll show you a little something about screwing around."

"Let her be," said Blackie, returning with a spade in his massive hand. "She'll tell us everything she knows once she gets a few shovels of dirt in her face."

"My God, he's going to dig a grave and bury me alive!" Dusty screamed inside her mind.

Marilyn backed away. "She damn well better, if she knows what the hell's good for her."

Blackie scraped away some leaves and began digging. "Not a problem, my dear. Not a problem."

"It better not be," snapped Marilyn, jamming her hands into her hips. "She knows too damn much, regardless of what the hell she says."

Blackie kept digging.

Marilyn said to Dusty, "One last chance, bitch. What the hell do you know?"

Dusty simply moaned.

Blackie dropped the spade alongside the hole he was creating. "Maybe she'll free up her damn tongue once she sees where the hell she's going to sleep tonight...and the rest of her worthless life."

He snatched Dusty by the ankles and dragged her several yards toward the hole. Her head bounced on the ground, hitting branches and rotted wood.

"Ouch!" she squealed.

169

Blackie chuckled. "Don't worry, snookums. It'll all be over for you very shortly. Trust me on that."

"I—I know nothing," begged Dusty, floundering like a hog-tied calf.

Marilyn said, "Uh-huh." She sauntered closer to the hole Dusty was now lying next to.

Blackie let go of Dusty's feet, which fell to the ground. He picked up the spade and looked at it. "Hell, there's no sense digging this thing any deeper. The bears or some other scavenging animal will dig her up anyway."

Marilyn said, "What's it gonna be, bitch?"

Dusty blew some leaves from her nose and shook her head no.

Blackie stared at Dusty. "Last chance, sweetie."

Marilyn added, "He means business, if you haven't realized that yet."

"Hell, she ain't gonna talk," said Blackie, lifting the spade above his head. "In fact, I honestly don't think she knows a goddamn thing."

Dusty closed her eyes and waited for the blow; she wondered if the spade would crush her skull or sever her head at the neck.

"Wait!" ordered Marilyn, holding up a halting hand.

"What? Why?"

"Somebody else might know something," answered Marilyn.

"Like who?" Blackie asked, lowering the spade. "Hell, she don't know nothing…and she ain't smart enough to be working for anybody."

"Just the same," retorted Marilyn, placing a hand on the spade's wooden handle, "we have to be sure."

Blackie snatched the spade free of her grasp. "Let go of the damn thing." He held it high once more. "I'm finishing her off, damnit! She ain't gonna tell anybody about me."

"I'm running the show here," ordered Marilyn. "Put down the damn shovel."

"You ain't runnin' diddly," he growled, glaring. "And you ain't ordering me around. I know too much about you that could send you to the damn chair."

"Really?"

"You got it, babe." He hoisted the spade above his head again.

Dusty was about to scream out when she heard a muffled noise.

The spade dropped from Blackie's hand and plummeted to the ground. It hit with a *whump*! His shocked stare widened as he placed a hand on a small hole in his chest. Blood oozed between his fingers. He glared at Marilyn. "Why?" he gasped. "Why'd you do that?"

"Nobody's going to threaten or...or blackmail me, damnit!"

Dusty shifted her gaze from Blackie to Marilyn, who was holding a small handgun. Smoke was spiraling from the silencer on the end of its barrel.

Blackie staggered toward Marilyn, who—without hesitation—put two more bullets into his heart. He stopped walking, collapsed to his knees, and fell on his face—his eyes never closing.

Dusty didn't know if she was going to scream, cry, wet her pants—or all three.

Marilyn knelt next to Dusty. "That's what going to happen to you if you don't tell me every damn thing you know about me...and what's been going down."

Dusty was about to say something, but Marilyn set the gun on the ground and began untying the knots at

Dusty's wrists. Dusty wondered what was going to happen next.

Marilyn picked up the gun and said, "They're loose enough. Finish taking off the rope, then untie your feet."

Dusty sat up, pulled the binding from her hands and undid the knots at her ankles.

Marilyn walked to the spade. She picked it up and said, "Come here and finish with this hole."

Dusty couldn't believe what she was hearing. Was she supposed to be digging the grave for both Blackie and herself?

God, help me, she silently prayed.

THIRTY-ONE

Dusty took the spade from Marilyn, who immediately backed away and pointed the gun at Dusty.

"Dig!" Marilyn ordered.

"What if I told you what little I know?" pleaded Dusty.

"Too late. Too damn late, gal." Marilyn motioned with the pistol. "You've seen and heard too damn much here. Keep digging."

Dusty stuck the spade in the hole and pressed her shoeless foot against the metal spade. It cut into her flesh. She wondered what had happened to her shoes; they weren't in the trunk of the car as far as she could recall.

Dusty kept switching feet as she dug, but it didn't help: both feet were cut—and getting worse with every push of the spade. It didn't matter because she was going to die anyway. She stopped digging and glared defiantly at Marilyn. "I'm through, damnit!" Dusty decreed.

"That's not big enough for the both of you," noted Marilyn, pointing the gun at the hole. "Dig deeper."

Suddenly a bus roared past on the highway about 50 yards away. The windows must have been open because loud yelling and laughing emanated from the bus and into the trees.

Marilyn looked up to see what the noise was all about.

Dusty didn't: She swung the spade up and caught Marilyn between her wrist and hand. The gun flew about ten yards into the trees. Both women gawked at it as it disappeared into the underbrush.

Marilyn glanced at Dusty.

Dusty glanced at Marilyn.

Dusty now had a weapon in her hand—the spade.

Marilyn didn't wait to see what Dusty was going to do with it: She scrambled toward the spot where the gun was last seen before being buried in the undergrowth.

Dusty thought about following Marilyn and hitting her over the head so she could retrieve the gun herself. But she had to catch up with Marilyn first, and that was next to impossible with the bottom of her feet all cut up. She spun around and headed toward the car as fast as she could, hoping she could get there before Marilyn located the gun and shot her in the back.

Dusty looked over her shoulder at Marilyn, who was on her hands and knees digging through the leaves and fallen branches. Dusty thought Marilyn resembled a squirrel digging up last year's acorns. It may have been a humorous sight at some other time—but not now.

Dusty reached the car and peered in the window.

No keys!

Damnit!

Dusty gave another quick glance at Marilyn—who was now practically covered with leaves—and then ran toward the highway where the bus with the noisy kids had been.

When she got to the highway, Dusty looked around for familiar landmarks; she didn't recognize anything in particular; but it was cooler, so she had to be in the higher elevation of the mountains. She and her father had gone camping a couple hours northeast of Atlanta at a place named Lake Chatuge at Hiawassee. She couldn't see any lake, but a stream or river could be heard in the distance. A river ran between Lake Chatuge and Murphy, North Carolina. Dusty wondered if that was what she was hearing.

A car coming down the highway caught her attention. Dusty looked in that direction but couldn't see anything because of the winding mountain road. She hobbled to the center of the highway and held up her hands as the car rounded the curve and approached her.

The driver jammed on the brakes, and the car squealed to a stop inches away from Dusty; who didn't move because she had just as soon die right there on the highway than at the hands of that evil Marilyn Kantel.

The tall and slender male driver hopped out of the car and ran toward Dusty. "Are you crazy?" he shouted, raking his fingers through his short blond hair. "I could have killed you!"

Dusty approached him, her blistered palms up.

His blue eyes scanned her shambled condition: dirty clothes, hands, arms, feet, and matted hair—no shoes. His jaw dropped.

"I-I need help!" Dusty gasped, and she then glanced over her shoulder.

The driver also looked in the same direction. "What is it?" he asked, turning his perplexed gaze to Dusty. "Is someone hurt? Are you hurt?"

Dusty ran to the passenger side of the car and grasped the handle of the door. "She's got a gun, and…and she killed a man," Dusty gasped.

The driver's head swung in all directions, obviously looking to see who the "she" was. He returned his wide-eyed stare to Dusty and exclaimed, "You can't get in there!" He rushed toward Dusty. "I-I'll call for help!"

Dusty had the door open and was about to climb inside. "You can call for help while we're driving…or you can leave me here and be an accessory to murder. Now, what the hell's it gonna be?" Her glare could have thawed a glacier.

Once again his head snapped between Dusty and the place where Dusty had been looking. He faced Dusty and said, "But—"

"It's all right," shouted Dusty. "I'm a private investigator. Now get the hell in the car!"

The driver gave another quick glance at the woods, tapped the strap holding the kayak on the roof and then got in the silver SUV. He snapped his seatbelt, slapped the car in gear and squealed down the highway. His eyes never left the wooded area where the "she" with the gun was supposed to be.

Dusty also gave another cursory glance in that direction.

"How the hell do I know there really is someone out there?" he asked, looking in the rearview mirror. "Hell, you could be the one who killed the guy, for Pete's sake." He glanced at the girl in the passenger seat, who was cowered down between the seat and door. Her petrified stare spoke volumes, but her lips said nothing.

"Get out your cell phone," ordered Dusty, "and call the cops. That's how you'll know who the hell is the victim here, damnit!"

He fumbled with the phone, opened it and checked the display. "No signal!" he exclaimed. "No damned signal!"

"Great," said Dusty, shaking her head in disbelief. "Just take me to where I can call, okay?"

"W-We're going down to where the buses park for white-water rafting. They should have a phone there."

"Where's that?" asked Dusty, looking out the rear window.

"Down on the Ocoee River…where the Olympics were held.

Dusty anxiously asked, "How far is that?"

"N-Not far…a few more miles, I think."

"Step on it!" said Dusty. "She'll be after us before we know it."

"Who the hell's this *she*?" he asked, turning to face Dusty.

"It's a long story," explained Dusty, looking out the rear window again. "You can get it from the cops later."

Their SUV came to a long stretch of straight road, and Dusty could see about a half mile behind them. A blue car was coming fast. Marilyn's car was blue—probably a rental.

"Hurry!" shouted Dusty. "I think she's behind us."

"I can't go any faster on this road," he explained. "We're sliding on these damned curves as it is. I could get us all killed!"

"You're going to get us *all* killed if she catches up with us, damnit!"

They rounded a curve, and Dusty could see the Ocoee River on their left. She twisted around and, once again, peered out the rear window. No Marilyn. Dusty let out a sigh of relief.

Their SUV popped over a hill, and a rustic-looking building with several cars parked in front of it flashed past on their left.

"Damnit!" he said, pressing the brake pedal. "We missed the Olympic Center." He shook his head out of frustration. "We were going too fast, and I didn't have time to slow down and turn into that narrow entrance." He flashed a quick glance to his left as they sped past the lot. "Damnit!" He smacked the steering wheel with the flat of his hand.

177

Dusty glanced at the place, then behind them—no sign of the blue car, but the hill they had just gone over limited her line of sight. She was sure Marilyn was not far behind and was probably gaining on them, especially since they had just slowed down. Dusty was also positive they would have had a telephone at the Olympic Center, but it was too late: The unique building, bridge and parking lot were long gone.

He said, "I'll see if I can turn around up ahead."

"No!" Dusty screamed, still looking out the rear window. "Keep on going! She'll...she'll be here before we can get back there!" Dusty returned her attention to the young driver and asked, "How much farther to that place where you were headed?"

He glanced in the mirror at Dusty. "The rafting place?"

"Yeah."

"About two or three miles, I think."

"Then," Dusty snapped, "get your foot off the brake and onto the gas pedal, damnit!"

They traveled the short distance—which seemed like an eternity to Dusty—to the rafting area with no sign of the blue car behind them.

The young man jammed on the brakes and wheeled into the gravel parking area. Buses filled the lot, and he had difficulty locating a spot to park.

"Hurry up and hide this thing," ordered Dusty.

"I can't find a place to—"

Dusty cut him short: "Then stop the damn thing, and I'll hop out. I don't want you to be seen with me. She might think I told you something and..."

No further warning was necessary: He slammed on the brakes and skidded to a halt.

178

Dusty opened the door and hopped out while the SUV was still rocking. She darted between two buses. She wanted to thank the guy and tell him to call the police, but he was already out of sight and heading down the highway. He apparently wanted nothing to do with Marilyn when she got there. Unfortunately for him, however, Marilyn might see his car and keep following him instead of checking out the parking lot.

Dusty glanced around and wondered if she should hide in one of the many buses; however, she decided against it, thinking it might be the first place Marilyn would search if she did stop and check the lot. Dusty thought about catching a ride with one of the departing buses or cars. The only problem was that nobody was leaving. It seemed they all had just arrived.

A sign caught Dusty's attention. She read it and noted that the water was only released from the dam at certain hours. She assumed that was about to happen.

A blue car raced past, then screeched to a halt. It backed up, wheels squealing against the asphalt pavement, then spun into the lot.

"Damnit!" cursed Dusty, after seeing the car. Her head snapped in all directions. She noticed that the buses had transported tour groups, and the people were donning their gear in preparation for a white-water rafting trip. A light went on in Dusty's head, and she ran to where the groups were assembled for their briefings. She eyed some extra helmets, life-vests and paddles a short distance away. She dashed to the pile and put on a helmet to hide her red hair. The vest was next, hiding her soiled green blouse. She picked up a paddle and disappeared into the crowd.

Marilyn hopped out of her car and scurried toward the buses.

179

Dusty could feel the panicky sensation building, and something had to be done in a hurry. She ran to where a raft was loading and pushed her way to the front of the line. The people didn't seem to care; they were too preoccupied with their gear and how to get into one of those colorful boats. And they may have been a bit intimidated or concerned about the Class 3 rapids that were ahead of them.

Nevertheless, Dusty clambered into a red rubber raft that was about 20 feet long and eight feet wide. She then noticed that all the other people getting into that raft were wearing the same colors: red helmets and red vests. Dusty glanced at her vest—red! She twisted the helmet slightly and saw that it was red also. A sigh of relief passed her lips because wearing the wrong colors would have made her stand out like a sore thumb at a bowling alley.

Dusty peeked over her shoulder and saw Marilyn racing from the buses toward the rafts. Dusty snapped around and lowered her head.

"All aboard," shouted a young, helmeted guide as he shoved the raft away from the beach. "Hang on folks and paddle when I tell you…it's gonna get a bit dicey!" He laughed.

Dusty snuck another glance at Marilyn, who was checking everyone who had not gotten into the other rafts. She then glanced at Dusty's raft and cupped her hands above her eyes to see through the glare of the bright sun reflecting off the water cascading over the dam.

"Paddle!" hollered the guide.

Dusty jabbed her paddle into the water with the rest of the seven rafters; however, she didn't exactly pull her share of the load because her head was still twisted around, and her eyes were staring at Marilyn.

180

That didn't last long. The raft plummeted and sped off like a bumpy rocket. Dusty's head jerked around, and she could see the raging river ahead. She paddled as hard as she could, following the guide's instructions. However, she periodically glanced at the highway paralleling them to see if Marilyn's car was following the gaggle of rafts.

Nothing.

Dusty relaxed and began planning her next move to escape. She figured if she had gotten away with melding in with the crowd, she could possibly get away on the group's bus also. After that, she would go to the police, and Marilyn would be *their* problem. She nodded in agreement with herself.

The guide was shouting out instructions: one side had to paddle forward, while the other side had to paddle backwards. Then, both sides would paddle in the same direction. The raft bounced and bucked like a wild bronco. And clear cold water sprayed over the side. Dusty used the spray to wash some of the dirt off her face and arms.

The raft finally sailed into some smooth calm water, and everyone relaxed and shook the soreness from their tired muscles.

"If you'll look up at that nest up on the ridge," said the guide, "you might see an eagle flying about."

Everyone, including Dusty, peered into the bright blue sky.

Suddenly, the bottom fell out, and the raft dropped about six feet. Dusty's heart flipped, and she smacked her chin on the paddle and was almost tossed overboard.

"Paddle, you land-lubbers!" shouted the guide, laughing about as hard as humanly possible at the startled rafters.

Dusty was about to say something to the smartass when she noticed Marilyn's blue car slowly driving along

181

the highway. Dusty tried to see if Marilyn was looking at any raft in particular.

It didn't appear so.

Dusty thought about her escape plan. It would have to be revised if Marilyn was waiting near the buses. Dusty would have to take off her helmet—leaving her plainly visible. Not good.

After several miles, Dusty peered down the river and saw another bridge crossing over it. The guide explained that the bridge was an access road to one of the several power plants along the river. Dusty wondered if the bridge had a controlled access.

As they were passing beneath the bridge, Dusty looked up at the structure. "No!" she gasped when seeing Marilyn peering down at them. Dusty jerked her head down and wondered if she had been seen. However, she had to be sure. She peeked up at Marilyn and saw a flash and smoke emanating from a gun—Marilyn's gun with silencer.

Dusty felt a strange sensation, like a white-hot searing spear, and she was flipped out of the raft when it hit some steep rapids.

"Abandon ship!" the guide shouted. "We hit a rock, and it punctured the raft! Everybody out!"

They hadn't hit a rock.

THIRTY-TWO

I, innocent little ole Buddy Bowers, was in big trouble. I mean trouble with a capital T, which sounds like P, which stands for Pool—where Harry Thomas' body was found, and where the cops think Dusty Diamond's body is now floating. Yes, sir; I'm caught between a rock and a slab of Georgia granite. Not good.

A little Divine Intervention wouldn't hurt here.

They—detectives *Curly and Moe*—had me in the police station interrogation room again. They were throwing every question they could think of at me. I wanted to tell them where Dusty was and what she was doing. But I honestly didn't know what the hell the girl was up to—or whether or not she was even alive. And there was no way for her to let me know, because the *two stooges* took her cell phone from me and locked it up some place. Probably somewhere safe—like a padded box where no one would ever hear the thing ring or buzz or whatever the hell it does. That's if there's any charge left in the doggoned battery.

Anyway, the detectives were about to start another round of questions when the station lieutenant came in. He was a tall, thin guy with gray hair and tired blue-gray eyes. He said something to Detective Biggs, who was standing next to the door with his arms crossed. As usual.

Biggs nodded his understanding then went to Small and whispered something to him. I wondered what they were up to. They had so much on me now, they were probably talking about who gets front row seats at my electrocution. Ouch!

The detectives nodded to the lieutenant and departed the interrogation room. The lieutenant held the door open while his stare bored holes in me, but he didn't say a word. A new approach, I thought. Maybe he expected me to make a run for it, and the detectives were lined up outside along the wall waiting to fill my body with slugs. That would save the state of Alabama a heap of money on trials and dumb things like that. Dumb?

The lieutenant also left the room. I interlocked my fingers and placed them on the table. I was going to hold my ground. If they wanted to shoot me, they'd have to do it from across the table—looking me straight in the eyes. That's if they had the guts to do it, which I doubted. However, you can never be too sure about things like that. Not with these guys anyway.

Instead of the lieutenant and his detectives returning to the interrogation room, a dapper young man in a dark three-piece suit came in along with the lieutenant. He nodded to the lieutenant, who shut the door and departed again.

Just the two of us—the dapper dandy and me—were now in that deadly-quiet place. It made me nervous. Especially with the door closed. Maybe I should have made a run for it. At least I would have gotten it in the back, and it would have been over quickly. And, I wouldn't be here waiting to face another onslaught of questions by this slick-looking fellow. I wondered if this guy was from the District Attorney's office, or if maybe he was my new attorney—one with plenty of experience in *multiple* homicides. Great.

Or, he could be a shrink. I think I could use one right about now. Especially after working with Dusty, and after being grilled by those two skanky detectives...and don't forget that little chat with Daddy Diamond. How could we not remember that? What a piece of work that guy is. Whew!

I wonder what the hell Daddy's first name is. I should have asked him while we were having our one-sided discussion. On second thought...I don't think so.

The "suit" approached the table.

If he offered a plea bargain, I decided I would take it rather than having to explain everything all over again—that's if I could, which I doubted. You see, even though it hasn't been that long, so much has happened since this whole thing started, I couldn't begin to regurgitate half the damned stuff. What I am able to recall, I can hardly believe myself. I think you know what I mean. That's if you've been paying attention at all.

Dusty, please come barging through that door with Lynn, Blackie and Mrs. Kantel and say, "Will the real killers please stand up."

Yeah, you're right—fat chance.

The smooth-looking guy took a seat across from me. He unbuttoned his blue serge jacket and dusted a fleck of dust off his lapel. He was about thirty, dark hair, bright blue eyes, maybe six feet or so—no wedding ring. The kind of guy my wife could fall for—after they hang me, or whatever the hell it is they do to murderers in Alabama.

I love you, Heather, honey. Always remember that—even when I'm dead and gone, and you're making mad passionate love to this suave and handsome devil.

"Mr. Buddy Bowers?" he asked in a soft, silky voice. It wasn't an angry blurt or anything like that. It was steady, calm.

Oh, man, my wonderful Heather is definitely going to go head-over-heels for this guy.

I nodded yes without realizing my mouth wasn't moving.

"I need a verbal response," he said, straightening his silky light-blue tie.

"Oh, sorry," I said with a sharp nod. "Yes, I'm Buddy Bowers."

"Mr. Bowers, my name is Wilson Roberts," he said, flipping open a black leather case and showing me his identification. "I'm a Special Agent from the local FBI office."

FBI? What the hell is the damned FBI doing on this case? Can't be a violation of the Mann Act. Dusty is twenty-two—more or less. She never did give me an exact age, however.

Doesn't the FBI have better things to do than to harass an innocent guy? Besides, I think this guy is a little confused: His name should be Robert Wilson instead of Wilson Roberts. He's probably more nervous than I am. Yeah, sure. He's as cool as a watermelon floating in a tub of ice. I wish I hadn't mentioned that word *floating*. Brings about memories of Harry Thomas, and that brings on bad vibes.

He slipped his ID case back into his inside jacket pocket and said in a reassuring voice, "I'd like you to tell me exactly what happened—starting at the golf resort. Okay, Mr. Bowers?"

Not again. Well, at least he didn't call me Mr. B.

I raised my palms and said to the agent, "I must have told the damned story a hundred times already."

"Humor me," he said without the slightest hint of a smile. "Tell it once more."

Well, I told him everything. I mean *everything*. Every minute detail. It was amazing how quickly and clearly it all came back. I don't know if it was this guy's

186

calm demeanor or what, but it felt like I was actually living the whole thing all over again. He made me relax and trust him. He was that kind of guy. Oh, Heather. Sigh.

He nodded his understanding and leaned back. "That pretty much coincides with what our Atlanta office said."

Atlanta office? Oh-oh.

How the hell did the Atlanta FBI get involved? They must have found Dusty's body and linked her to me. Did I give her a business card? I don't remember doing so. Maybe she had some things written in a notebook, and they found it on her body. Yeah, that's got to be it. Poor kid. I was beginning to like her too.

I faked a smile. "Atlanta?" I asked, hoping for a good response.

The agent explained, "They were contacted about your case."

Man, this has gotten out of hand. It must have been that dummy Dusty who did it. Did she get her goofy ass thrown in jail for breaking and entering? Good grief.

He nodded again. "Seems your investigator... Diamond, is it?" He pulled out a little black book and glanced at some notes.

I beat him to it. "Miss Dusty Diamond."

"Right," he said, looking up from his book. "Well, the Atlanta FBI office was called in for assistance, and—"

I cut him short. "Thank God."

His eyebrows pinched together. "What's that?"

Thank God she went to you guys instead of another PI firm that charges a million bucks a day...plus expenses.

I said, "I'm glad Miss Diamond asked the FBI for help. I think she was getting in a little deeper than she could handle."

"You're correct about that," the agent said, shaking his head in despair. "Unfortunately, *she* didn't call us." He gazed at me for a moment. "We should have been brought in sooner."

Unfortunately? Sooner? What exactly did that mean? Did something happen to poor little Dusty? Was she dead by the time the FBI got to her? Oh, no. It was all my fault. I shouldn't have bought her that damned ticket to Atlanta. Or, I should have said the hell with Detective Small and gone with her. *I'm so sorry, Dusty. Please forgive me, because I'll never forgive myself.*

The agent interrupted my thoughts by saying, "Miss Diamond was on the right track, however. Bruno Grimes was the one in Atlanta with Mrs. Kantel, and we're pretty sure he's the one who did the killing for her. We're checking that out."

Killing? Grimes? That's a new one.

I prayed Agent Roberts wasn't referring to Dusty being the victim.

I blurted out, "You mean this Grimes fellow killed Harry Thomas and Hans Kantel, right?"

Instead of answering my question, he asked, "Did you know Mr. Grimes?"

"Me? Well, no." I shook my head emphatically. "I mean, hell no."

He stared at me with those piercing blue eyes. It appeared he was holding something back. Why wasn't he telling me everything? Did he suspect I was involved with that greasy Grimes guy? However, Dusty did say she had a bit of a run-in with a guy dressed in black. Same guy? Hell, I never even got a glimpse of the damned goon.

Speaking of Dusty, I really wanted to know what was going on with her right now. I leaned forward and asked Agent Roberts, "Did this Bruto Grimes also kill—?"

"It's *Bruno*," he corrected me.

"Right," I said, straightening up. "Who is this...this Bruno Grimes, anyway?"

"Grimes was a two-bit contractor hired by Mrs. Kantel. And he—"

"Contractor?"

"Yeah," Roberts said, nodding once. "That's a term used to describe a person paid to do someone else's dirty work."

I was catching on. I said, "Like killing?"

He nodded yes. "Killing is high on the list." Roberts stared at me for a long moment. "You're fortunate they didn't get you also."

That made my knees knock. I knew those rotten scoundrels needed a fall guy, but I honestly didn't think I was that close to dying. I closed my eyes. Oh, Lord.

He went on: "Mrs. Kantel isn't one to leave any loose ends."

I said, "She didn't think she'd get away with it, did she? I mean the FBI would track her down, right?"

"She almost did get away."

My eyebrows arched. "Almost?"

"Mrs. Kantel didn't plan on sticking around very long. She had a ticket for a direct flight to Germany the same evening we were called in."

Germany? That figures—being married to Hans and all.

I said, "Germany, huh?"

The agent put away his notes. "Yes, and Mrs. Kantel would have fled the country without suffering any consequences."

My voice was sharp and quick. "That didn't happen, did it?"

"Fortunately," he said with a certain cockiness FBI agents possess, "that did not happen. She was apprehended by the state police at a bridge near the Olympic Center on the Ocoee River. She had a pistol that had just been fired."

Pistol? Olympics? Ocoee River?

I asked him, "Where the hell is that?"

"Near Cleveland, Tennessee; northeast of Chattanooga. The Ocoee River was the site of the 1996 Summer Olympics."

Swell. That really clears it up.

I asked him, "Where is she now...Mrs. Kantel?"

"Mrs. Kantel's in custody in Atlanta," he replied. "She'll be escorted back here and tried in an Alabama court for murder...and being an accomplice in arson, embezzlement, tax evasion and fraud...for starters."

Good grief!

I asked, "Was Grimes the guy dressed in black?"

The agent cocked an eyebrow as if wondering how I knew about Blackie, then he slowly nodded yes. That same accusing stare resurfaced.

I ignored it.

I slid to the edge of my seat. "How about Mrs. Kantel's accomplice: Lynn...Lynn Smith? Did she leave the country? Or, did Mrs. Kantel do her in also?"

He pushed away from the table. "I'm afraid that's all I'm authorized to say about the case."

"What? Why?"

"As I said," Roberts replied, getting to his feet and buttoning his jacket, "there's still Mrs. Kantel's trial."

I also stood. "Is Miss Diamond all right?"

He shook his head no and slid his chair against the table. "I may have divulged too much already,' he said in a stern voice. "You'll have to speak with Mr. Diamond about that, I'm afraid." He stared at me with empty eyes. "I'll say

190

one thing though…Miss Diamond did one hell of a job…and we wouldn't have caught the perpetrators without her help."

What the hell did that mean? No—Dusty wasn't all right? Or, no—he couldn't say what happened to her for some stupid reason of his?

I went numb, as if someone had just punched me in the stomach. I simply stood in shock. Speechless.

After a moment, I said, "Wait a minute, damnit!"

He pulled his chin back and glared at me. He may have been insulted—or he may have noticed the veins popping out of my neck. Whatever, I got his attention. "Miss Diamond's got nothing to do with your lousy trial!" I practically shrieked. "What the hell happened to her for Chrissake?"

He seemed to evaluate the situation for a minute before finally saying, "She was shot by Mrs. Kantel, according to witnesses. And she fell into a raging river. I'm afraid she—"

"Did she drown?" I asked fearfully, cutting him off. "I mean…was she dead when she fell in? Did they recover her body?"

He shook his head no again. "That's not my department. You'll have to—"

"Talk to me, damnit!" I practically yelled at him. "Please tell me," I pleaded with uplifted palms.

"I…I can't," he said in a low, humble voice as he turned away.

I collapsed in my chair.

He began walking away. "Oh, by the way," he said, turning his head slightly, "you're free to leave."

I didn't know what to say or do. I simply stared at his departing back.

After Agent Roberts was gone, I buried my face in my hands and felt hot tears burning my eyes. I should have felt relieved, but I didn't. All I could think about was Dusty getting killed because of me. And getting killed by that no good, sadistic Godzilla—Grimes. Damn him!

Damn them all, damnit!

THIRTY-THREE

Believe me when I say I have never felt so low in my entire life—not even when I thought they were going to hang me. I believed I was totally responsible for Dusty's death. A whole bunch of coulda-shoulda stuff was swirling around my brain. I kept thinking I should have spent the extra money and had one of those more experienced firms handle the case. But, would all that extra money ensure that I would have been found innocent? And, would the real murderers have been caught without Dusty's assistance? I don't think so. Dusty, despite all her quirks, was something special.

You know, I really liked that kid. And, no matter what happens to me the rest of my life, I will never forget what she did for me—and I'll be eternally indebted to her. I only wish she were still alive today so I could personally thank her. *Sorry, kid.*

Now was the tough part: meeting with Mr. Diamond and trying to explain what had actually happened and how much his daughter truly meant to me. *Good luck, Buddy.*

I parked my car and left it with my wife in the hospital parking lot. After I had explained to Heather that Dusty was the one actually working on my case and then what had happened to the kid, Heather wanted no part of this. No, sir. Oh, it wasn't that she didn't care—but under that hard shell of hers was actually a tender and emotional heart. She said there was no way she could keep it together when I talked to Dusty's father about his daughter's untimely demise. I honored her wish and didn't press the issue. After all—and you know what I'm talking about—Heather had already gone through more than a wife should have to endure.

I entered the hospital alone, stepped into the elevator and thought about what I was going to say to Mr. Diamond. I knew there was really nothing I could say or do that would lessen his grief. What could one say to a father who has lost his only love in life? I mean, after all, if I hadn't shown up at Diamond and Diamond, sweet little Dusty would still be pushing papers around Daddy's large cluttered desk.

I punched the button for Mr. Diamond's floor and stepped back and crossed my arms. When the elevator arrived, I entered and slouched against the stainless steel wall. Thank goodness no one was in there with me. I was a mess, and it showed. I needed my solitude. My privacy. Needed time to think. Ponder my thoughts and what I was going to say to Dusty's dad.

I rehearsed several scenarios as the floors slowly passed, but nothing seemed appropriate. Even though Mr. Diamond displayed the armor of an old snapping turtle, underneath that disguise was a truly caring man. Anyway, that's what Dusty had told me. He didn't show it openly, but I guess he loved her in his own private way. And she obviously adored him.

When the elevator reached Mr. Diamond's floor and the doors opened, my courage melted away like a piece of ice in the hot sun. I couldn't get out of the cab. Couldn't move.

I stood there huddled in the corner of that shiny steel box until the doors eventually closed. The elevator began moving downward from someone obviously having pushed the demand button. A sigh of relief escaped my body. But I also felt like a spineless wretch for not being able to face Mr. Diamond in his time of need.

I would return to the car, discuss it with Heather again, and maybe she would have some magic words that would somehow give me the courage to face Mr. Diamond. Heather was good at those things. If she couldn't come up with something, a letter offering my condolences would have to do. *Sorry, Dusty.*

When the elevator finally bottomed out, and the door opened, I lowered my head and stepped out. I didn't want anyone to see my cowardly face.

"Mr. B?" a familiar voice asked.

I couldn't believe the sound. It had to be a coincidence. I was afraid to raise my eyes for fear it might be someone else. But who the hell else calls me Mr. B?

With tears welling in my eyes, I looked up at the grandest sight I had ever seen. A skinny, green-eyed, carrot top with six earrings in her left ear was standing with her hands on her bony hips. She looked different though: Her hair was all curls. Cute.

Dusty flew into my arms and hugged the hell out of me. And that was okay.

"Dusty," I said when I was finally able to speak. "Dusty, I thought you were dead. Thought they had killed you too." I swiped at a tear trickling down my cheek.

She pushed away from me and stared unbelievingly into my watery eyes. "Didn't the dang FBI tell you what the heck happened?"

"Well…they led me to believe you were killed by Marilyn Kantel and some guy named Grimes who worked for her. I think you called him Blackie."

"No way, Mr. B." Her left eyebrow arched high. "Seriously?"

I nodded yes. "They said they couldn't talk about the case until after Mrs. Kantel's trial."

"Hogwash!" she said, shaking her head in disgust. "Ain't so, and they dang well knew it, damnit!"

All I could do was smile. Dusty was back.

"C'mon," she said, grabbing my arm and dragging me back to the elevator. "We're gonna go see Daddy, and then we're gonna hafta give 'em Fibbies a piece of our minds."

That might not be such a good idea, kid. I don't want to end up in jail again.

Funny how priorities change, eh? A few moments ago, jail didn't matter a fiddler's damn to me.

Nevertheless, I was now thrilled to death—no pun intended—that I didn't have to tell Daddy Diamond his daughter was dead.

Dusty jammed a finger into the elevator call button so hard I thought the plastic was going to crack. "Damn fools!" she said, shaking her head in disgust again. "Scaring the hell outta you like that. I hope they didn't lead Daddy astray too, damn 'um."

I hoped not also.

Dusty backed away from the buttons with a slight limp.

I pointed to her hip and asked, "What's that all about?"

She looked down. "Oh, heck; ain't nothing but a dang scratch."

"Well, they told me you were shot, and they led me to believe—"

Dusty cut me off. "That dang Marilyn Kantel shot our raft, and we all got dunked. Boy, that dang water was cold! Luckily we had only a couple hundred yards before we were at the goldarn pickup point."

196

Man, you can't get a straight answer from this kid.

I said, "But you did get shot, right? I mean, that's what the FBI agent said."

"It's just a little nick," she said, hoisting her dress to show me the bandage wrapped around her skinny thigh. "The dang tape caused more trouble than the doggone wound."

My head jerked around to make sure nobody had seen Dusty flashing her leg at me. Fortunately, we were the only ones waiting for the elevator.

"See?" she said, holding her dress hem up as if it were an apron.

I raised my hands to block the view. "Put your dress down, Dusty. I get the picture." I rolled my eyes at her being so naïve and innocent.

She studied her thigh for a moment, nodded in agreement with her assessment, then let go of her hem. The light green dress fluttered down like a grasshopper landing on a blade of grass.

I gave another look around before exhaling a sigh of relief. Nobody was there; however, the way things had been going for me, I wouldn't have been surprised if Daddy Diamond himself had been right there in the hallway leaning on his crutches; watching and snarling. God forbid!

The bell *dinged* and the elevator door opened. Dusty charged inside, dragging me with her. The people getting off the elevator had to jump aside to keep from getting trampled. They looked at us as if we were crazy or something.

Who, us?

I tried to think of something to get Dusty's mind off the feds. I was quite familiar with her antics by now and knew it would be quite a tasking. Stubborn? No— persistent.

197

"Dusty," I asked with as calm a voice as I could muster, "what the heck actually happened in Atlanta?"

Dusty shook her head in disbelief. "You wouldn't believe it, Mr. B. I spotted that dang Mrs. Kantel…as I told you over the phone and—"

Dusty was interrupted by the elevator stopping at the second floor and people getting on. Holding my hand now, she leaned close to me and whispered, "Tell you the rest when we get offa this dang thang and into Daddy's room."

I tried to let go of her hand, but it was like flicking wet toilet paper off the heel of a shoe. No luck. I glanced around to see if anyone had noticed.

They had.

All kinds of weird stares came our way. And even though I was blushing, I really didn't care what they thought. They had no idea what was going on between us or what we had been through.

I simply smiled, and my face slowly returned to its usual ruddy complexion.

Screw 'em! as Dusty would say.

THIRTY-FOUR

We had to gather in Mr. Diamond's hospital room of all places. Believe me, it wasn't my idea. The last time I met with that guy, he scared the bejesus out of me. However, Dusty insisted that Daddy be part of the final get-together. I guess he had more to do with solving the case than I had figured. Therefore, I thought I would give him another audience—as painful as it might be. At least it was better than having to tell him his daughter was dead.

Dusty, no longer holding my hand, limped into his room ahead of me. Her father was sitting in bed reading a newspaper. I couldn't see his face, so there was no telling what kind of mood he was in. Dusty looked at me and shrugged. Her green eyes cut from me to her father. She hesitated for an instant, then hobbled over to him and kissed him on the forehead. He lowered the paper to his lap and said something I couldn't hear, but it certainly wasn't anything about her being dead or anything like that. There wasn't enough emotion from either of them. However, Daddy did hold her hand. Yes, you heard right. He actually held his daughter's hand.

Hey, that may not be such a big thing for you and me—but for Daddy Diamond—it's a gold star. I guess that was his way of congratulating her for solving my case.

She let go of Daddy's hand, walked gingerly over to me and gave me a big hug.

"Dusty!" scolded her father. "He's our client, for Chrissake!"

Dusty ignored him. "We done it, Mr. B! We done it!"

She hugged me again.

I gently pushed her away before she got too attached and possibly wanted to go home with me—you know, like one of those stray puppies that takes a liking to you after you've scratched it behind its ears. Anyway, I didn't think Daddy would remain in that hospital bed much longer if I continued to hold her. And Heather, my less-than-understanding wife, if you recall, wouldn't think too fondly of my bringing home a cute little puppy...named Dusty.

Now don't get me wrong. I actually got to love that little gal—not in a sensual way—but more like a father loves his child. However, I'm not nearly old enough to be her father—and that's part of Dusty's problem, you see. She seems to have forgotten the age thing...and the fact that I am happily married.

She'll get over it.

"Not *we*, Dusty. *You're* the one who did it all," I said, still trying to fend off the little octopus. "Believe me, I had nothing to do with solving the case."

"Oh, yeah, you did, Mr. B. You kept leadin' me in the right direction every time I got off track. We were a danged good team."

I did? We were?

She stepped back, took my hand and led me to her father, who was staring at us with doubting eyes. "Daddy, this here's Mr. Buddy Bowers, the most understandin' and patient man I've ever met."

More BS.

That's how she feels about me—only because she's comparing me to Daddy. And that's not much of a compliment, is it?

I said to Dusty, "We've met."

"Helluva guy," said Daddy, reaching his huge paw out for my hand. "Helluva guy."

Now if you recall, he just about broke my fingers the last time we shook hands…and that's when he *wasn't* glad to see me. Can you imagine what he would do to my hand now that we're…uh…friends? Yow!

"Thank you," I said, shoving Dusty between us so he couldn't get to my hand again.

Dusty said, "Too bad he's married, huh, Daddy?"

Oh, boy.

Daddy's eyes narrowed again, and he glared at me. His huge hand slapped the bed. "Sonofabitch!"

I raised both my hands, palms toward him, as if to say, *"Wait a minute! It's not what you think, sir! Nothing at all like that!"*

However, I never got the chance: Dusty came to my rescue—again. "Good heavens, Daddy, he's been as much a dang gentleman as a guy could possibly be."

My grin was quivering. "She gets carried away sometimes," I attempted to explain. I looked over my shoulder to see if Heather had come into the hospital and accidentally entered the room. Man, that's all I needed right now.

She hadn't; thank God.

I returned my attention to Mr. Diamond. Daddy's stare told me the big man didn't fully accept my explanation. And you know what? For some reason, I was glad he was still connected to the bed and all that paraphernalia.

I let out a sigh of relief and, keeping one eye on Mr. Diamond, turned to Dusty. "Tell me about the two girls, Lynn Smith and Marilyn Kantel. How'd you figure it out?"

Dusty blushed, believe it or not; she actually blushed.

"Ahhh," she said, wagging her head in embarrassment. "It really weren't nothin', Mr. B."

I wanted to tell her to call me Buddy or Mr. Bowers …but you know what? That Mr. B stuff had a nice ring to it when it came from her…and I decided that I kind of liked it. It grows on a guy.

"Go on, sugar," Daddy growled. "Tell 'im what the hell you told me over the damn phone."

So, Mr. Diamond already knew about the girls and Bruno Grimes. Or, was Daddy the one who figured it out?

I wondered.

Dusty's green eyes lit up when she looked at me. "Remember when I hung up on you so I could follow Mrs. Kantel?"

"Uh-huh."

"Well, she caught a taxi and sped away," Dusty went on, motioning with her hand as if flinging it down the street. "By the time another taxi came along…well, Mrs. Kantel, that crafty little sucker was long gone."

Sucker?

I said, "So that's when you called in the FBI, right?"

"No. That's when I broke into her dang room."

Why don't I want to hear the rest of this?

I placed my hand on my forehead and said to her, "And someone caught you and reported you to the FBI?"

"No," she said, shaking her head. "That's when I searched her room."

No warrant. Illegal search. That's after breaking and entering. Good grief! *Oh, Dusty.*

I asked, "How did you get away with it?"

On second thought, I really don't want to know that either.

"You see," she went on, "a bellhop kinda ran interference for me."

Kinda? Interference?

I asked her, "What did he do...and what did you find in her room?"

"That's where it got kinda confusin', Mr. B. I thought I was in the room registered to Mrs. Kantel. However, the things I found in the dang place didn't make sense to me." She stared at me with one of her dumb expressions, this time with her fingers tugging on her six earrings. "What's it called, Mr. B, when you expect somethin' but get that thang...plus somethin' else by accident—a bonus, so to speak?"

"Serendipity."

"Wow!" she said, her green eyes flashing. "Yer so dang cool, Mr. B." She turned to her father. "Ain't that right, Daddy?"

"Yep," he said, nodding. "That man be smart as a damn dingo."

Dingo? Are they smart? Did I just get a compliment or what? Beats me.

However, Dusty's procrastination was driving me nuts. I was so anxious to find out the connection between the two girls, I thought I would split right down the middle if the darned kid didn't get on with it. But it seemed all Dusty wanted to do was sidestep the issue.

"Getting back to the things you found in the room, Dusty," I said with a voice a little less than patient, "would it be too much for you to elaborate further?"

A sharp nod. "No problem, Mr. B."

Thank God for small favors.

THIRTY-FIVE

Daddy Diamond picked up the newspaper and pretended not to be interested in what his daughter had to say. I say pretended because I could see his blue-green eyes peeking over the paper. Maybe he was familiar with what had happened but didn't know the entire story. Or, maybe he knew the whole thing and wanted to make sure Dusty got in all the details so it would show they did a professional job—and he could therefore justify additional charges. Ouch!

Whatever. He nodded to Dusty as if giving her permission to lay it all on the table. He returned his attention to the newspaper.

Dusty turned to me and finally explained everything: "There never was no Lynn Smith."

I was dumbfounded. Don't tell me there was never a Lynn, because I actually held her in my hands. I mean, that's how this whole darned thing got started, right?

My jaw dropped. "What?" I asked with a dumb expression on my face. "What are you talking about?"

Dusty nodded slowly. "They was one an' the same."

I sucked in a deep, calming breath. "Who was… were…?"

"Lynn and Mrs. Kantel."

My fingers raked through my hair. "What? The same person? You've got to be kidding, Dusty."

How was that possible? I mean, Lynn was a brunette with brown eyes, and Mrs. Kantel was a blonde with blue eyes. Besides, Lynn was Harry Thomas' lover; whereas Mrs. Kantel had her husband, Hans, and her handyman dressed in black. No way the two girls could be the same person.

"There must be some mistake," I told Dusty. "The gals didn't look anything alike...and they had completely different interests."

"Oh, the dang interest was the same," Dusty said, her head bobbing up and down. "It's always the same: envy, lust, greed, money."

"You mean to tell me, Dusty, they're the same person, when I personally have first-hand knowledge —"

Interrupting (as usual), Dusty said, "Oh, they're definitely one an' the same, that's fer sure, Mr. B."

"What about the different color hair and eyes?"

"That's the cool part, Mr. B," she said, grinning. "As you know, Mrs. Kantel's first name was Marilyn."

"Uh-huh."

She looked up at me and stared for a moment as if waiting for me to pick up on the rest.

I didn't.

"Well," Dusty went on, "I found a pair of brown-colored contact lenses in the hotel bathroom. And in the closet was a small leather bag that contained a brown wig. It was obvious Mrs. Kantel—the blonde—wore the dark wig and brown contacts when she wanted to be Lynn Smith...or your Lynn Thomas. That was to keep from bein' recognized...and to throw us off."

I nodded my understanding. "So you figured Mrs. Kantel was Lynn."

"No, I figured Lynn was Mrs. Kantel."

Whatever, Dusty.

I asked her, "Find anything else there?"

Dusty shook her head. "Nope. I was too busy straightenin' up thangs I'd knocked over and then gettin' the heck outta there before I got caught."

"That was wise...very wise," I said nodding in total agreement. "Then what did you do?"

"My new bellhop friend ran interference for me again and let me check the front-desk register."

"Uh-huh."

"And when I was lookin' for Lynn Smith's name, I saw Mrs. Kantel's signature. It was hard to read. She doesn't have very good penmanship, you know. She probably has someone else do all her writin' for her. Dumb blonde."

Get back to the point, Dusty.

I curled my lip and said, "Go on."

"Oh, yeah," she said. "Well, you know how you sometimes get when yer not asleep but not quite awake either?" she said with forehead furrowed. "What's that called?"

"Reverie."

"Right. Well, my brain began clicking on all five cylinders, and I took a closer look at Mrs. Kantel's signature. It was a mess. However, when I studied it carefully, the first part was more or less a blur. But the endin', Mr. B, well, that was pretty dang clear...lyn."

I nodded and said, "And?"

Dusty raised her palms in frustration. "Don't you get it?"

I displayed a dumb stare.

"Marilyn," she said slowly and methodically. "Mari...**lyn**."

The light in my head finally flashed on. I'm pretty quick once everything's explained to me and all the facts are known. Uh-huh.

I asked with a cocked eyebrow, "You mean Marilyn used the name Lynn for short?"

"Yep."

I smiled, knowing what was coming next. I hate to be right all the time. But, as I said, I'm pretty quick.

"So," she said, grinning proudly, "I asked myself... 'lyn' as in Lynn? Yeah! That's when it all came together: how she set you up and trapped you so you'd take the fall for her, Mr. B. And how she had her Ninja—the guy dressed in black—do her dirty work for her." Dusty's grin spun into a look of satisfaction.

"Bruno Grimes," I informed her.

Her tiny nose rose slightly. "Huh?"

"Grimes," I explained. "He was your guy in black."

"How'd you know that?"

"The FBI."

"The Fibbies?" She jammed her hands into her bony hips. "Did they also tell you how I found 'im?"

"Nope. Just that—"

"Well, hell, Mr. B," she said, cutting me off. "That's the best dang part."

"It is?"

"Yep. After checking the register, somethin' kept gnawin' at me. You see, there was more to it than what meets the nose."

I thinks it's eye, Dusty. But who's going to correct the kid now? She's on a roll.

I asked her, "And what did your nose detect this time?"

"It wasn't my nose, Mr. B. It was my eyes. Yep, I saw 'im with my very own eyes."

There she goes again.

"Who, Dusty?"

"Blackie," she replied with a sharp nod. "Yer...yer Mr. Grimes fella."

"You saw Grimes?"

"Yep. Thought he was gonna kill me for sure."

"What?"

"Uh-huh."

I could feel my pulse quickening. "Where was he, Dusty?"

She looked down and stared at the floor, as if actually seeing him at that moment. "He was just sittin' there." She waved a hand. "Dead as a doorknob...I thought."

*It's **doornail**, sweetheart.*

I asked, "And where was that?"

"Right in front of my own doggone nose," she said, shaking her head and showing a look of pure disdain.

Are we going in circles here or what?

"Could you elaborate a little, Dusty?"

"How I missed 'im the first time I checked the closet; I haven't the slightest, Mr. B." She shrugged. "Maybe he hid in there when we knocked on the door, or maybe he wasn't there then but came in *after* to get his gun...or to scare Mrs. Kantel...or do somethin' kooky. I dunno."

Does this girl keep you in suspense, or is it just me who's frustrated?

"Well, where the hell was he, Dusty?"

"In the dang closet!" she finally answered with a burst. "The very same closet where I found the leather bag with the dark wig Marilyn Kantel wore. Boy, that dang woman sure had it all figured out, didn't she? She's slicker than a hog in a mud pit."

Sidetracked again. What's new?

I asked her, "Was this before or after you found Grimes?"

"Huh?"

"When did you find Grimes?" I asked in a firm voice; my patience about at an end. "Before or after you found the wig?"

"The second time," she replied. "I found the wig and contacts the first time I checked, but I didn't see him then. I don't know how the heck I didn't see 'him right away. Maybe he was scrunched into the corner and covered with a dang coat or something."

That would do it, Dusty.

"In fact," she went on, "when I did spot him, all I saw at first was the tips of his black boots."

"I wonder what—"

She cut me short again. "Marilyn Kantel had Blackie…that Grimes guy…shoot her husband, Hans."

"You don't say."

"Yup," Dusty replied, nodding. "She then shot Grimes to make sure there was no witnesses."

"Really."

"Uh-huh," said Dusty, nodding again. "In fact, it was Grimes' gun—silencer and all—that Marilyn Kantel used to shoot the dirty bugger." A hint of a grin creased her lips. "Grimes musta—"

I cut her short. "I wonder why Hans said he wasn't married."

"Oh, they was still married," Dusty explained. "But Hans had filed for divorce after finding out Marilyn was screwin' around with Harry Thomas. Don't thank he knew about Blackie though. However, she never signed the papers. Wanted the insurance money instead of the divorce settlement, I guess."

"And how did you find out all this, Dusty?"

"Got it from the Fibbies."

Albeit, I was still a bit confused and wondered how the FBI even got into the picture.

I said to Dusty, "That's when you called the FBI, right? I mean...when you found Grimes' body in the closet?"

"Noooo!" she explained, wagging her head adamantly, as if I had missed the point. "Grimes was in the closet, but he wasn't *dead* in the closet."

What now?

I arched an eyebrow. "Dusty, I need a little explaining here."

"Mr. B," she clarified, rolling her eyes as if I should have guessed what really happened, "that Grimes guy was waiting in the back of the dang closet—not wanting to be seen, I guess—until he realized it was me snooping around in their hotel room. Then, he sprang at me like a goldarn Gila monster snatching a bug. He grabbed me by the dang throat, and...and I passed out."

"How in the world did you get out of there?"

"I'm not sure," she said, shrugging. "I suppose he carried me out when Mrs. Kantel returned. They then tossed me in the trunk of a rental car and hauled me to the mountains where they planned on killing me."

I couldn't believe what I was hearing. However, knowing these people like I now do, I wouldn't put a thing past the loathsome lot.

I asked her, "How did you escape?"

Dusty explained to me about her spending the night in the trunk of their car, digging the grave, the argument between Grimes and Marilyn, and how Marilyn shot him with his own gun. Dusty told me how she smacked the gun out of Marilyn's hand with the shovel; and she also relayed the story about the young kayaker picking her up and taking her to the white-water rafting area on the Ocoee River. She also told me how she saw Marilyn shoot at her from a bridge downstream from the Olympic Visitor Center, and how her rubber raft deflated when the bullet that grazed her leg also punctured the raft. She said she didn't recall much after bouncing head-first off the rocks and then sucking a few gallons of the raging white water. I wonder why…

After Dusty had time to catch her breath, I said to her, "I guess you had a life vest on and that saved you from drowning, huh?"

"Yep," she replied, nodding. "And, thanks to a passing raft where somebody yanked me outta the dang river."

"I wonder how Marilyn got caught," I said, my forehead wrinkling. "I mean, she's a pretty shrewd cookie."

"Oh, yeah," added Dusty, "the cops said the young kayaker who picked me up made a call to the Highway Patrol when he was able to get a signal on his cell phone. They were able to get to Marilyn before she got off the bridge."

"You're lucky you just got shot in the leg, otherwise—"

"I'm lucky she didn't get to the end of the run where they take the boats outta the river—she woulda been waitin' for me and shot me in the dang head for sure."

It was funny—but it was too serious to be funny.

I said, "I guess they found Grimes' body too, huh?"

"Yep. The kayaker knew approximately where he had picked me up, and he took the cops there. They found that dadgum killer's body lying next to the dang grave they had intended for me." She shook her head in disgust with it all.

211

"I can't believe they would kill you just for following them."

"They really wanted to know all I knew about what they'd done...and who the heck I'd told." She nodded in agreement with herself. "They woulda come after you, Mr. B, if I'd squealed on ya."

"You should have, Dusty. At least they would have been chasing me...instead of trying to kill you."

"Get real, Mr. B," she said with one side of her lip lifting a bit, "they woulda killed me anyway, then gone gunnin' for you."

I shrugged. She was probably right, as usual.

"So," I said after a moment, "I guess after they patched you up and the cops finished questioning you, that's when you called the FBI?"

"Nope. That's when Daddy called the FBI."

Huh?

She continued, "Daddy was the one that called the FBI."

I glanced at Daddy, who was once again peering over the newspaper.

He simply grinned. "Helluva job, kid," he said to Dusty with a quick, sharp nod. "Helluva job."

Dusty smiled at her father, then hobbled over and gave him a kiss on the forehead.

Daddy waited a moment, then pushed her away and said, "Cut the crap, girl."

I honestly think the guy was blushing. Blushing!

What could possibly happen next?

THIRTY-SIX

So, the case was solved—thanks to a most unlikely duo. However, I never for one moment had any doubt about the kid's...and her father's...abilities. You believe that, don't you?

A couple weeks had passed, and I was able to get my life back to where it once was—more or less. I also had time to take care of a few things that had been awaiting my attention—like setting things straight with my golfing buddies...and smoothing things over with my wife, Heather, for starters. I also had to meet with Mr. Diamond and settle up with him.

Daddy Diamond looked up at me from his hospital bed when I walked into the room. Dusty was sitting in a chair next to him. A bright smile lit up her face.

Mr. Diamond rubbed his fingers together in the international sign language of "money" and said, "There's a little matter what still needs settlin'."

"Oh, the payment," I said, nodding in agreement.

"Yup," he said, an evil eye piercing my soul. "I'll have it all tallied up...daily fees, all the dang expenses, and the like. And don't fer a goldarn minute thank you kin snooker the kid either."

"Well, Mr. Diamond, the daily fees won't be a problem. However, the...expenses...well, they might be."

"Hey," he said in that growling voice of his, "a deal's a damn deal, goddamnit! You sent the kid to

Atlanta…which you had no business doin' in the first damn place…so you have to bite the damned bullet and pick up the goddamn tab! Cain't leave her holdin' the short end of the damn stick fer somethin' that you caused." He adjusted himself on the bed to face directly at me. "And you damn well better know it."

I grinned at Daddy Diamond even though it looked as if he was about to jump out of that hospital bed and grab me by the throat. I took a step back and said, "Atlanta's not the problem, sir." I looked at Dusty, who was waiting with a perplexed look on her face. "It's your daughter here. She seems to think I might be responsible for some irresponsible act of hers."

"Oh?" asked Daddy, turning to Dusty. "And what the hell might that be, girl?"

Her lips pursed. "I thank he means my Jeep, Daddy," she pouted. "I lost my Jeep."

I thought the poor kid was going to burst into tears. After all, that Jeep of hers was the only thing of value she possessed in this world…other than that damned pellet gun, that is. It makes you feel kind of empty deep down inside.

"Lost it?" Daddy asked, arching a bushy brow. "How the hell did you manage a thang like that, girl?"

"Well, I didn't actually 'lose it' lose it."

"Huh?" he said, his thick reddish eyebrows now pinching together.

She shrugged her slender shoulders. "It got burnt up," she said in a mousy voice. Then, she explained to him what had happened.

He didn't look very surprised. I surely would be, if something like that happened to me. But, I guess when you're in their line of work, stuff like that happens.

Daddy simply nodded his understanding and turned to me. "Don't hardly seem fair, does it?" he said, again cocking one of those furry eyebrows. "But I cain't see how the hell we kin charge you fer it, 'cause the kid shoulda took better care of the damn thang." He shook his large head in disgust. "Besides, she kin use my car till I get outta this godforsaken place...then we kin ride together. In fact, she'll hafta drive me 'round fer quite a while, I reckon." He glanced at Dusty, who was counting the gray vinyl floor tiles. "Ain't that right, girl?"

"Yes, Daddy," she said in a voice just above a whisper. She turned away while she sniffed and dabbed at her watery eyes.

I thought I was going to start bawling myself. I took a deep breath to recapture my composure and walked over to the window and looked outside. The sky was a brilliant blue, and the sun was shining brightly. I turned and held my hand out to her. "Come here, Dusty."

She looked at me with those sad puppy-like green eyes, got to her feet, and slowly moved next to me and slipped her fingers into mine.

"Look outside," I said, guiding her gently to the window.

She followed but didn't show much reaction.

I said to her, "Remember this, Dusty, no matter how bad things seem to get, there's always a bright side hidden in it. It's like having your own personal rainbow with you all the time. You just have to look into your heart and find it."

Listen to me—the big philosopher. Like I know what the hell I'm talking about.

"I know," she whispered, wiping away a tear. "I don't thank I've ever seen the sky that blue before. Maybe it's a sign."

"Maybe it is, Dusty. Maybe it is." I nodded and swallowed hard. "Look down, and tell me what you see."

She slowly lowered her gaze. "The parkin' lot," she said, her trembling voice trailing off.

"Now do what I said and try to find the rainbow."

Her eyes, still watering, scanned the lot.

I asked, "What do you see?"

"Cars."

"What kind?"

"All kinds," she said with a slight sob.

"Like what exactly?"

"I dunno," she replied, shrugging. "Cars, trucks, vans…and a Jeep."

"A Jeep?"

"Yep. A shiny new Jeep."

"What color Jeep?"

"Green."

"Like the color of your eyes, maybe?"

Another shrug. "Sorta, I guess."

"Do you like it?

She studied it for a moment and said, "I guess."

Daddy broke in. "Hey," he growled, "whacha doin' to my little girl, damnit?"

Ignoring the kid's father, I said, "Then it's yours, Dusty."

Her liquid green eyes turned and stared at me for a second or two. "Really?"

I could feel my eyes filling also. "Really," I said with a truly satisfying smile.

"No joke, Mr. B?"

I shook my head. "No joke."

She looked at her father. "Daddy?"

He shrugged his massive shoulders. "If that's what the hell the man says…then that's what the hell he means, I guess."

216

Dusty turned to me and stared at me for a long moment. I guess she wanted to see if I was going to tell her it really was just a prank or something. But when I smiled openly, she gave me another one of her smothering hugs.

"How can I ever thank you, Mr. B?" she said, pressing those six earrings into my chest. "You have no idea what this means to me! You're just the greatest! Really awesome."

She squeezed me harder than ever. You know, the little pip-squeak was pretty darned strong for her size.

I said, "I think I do, Dusty. I think I do." I hugged her back. "And you can also thank my golfing buddies who chipped in for it."

"Awesome!" she said, leaning back and looking into my watery eyes. "That's like...totally cool."

That brought out a big grin from me.

"Thank you, Mr. B," she said, squeezing me again but still looking up at me. "The next time yer in trouble and need some help, look me up. I'll give you a freebie."

A freebie?

Oh, jeez.

Heather, where are you?

I glanced at Daddy, who was now scowling...again.

I turned to her and said, "Thank you, Dusty, but I hope that won't be necessary." I managed to break free and step away from her. Phew!

She grinned and said, "It won't be necessary, Mr. B...that's if you stay the heck outta those dang sand traps."

Daddy appeared confused. His bushy eyebrows pinched together again.

However, Dusty and I knew exactly to what she was referring...both ways.

I smiled, then began walking out of the room. "Uh-huh," I said over my shoulder. "No more sand traps, Dusty."

A huge smile smeared my face, but they couldn't see it of course. I wasn't so sure about missing Daddy, but I knew for certain I was going to miss the hell out of that doggoned kid of his.

Thanks, Dusty.

THIRTY-SEVEN

While I was in the hallway waiting for the elevator, I thought about the myriad of weird things that had transpired with Dusty during the past several weeks: the way I tried to dump her in the beginning; how she transformed into a sophisticated lady when meeting Hans Kantel; the incident when she knocked her Jeep out of gear and the cops found it…and nearly me; her Jeep getting burned up; and finally her puzzling together the situation with the (two?) girls…while almost getting wasted by Bruno Grimes and Marilyn Kantel.

Man, did I almost screw up by not hiring the kid. I'd be hanging by a hemp necktie if it weren't for her persistence and tenacity. Thank God for the little rascal.

Dusty suddenly grabbed my arm, scaring the hell out of me. "Mr. B!" she gasped, after hurrying to catch me. "I thought I'd missed you."

I stared at her for a moment. I never expected to see the kid again, much less right there and then.

"Dusty?" was all I could manage in my surprised and confused state. "What—?"

She cut me off again. What's new?

"We've some unfinished business," she said, still holding onto me. "Really important stuff."

I looked around to see if anyone was watching. Sure enough, two nurses—who were pretending to be reading charts—gawked at us over their clipboards. I attempted to shake Dusty's arm free, but it was like fending off a fouled-up fish net.

"Dusty," I bent over and whispered, "people are looking."

Without looking at the two nurses, she said, "Screw 'em!"

Now why didn't I know that was coming?

Still trying to shake free, I asked, "What exactly is this unfinished business of yours, Dusty?"

"The dang FBI!" she replied, cocking her head to the side. "Don't you remember what we talked about?"

Oh, yes, the feds. How could I forget something as important as that? We were—I should say Dusty was—going to give them a piece of our minds, if you recall.

The nurses no longer kept up their charade; they simply stood there—clipboards hanging at their sides—staring and listening. I guess we got their undivided attention when they heard Dusty say *FBI*.

I was saved by the bell—the elevator bell *dinging*, that is. The doors opened, and I quickly stepped in. Well, *I* didn't step in. *We* stumbled in—Dusty and I together—locked arm-and-arm. I'm sure we looked like a couple of drunks returning from a Friday night binge—rather than two entangled friends. But who the heck cares besides those two nurses, right?

When the door closed and Dusty and I were alone inside the cab, I managed to unwrap myself from her grasp. "Dusty, you can't do that. I'm a married man, remember? What if—?"

She cut me off. "Aw, shucks, Mr. B, we're just a coupla simple folks havin' a little innocent fun, that's all."

Fun? Innocent?

I did, however, enjoy the kid's company and friendship. But I had absolutely no desire to let it go beyond that. I smoothed the sleeve of my blue shirt and attempted to compose myself.

I said, "Dusty—"

She cut me short...again. Boy, am I going to miss that. Ha.

Her normally beautiful green eyes narrowed. "Mr. B," she said in a stern voice, "we've got somethin' very important to say to 'em dang idiots down at the damn Bureau."

I stepped back and widened my eyes at that. "Don't you think we should let bygones be bygones, Dusty?" I said, raising my palms. "I mean...it all ended up okay, and—"

Interrupting—as usual—she said, "No way are they gonna scare the hell outta you, Mr. B." She shook her head like she meant it. "Not without gettin' a snootful from yours truly."

*I think it's **earful**, Dusty.*

I took a deep breath out of frustration. It seemed useless trying to convince Dusty not to do it. However, my good sense told me not to start anything we couldn't finish. And starting something nasty with the feds never finishes; it's just a beginning.

"Dusty, antagonizing the feds really isn't necessary...or very prudent." I took her hand in mine and looked straight into those green eyes of hers. "Everything turned out all right, and...and I truly appreciate what you did...and what you're trying to do for me now. But—"

Another interruption.

"You do?" she said, perking up. "Then maybe we should just let it slide like you said, Mr. B."

That wasn't so bad now, was it? I mean, she could have kept insisting and such. Bless her little heart.

I nodded. "You betcha, kid. You were great, and I'll be ever grateful for all you did for me. And, there's no way I could ever—"

Damnit, she cut me off again.

"Dang, Mr. B, that's the nicest thang anyone's ever said to me."

Could she be blushing? I honestly think she was blushing.

I smiled—and it wasn't just from my lips—it came from deep within my heart.

She returned my smile, and her green eyes sparkled like the brightest emeralds ever polished. Dusty was certainly something special.

"Mr. B?"

"Yes, Dusty?"

Her innocence was reflected in the warmth of her delicate smile. She said, "Would you come clean with me on somethin'…I mean, straight up?"

"Sure, Dusty. What's on your mind?"

She cocked her head slightly. "You know that shiner you said you got when you slammed yer head on the handrail at the motel when you first met that Lynn gal?"

Something's coming.

"Yeah," I replied.

"You really didn't get it that way…I mean the way you said, did you?"

Oh, boy.

I cocked an eyebrow and gave her a confused look that offered, *What the hell are you talking about?*

She must have gotten the picture because she looked askance and pierced my soul with an accusing stare.

It was so quiet in that elevator, one could have heard a flea flop on the floor and pump out a plethora of push-ups.

Fortunately for me, however, I didn't have to answer Dusty's question about how I got the black eye; I was saved by another *ding* of the elevator bell before I could think of a response that wouldn't get me in too much trouble with the kid. The elevator came to a stop with a slight joggle.

Dusty motioned for me to come closer.

I prayed she wasn't going to ask me again about the shiner, or worse yet, get back on that darned FBI thing again. That would not be a good way to end our relationship.

I leaned over to hear what Dusty had to say that was so important. However, instead of her whispering something significant to me as I had expected, her little lips clomped onto my cheek like a saltwater snail sucking a slimy stone.

"Dusty!" I exclaimed, getting my arms entwined with hers as I attempted to push her away.

However, before I could do anything about untangling our arms and getting the persistent little squid separated from my face, the elevator door opened, and... and you won't believe who was standing there.

Heather.

HEATHER!

Heather, my not-so-understanding wife, was waiting to get into the elevator.

God help me.

"Heather," I pleaded, finally breaking free of the cute little green-eyed redhead. "It's not what it looks like." I reached out to her as she turned away. "I can explain, sweetheart."

Yeah, right. Lots of luck, Buddy.

"Heather, wait!"

"HEATHER!"

"HEATHER?"
Oh, nooooooo!

THIRTY-EIGHT

Believe me when I say that my wife, Heather, seeing Dusty draped all over me was the least of my problems. You see, after my furious—no, incensed—wife fumed off, my eyes shifted to the two men waiting in front of the elevator. You won't believe it when I tell you who was there. Detectives Small and Biggs were standing near the elevator doors and grinning like two foxes facing a cornered canary.

I glanced at Dusty, who didn't appear the least bit surprised. She simply shrugged and drifted aside like I had the plague or something just as nasty. So, she was in on it. She knew.

Swell.

My gaze shifted back to the detectives. I had one last hope: Maybe they were there to congratulate Dusty on doing such a fine job solving the case for them.

Yeah, sure.

Dusty and I stepped out of the elevator, and Detective Small walked up to us. Detective Biggs stood behind him, arms folded at his chest. What's new?

"Mr. Bowers," Small said, "you're under arrest for the murder of Harry Thomas."

Not again!

I turned and glanced at Dusty.

"Sorry, Mr. B," she said, lowering her head.

From her reaction, I gathered she must have set it up. How could she do something so devious after all the things I did for her…and the great relationship we had? Women!

Detective Small read me my rights and slapped handcuffs on my wrists. The three of us—Small, Biggs and I—got into the squad car and drove off.

Dusty had disappeared during all that. I guess she didn't want to get involved again. Hell, can you blame the kid?

When we got to the interrogation room at the jail in Gunter, Detective Small informed me that Marilyn Kantel told them she saw me kill Harry Thomas. Can you believe it? That little rat, Lynn—Marilyn, that is—still wasn't through with me. I suppose she wanted her pound of flesh for my rejecting her invitation to join her in the pool and then getting away unscathed.

I asked Detective Small, "Why would Marilyn Kantel do a thing like that when *everybody* knows she and Grimes did in Hans and Harry?"

"Apparently she thinks all the pieces of this puzzle aren't quite in place yet."

I asked, "Does that FBI guy, Special Agent, um—?"

Small helped me: "Roberts?"

"Yeah, Roberts. Does he know about this?"

Small nodded in the affirmative.

I leaned back in the metal chair and folded my arms across my chess and asked, "Then why the hell did Roberts tell me I was free to go?"

"To see if you would lead us to the rest of the damned dough."

"The dough?" I asked, my left eyebrow arching. "You mean there's money stashed someplace?"

"Yep," replied Small. "And don't try to tell us you know nothing about it, Bowers."

I faked a smile and said to him, "So it's really just the money...and not the murder I'm suspected of being involved with."

"Both," answered Small.

Both?

Hey, you know as well as I that I didn't kill Harry Thomas. And as far the money goes, Marilyn Kantel is just guessing. She's just throwing out some damned darts to see if they hit anybody when they land. She most likely made that up about the money, so they'd have something else they could pin on me. You've got to believe that—even if I didn't tell the whole truth to begin with.

What?

Okay, let's talk. Maybe I didn't exactly come clean earlier. But I didn't lie to you. Honest. I just twisted the truth a bit. Just a little fib, more or less.

Don't look at me that way.

Damnit! Now you think I was in cahoots with that baneful bunch. Well...I was a little with Lynn; however, you know pretty much all about that. But, hey, I promise you, I didn't kill anybody—I don't think.

Okay, I'm going to come clean and level with you. Here's the deal in a nutshell. You see, when I left Lynn at the pool that dark, moonless night at the resort, I didn't go directly to my room like I had said. I sort of ran into somebody in the dark. Sort of?

Remember the shiner and welt I had on my eye that Detective Small asked about? Well, I didn't whack my head on the railing like I told him. And now that I think about it, I believe Detective Small—and Dusty—knew my story was a lie all along. Anyway, the shiner I got was from saying hello to somebody's fist in the shadows. I didn't see who it was because I was knocked out colder than an Eskimo in an icy igloo. And when I woke up, nobody—and

I mean nobody—was around. Anywhere. Nobody. Not even in the pool. How do I know that? Well, after I regained consciousness, I went to the pool and splashed water on my face. If someone were there, I definitely would have seen him or her.

I leaned forward and said to Small, "You didn't believe me when I told you how I got the black eye, did you?"

"Nope," he said, slowly wagging his head. "And I didn't believe you when you said you weren't part of their slimy scheme neither."

There he goes again, trying to tie me in with that bunch of hooligans.

I asked, "What makes you think I was in on it?"

Small pushed back from the table and crossed his arms. "Marilyn Kantel saw you scuffling with Harry Thomas when she was heading back to her room from the pool."

Okaaay.

"Is that what she told you?"

"Nope. That's what she told the feds."

The feds? Great.

I asked Small, "Well, how in the world did she know it was Harry Thomas who slugged me? She was still in the pool when I left...and it was darker on that hotel walkway than the inside of a closed clamshell."

Small sucked through his teeth to dislodge some food before he said with confidence, "Said she ran right past you and Harry Thomas."

I asked, "Was Marilyn staying in Thomas' room? Were they having an affair?"

"Whatever," answered Small. "All we know and care about...is that she made you."

"Made me? We didn't...I mean—"

Small interrupted my thought, "Identified your ugly face."

That really got my dander up. "Hey," I said, looking as defiant as I could, "it was so damned dark out there, I couldn't tell who the hell it was at the other end of that fist. I mean, I was an arm's length from the damned guy and couldn't see his freaking face. How in the hell could Lynn—I mean Marilyn Kantel—have identified him from where she was...some twenty yards away in that damned pool?"

Small ignored my question. Instead of him analyzing my rationale, he said, "That's when you got that shiner, ain't it?"

See, I told you he knew about the black eye. The guy's not nearly as dumb as I thought.

I nodded slowly. "Yeah, I guess."

"And I'll bet Biggsie's paycheck that your knobby knees buckled...and your damned lights went out. Am I right or what?"

How'd he know that? Based on logic? Hardly. Just guessing, I'm sure.

My head twisted slightly, and I peered at Detective Biggs. He was grinning like a grazing goose.

I returned my stare to Detective Small but didn't answer his question. I said to him, "It's a damned set-up. That screwy Kantel gal had to know someone was hiding in the shadows—probably that thug she hired. They must have had the whole thing planned."

"Don't think so," interjected Biggs.

I shifted my gaze to Detective Biggs. He wasn't smiling this time.

"Your story don't hold no water," Biggs said in his deep voice.

229

"What Biggsie here is trying to say," explained Small, "is that Harry Thomas wasn't in their motel room when Marilyn Kantel returned."

I glared at Small. "Hell, just because Harry Thomas wasn't in his room doesn't mean he was the one who slugged me, does it?"

Small nodded a couple of times. "Odds are pretty good."

"I don't think so," I retorted. "It could have been anybody—particularly that goddamned goon—Grimes."

Biggs said, "You're grabbing for straws, Bowers."

Ignoring the large detective, I said to Small, "There's no way Marilyn Kantel could be positive who it was unless she was in on it. She's trying to frame me." My bewildered gaze shifted from detective to detective. "Don't you see?" I raised my hands, palms up.

Small shrugged and said, "Hey, that's what the lady told 'em."

I asked him, "The FBI?"

"Yup."

I shook my head in resignation. "Well, she's either guessing...or she knew all along who the hell was hiding in the shadows, and the two of them were in it together...thick as thieves, as they say."

"Think what you like, Bowers," said Small. "But she's our eyewitness, and it's her word against yours. And she doesn't have anything else to lose."

Biggs added, "She's going away for a long time...a very long time."

Small scrubbed the short, thinning hairs on top of his head. "Besides, you seem to have trouble keeping your damned stories straight, son."

My anger was turning my face magenta again. "And you're going to take Marilyn Kantel's word over mine—

the word of an embezzler, an arsonist and a murderer? You've got to be kidding, Detective."

Small said, "Pretty much a draw, I'd say."

"'Specially when you got *two* killers," added Biggs. "Mrs. Kantel may have killed her husband, but you killed Harry Thomas because he caught you messing with his gal, Lynn—or Marilyn, that is."

I glared at Biggs. "I'm no killer, damnit!"

"Uh-huh," he offered, folding his arms across his massive chest.

I returned my attention to Small. "Think about it for a minute. If Thomas punched out my lights, how the hell did I kill the damned guy?"

"You coulda got to your feet and clubbed him when he wasn't looking."

"If I did, where the hell's the murder weapon?"

"We got the club," interjected Biggs.

I asked Biggs, "Any fingerprints on the thing?"

Biggs wagged his head back and forth. "Nope."

"See, that proves I didn't do it."

Small said, "That *doesn't* prove you didn't do it."

Huh?

I gave him a screwy look.

"You coulda wiped 'em off," continued Small, "or been wearing gloves at the time."

"Maybe your *golf* gloves," added Biggs with a snicker.

Very funny.

I asked Small, "Where'd you find the club?"

"Right where you pitched the damned thing—over the wall and down the hill."

I figured I had him: "What kind of club was it?"

231

Biggs interposed, "You should know, Bowers. A *pitching* wedge, maybe?" He let out a howl that made the bars on the window rattle.

What a comic.

I shook my head in frustration. These guys had their bird-sized brains made up and were not about to listen to a word I had to say—especially after catching me in a lie...or two.

Small finally explained: "The club was a piece of wood—probably firewood."

"Any blood on it?"

"Plenty," he replied, nodding. "All belonging to Harry Thomas."

"So you think that after I got punched...I got to my feet, clubbed Thomas over the head, tossed the weapon over the wall, dragged his bleeding body to the pool and dumped him in it, right?"

"Uh-huh," replied Small, nodding once. "That pretty much sums it up."

"Then why the hell wasn't I covered with his blood when you found me?"

"You may have washed it off in the pool."

Did this guy read my mind, or does he know more than he's letting on?

"How about my clothes?" I asked Small. "There would have been blood on them if I had done it; isn't that correct?

"You probably ditched your duds."

"Coulda burnt 'em," added Biggs.

Small nodded in agreement. "Got fireplaces in those cottages, I hear."

I asked, "Did you check them—the fireplaces, that is?"

232

"No use," replied Small. "They're cleaned out every day."

Okay, fine.

"You saw my clothes in my room the next morning," I explained. "They were still damp from the night before." I glanced at both detectives. "You saw them, right?"

Biggs said, "Coulda washed them, and they didn't have time to dry."

"Or you coulda got new ones and wet them," Small said. "Easy to make the switch, Bowers."

"Had it all thought out, I'd say," added Biggs. "You got the new ones just wet enough to make 'em fit your story."

They had me backed into a corner, and there was no way out as far as I could tell. See what a couple of frigging little lies will do to you?

"I want a lawyer," I snapped. "And a good one this time, damnit!"

Small nodded slowly. "You're gonna need one, son; you're definitely gonna need one."

THIRTY-NINE

When I entered my all-too-familiar jail cell, I crumpled onto the hard, musty bunk that smelled like Grandma's vegetable cellar and rested my head back in my hands. I stared at the drab concrete ceiling. I was mentally exhausted and totally confused about how the hell I got caught. My brain was spinning like an out-of-control carousel. I kept asking myself why Marilyn Kantel wanted to take me down with her. I hadn't done anything to her—that I was aware of. That is, other than turning her—or Lynn—down that day at the lodge and the pool. I was also wondering how Dusty knew I had lied and how long she had known. But the thing that really got to me was that I was beginning to have doubts about myself. You see, the possibility exists that after I regained partial consciousness; I actually could have whacked Harry Thomas over the head and didn't remember doing it. Damn!

I had a visitor. No, it wasn't my wife, and it wasn't my two detective friends; it was Dusty Diamond—my Judas gumshoe.

I didn't want to see the kid ever again, much less talk to the little snit. I had a lot of unpleasant feelings harbored inside me, and I didn't want them blurting out. Just let it go, I figured. She was only doing her job, and doing it as a pretty damned good private eye, I suppose.

However, the jailer didn't give me any choice about seeing her: He unlocked my cell door, grabbed my arm, yanked me out of my cell, and practically dragged me to the visiting room where the all-too-familiar old gray table and metal chairs were waiting.

Dusty was pacing and not making eye contact. Guilt maybe?

I sat on the cold hard chair and watched her for a minute or two while I pondered why the hell she was here.

Just as I was about to ask how in the world she could betray me, she flashed a horrific piercing stare at me and shouted, "WHYYYY?"

Her shout echoed off the cold, hard walls. I cringed as if a rifle had just been discharged. I then looked around to see if it were me she was addressing. "Why what?" I finally asked when my startled stare returned to her.

She moved to the table and flapped her palms on the Formica top. A stare I couldn't begin to explain drilled deep into my soul. "Why the hell did you do it?"

"Dusty, I—"

"I trusted you, damnit! And you made a goldarn fool outta me." She straightened, jammed her hands into her hips and once again stalked around the small room.

I swear I could see steam coming from her ears.

"Dusty, please lis—"

"You even snookered Daddy," she snapped at me over her shoulder. She stopped walking, turned, and locked her glare on me. "What the heck am I gonna tell 'im? He trusted you just about as much as I did."

I didn't interrupt her. I'm pretty sure I couldn't have spoken anyway: Her suffocating stare gave me lockjaw.

She began walking again and then started a two-way conversation with herself: "Daddy, you know that nice man, Buddy Bowers? *Yeah.* Well, he pulled the dang wool over our heads. *No way.* Yep. He lied to us. *Yer kiddin', girl.* Nope. Just when we thought we got 'im off the dang hook, we find out he was in on their dadgum little scam. *I can't believe it, Dusty.* You had no way of knowin'…had no say 'bout it, Daddy. He made you open wide and then rammed it down yer dang throat. *Really embarrassed us, huh? Embarrassed* ain't a strong enough word, Daddy. The low-down rotten scoundrel reeled us in like a coupla dead fish."

I raised my hands in surrender. "Okay, Dusty, that's really cute, but—"

"Cute? Cute?" she screamed, practically running at me. Is that what the hell you thank? Cute? I'll show you cute!" She grasped the other metal chair and flung it into the corner. It sounded like the Liberty Bell clanging when the chair hit the cinderblock wall. She glared at me. "How 'bout that for cute?"

I think she was a bit upset, so I kept my mouth shut. Smart move, Buddy.

She leaned on the table and those once-pretty green eyes glared right through me. "I'd choke you if I could reach yer dang throat." Her eyes narrowed, and she lunged across the table toward me.

I pushed away just in time. Don't laugh; Dusty may have been skinny, but I'm sure she would have strangled me if she could have gotten to my neck. I think the kid had a little too much adrenaline flowing; I was glad it was a long table.

The guard didn't bother to stop her…or help me. He simply stood near the door with his arms folded across his chest and smirked. Where are the damned police when you need them?

She was actually lying prone on the table now. "I swear I'll get back at you one way or another." The words exploded from the irate kid as if she had swallowed a Gatling gun.

236

"Dusty, please," I pleaded, backing away as far as I could. "Get off the table. You're making a fool of yourself."

She scrambled backwards, sparks still shooting from her eyes. "I'm makin' a fool of myself, you say? Hell, you already done that ten times over. In fact, ten times ten—if you count Daddy, damn you!"

Now I was totally confused. It was quite obvious she was upset—livid. But there was something deeper there. She was acting more like the way my wife, Heather, would under the circumstances. It sounded to me as though Dusty was angrier about me lying to her than my committing a crime—which I hadn't—I don't think. Maybe when she calmed down a bit, I could get a better read on it.

She slithered off the table like a coiling cobra. Her eyes glared at me while she went to retrieve the upside-down chair. She appeared to take a deep breath to gather herself before picking it up and carrying it back to the table. She calmly sat down, pursed her lips and stared at me for a long time. I think she was waiting for an explanation.

"Dusty," I started, expecting to be interrupted again.

However, she didn't: She simply crossed her thin arms over her lime-green sweater and remained quiet. That's right—Dusty Diamond, for the first time since I met her, didn't have a thing to say.

"Dusty," I continued in a soft voice, "I'm sorry for causing any embarrassment to you and your father. I had no intention of doing any such thing. In fact, I would never do anything to intentionally offend or hurt either of you."

Still no reaction from the stoic-faced kid.

"You've got to believe that, Dusty. And you've got to believe, if you can reach deep into that big heart of yours, that I was not involved…in any conceivable way…in their slimy little scheme."

Her eyes narrowed. "Then why'd you lie, damnit?"

She speaks.

My head lowered. "I truly am sorry for that, Dusty," I said, slowly raising my gaze to her. "But I really didn't know exactly what happened. And somehow I was hoping you might find out more about what went down and come to me with it—instead of going to the damned FBI."

Now I was the one getting my dander up.

"I didn't go to the dang FBI."

"No?"

"Nope. They came to me."

"Why?"

"About something Marilyn Kantel had told them."

"And you're going to take the word of that good-for-nothing, back-stabbing, murdering feline over mine, Dusty?"

"Of course not, you dang fool," she replied, appearing to be softening. "But you shoulda come clean straightaway, and none of this woulda been necessary. I coulda covered for ya."

"I didn't need anyone to cover for me, Dusty. I didn't do anything wrong...except leave out a few minor details. And if you recall, it was I who was on the receiving end of the fist thrown by Harry Thomas...or Bruno Grimes...or whomever."

"Then why the heck didn't you say so in the first dang place? You coulda made things a lot simpler for yerself and me...and Daddy."

"I know, Dusty." I shrugged. "What else can I say?"

She wrapped her arms around her small chest. "You got anymore of 'em lies tucked away someplace?"

I shook my head emphatically. "No. Hell, no, Dusty. And you've got to believe me because you're the only one around this damned place who will."

And that included my wife, Heather. However, I didn't share that little bit of knowledge with the glaring green-eyed kid.

She stared. STARED!

"Dusty, don't look at me that way. It gives me the heebie-jeebies. And besides, it doesn't become you the least bit. You're much too nice a girl."

Her stare lost some of its hardness. "I don't know what the heck I'm gonna do with you...or for you, Mr. B," she said in a softer voice. "You got us all so danged bamboozled nobody even wants to talk to you."

I knew that to be a fact: None of my friends—or my wife—had been in to see me this time around. I wonder where Heather went after seeing Dusty kissing me in the elevator and then the detectives handcuffing me. Probably went to call that suave FBI guy—Robert Wilson—or Wilson Roberts—or whatever the heck his name is. Why can't a guy have a simple name, so it would be easy to remember? That way, Heather could...

What the heck am I saying?

HEATHER!!!

"Mr. B?"

I shook my head to clear away those nasty thoughts. I focused on Dusty's prying stare. "What?"

"What am I supposed to do, Mr. B?"

"Believe in me for one thing, Dusty."

"That's kinda tough to do right now."

"Dusty, you're young...and you may not be as sophisticated as some of those high-powered lawyers...but you've got more tenacity and persistence than any ten of them. Plus you've got something even the best of them don't have."

"What's that?"

239

"Instinct, Dusty. Instinct. You—with your kitchen-sink methodology—have a gift that enables you to see through all the smoke and mirrors hurled at you. And you have a heck of a knack for getting to the truth—just like you did when you knew I wasn't telling the complete truth."

I thought I saw her blush. Or, maybe she was still red from being so inflamed when she was screaming at me. Whatever, she was coming around—I think.

"Are you pullin' my foot?" she asked with an arch to her eyebrow.

*I think it's **leg**, Dusty.*

I said, "No, it's the God's-honest truth, Dusty. I sincerely mean it."

"And yer tellin' the truth. You didn't kill nobody?"

"Right." I nodded emphatically. "I didn't kill nobody …anybody, Dusty."

She lowered her head, unwrapped her arms and entwined her fingers on the table. After a moment, she raised her narrowed eyes and said, "Level with me, Buddy. Did you take the danged dough?"

Oh, hell.

FORTY

Here I am in a bad situation again: Should I tell Dusty something she may not be able to handle, or keep on avoiding the inevitable? I stared at the kid for a long moment, wondering. Speculating.

"Dusty," I finally said, "can you keep it together if I tell you something? That is, something you may not want to hear?"

She rolled those bright green eyes of hers. "You got more lies to confess?"

"It's not a lie, Dusty. I just haven't got around to telling you about it, that's all."

"Yeah, sure. Just like when you didn't git around to tellin' me 'bout the dang brawl you had with Harry Thomas."

"It wasn't a brawl, Dusty. I just ran into some guy's knuckles—most likely Bruno Grimes'—in the damned—"

"Or, like when you was smoothin' with Marilyn Kantel, maybe?"

"I wasn't *smoothing*, or whatever, with Marilyn Kan—"

"Yeah, right." Dusty wagged her head in disgust. "I'm not overlookin' the fact that Marilyn Kantel was *your Lynn* in the danged bedroom at the motel, you know."

And this is true. I almost forgot about that. She had me there.

"She wasn't *my Lynn*," I attempted to explain. "And, Dusty, I sure as hell didn't—"

"More danged lies, Mr. B?" She got to her feet.

"Dusty, I haven't lied about anything. I merely haven't told you—"

"What's this shockin' and earth-shatterin' thang you have to lay on me now?" she asked, glaring and jamming her fists into her hips. "More of your dang shenanigans?"

"Sit down, Dusty," I said, glancing at the guard. "You're making me nervous, for crying out loud."

She yanked the chair out and plopped onto it. She folded her arms and gave me another defiant stare. "I'm making *you* nervous? Well, ain't that a danged shame. I guess you want me to feel *sorry* for you too." She shook her head slowly in antipathy. "Pardon me iffin I don't feel a whole heckuva lot of sympathy for you right now, Mr. B. But you see, I'm the one who's been jumpin' through hoops and dancin' around on the dang griddle tryin' to get to the danged truth before they snap a damned rope around yer lyin' neck." Her eyes resembled a Persian cat's. "So...so I'm the one who should be nervous around here, dang it all."

I guess she had a point. Fair enough.

"I'm sorry, Dusty. I wasn't looking for sympathy, you know," I said in a low voice. "I was simply trying to keep you from drawing too much attention from the guard while I told you—"

"Oh, malarkey," she said, cutting me off and shaking her head in disgust. "I don't believe that crap, and you know it."

"It's the God's honest truth, Dusty—I swear."

She stared at me for endless moments. When she finally spoke, she asked, "You finally gonna tell me the whole danged thang now?"

Perseverance pays.

I nodded in defeat. "Yep, the whole thing, Dusty."

Dusty leaned forward in the hard metal chair and squinted. "Well, I'm waitin'."

I rested my folded hands on the table. "Dusty, unlock your jaw, and come close, okay?"

She glared at me, and I hate to think what was whizzing around in her little mind right then.

After a moment, she moved her chair to the table and placed her elbows on the gray surface. "'Fess up," she demanded.

'Fess up? I'm not confessing anything. Well, if telling the whole story is confessing, then I guess she had me there.

She continued: "I'm all ears, Mr. B."

"Actually, Dusty, there was in fact some money involved," I whispered. "You see, Marilyn Kan—"

"I knew it, dang it!" She clapped her hands together and pushed away from the table. "I knew you weren't tellin' the danged truth all along." Her head rolled in disgust.

"Dusty, look at me."

She finally grounded herself and gave me another defiant stare.

"I was telling the truth, Dusty. I mean what I told you was the truth. I just didn't tell you all the things that—"

"But now that yer about to hang, yer gonna tell me where you buried the danged dough, right?"

Hang? I hadn't thought about hanging—for real, that is.

I swallowed and said, "I just want you to know what the heck Mrs. Kantel is talking about, that's all."

Her green eyes narrowed and glared again. "I knew the two of you were into something all along," she snarled.

"The two of us weren't into anything, Dusty. I had nothing to do with that diabolical dame."

"Other than messin' around with her in Harry Thomas' hotel room, you mean."

"Look, Dusty, will you please drop that thought for a minute? I mean...get over it, girl." It was my turn to shake my head. "Man, you're beginning to sound like my wife."

"No wonder she left you."

"She didn't leave me, Dusty. She—"

"Then why the heck ain't she been to see you?"

Another good point. I wondered what that suave FBI dude was up to right then.

I returned my attention to Dusty and said, "She... she's embarrassed, that's all."

"Cain't blame her none," Dusty snickered. "Heck, I'm embarrassed, and I ain't even related to you,."

I took in a deep, calming breath. "Do you want to hear about the money or not, Dusty?"

"Of course I do. I don't know why you just don't come right out and say what the heck yer hidin' from me."

Is it me, or am I getting tongue-tied trying to enlighten this kid?

I cleared my throat and said, "I'm not hiding anything, Dusty. I simply haven't had a chance to get to it yet. You keep inter—"

"Well, why the heck not, Mr. B? I mean, you keep messin' around instead comin' to the danged point."

What can I say?

She shrugged her slender shoulders, which I think meant she was waiting.

I shot a quick glance at the guard then shifted my attention back to Dusty. "Remember when I was in Hans Kantel's office?" I asked quietly.

244

"You mean, when you got conked on the head, and I had to patch up the gash in yer head?"

"Right." I snuck another quick peek at the guard, leaned toward Dusty and whispered, "Well, before I got hit on the head, I found some numbers on a card in Kantel's desk."

"Numbers?" she practically shouted.

I raised my hand to caution her. "Uh-huh," I whispered, checking to see if the guard was paying close attention. He wasn't. I returned my eyes to Dusty. "I stuffed the card with the numbers into my pocket and later checked them out."

"And?"

"And the numbers were to a Swiss bank account. So when Mrs. Kantel was in Atlanta, and I thought she was about to leave the country; I, uh…well, I didn't want her getting away with all that darned money she took from Hans' company…and what she also connived out of the insurance company. And—"

Dusty cut me off: "And you didn't thank I could catch her, and so you filled your dang pockets with the damn dough."

"Not exactly, Dusty."

"Well, what the heck did you do with it?"

"I transferred it to another account."

"So, yer gonna die a rich man, I guess, huh, Mr. B?"

"I may die, but I'm not going to die rich, Dusty."

"What?" She straightened, and her green eyes glistened like watery emeralds. "What the heck did you do with it?"

After another quick gander at the guard, I said, "I put it in *your* name, Dusty."

Her eyes widened to the size of two Hummer hub caps. "Huh?" she gasped.

FORTY-ONE

Dusty had argued with Buddy for over half an hour. She was furious that he—regardless of his intentions—had illegally taken Kantel's money. She was even more infuriated that he had put the new account in her name. She figured that the two dumb detectives probably wouldn't make any connection between her and Buddy; however, the FBI would surely suspect something—especially if and when they dug deeper.

Dusty had grilled Buddy time and again about his taking the money. Whenever he attempted to explain, she wouldn't listen: kept cutting him off. And when Buddy finally managed to finish a sentence, she wouldn't accept his answer; she hammered him like a roofer setting singles.

She also didn't let Buddy forget about his lying to her earlier. She wavered between the lying and why he took the money and why he put it in her name. She was confused and perplexed. She didn't know what to do. Her mind was spinning like a top: going faster than her mouth—for a change.

Dusty continued lecturing Buddy until the guard intervened and dragged her away. She gave Buddy one last piercing stare with her glaring green eyes, shook herself free of the guard, brushed the wrinkles out of her light green sweater, and left the jail in a huff.

Buddy simply sat on the metal chair in total shock.

After Dusty left Buddy, she felt she should visit her father in the hospital to see how he was doing and to get his advice on what to do with the new situation she was now deeply engrossed in. However, she didn't know how to explain everything to her father—especially about the money being in *her* name. Dusty also couldn't get a handle on the way she was feeling: Her emotions ran the gamut. Therefore, instead of driving to the hospital to see Daddy Diamond, Dusty stopped to see a friend about a new type of cell phone; then she sped to the jail in Huntsville.

The Huntsville jail was much larger than the one in Gunter where Buddy was confined. It was also more like a *real* jail: The security system had the latest technology, and the rules were much stricter. The visiting area was also more secure. Visitors had to sit on the opposite side of a wire screen instead of being at the other end of a table like it was at the Gunter jail. There could be no physical contact between inmate and visitor.

Dusty sat on the hard metal chair and adjusted her dark brown wig. She straightened her horn-rimmed glasses with tinted lenses that hid her green eyes. She then pushed up her heavily-padded bra under the tight pink sweater. She hoped the disguise would fool Mrs. Kantel.

Dusty was in no hurry; her mind was still spinning. She still could not accept the fact Buddy had taken the Kantels' money; and to make it worse, she didn't know what to do with it now that it was stashed away in her name. She wanted no part of the darn dough. However, if she told the FBI about the money, that bit of evidence would probably be all they would need to make Buddy an accomplice of Marilyn Kantel. And once that was done, Buddy Bowers would undoubtedly be put away for a very long time.

Dusty's thoughts were interrupted when Marilyn Kantel was led into the visiting area. Mrs. Kantel appeared tired and distraught: Her blue eyes had dark circles under them, and her blonde hair looked like it had been styled with an eight-pound Oreck vacuum cleaner. The oversized and frumpy blue-gray dress did little for her once-proud ample breasts. The dress fit like a sack half-full of onions.

Marilyn Kantel stopped walking and stared at Dusty for a moment. Dusty wondered if the woman had any idea who the private investigator was or what she was doing there. Marilyn turned to the expressionless female guard but was quickly directed to sit across from Dusty. Marilyn glared at Dusty before sitting. The disgusted look on the prisoner's face told Dusty the lady had no desire to be there, nor had any intention of speaking with her visitor.

Dusty nodded a greeting.

Marilyn leaned forward and gazed closely at Dusty. After a moment, she cocked an eyebrow and asked, "Don't I know you?"

Dusty's face flushed; she hoped Marilyn hadn't noticed. She took in a slow deep breath and said, "I don't think so." She looked down at her bulging breasts. "I think you'd remember me if we had met."

Marilyn gave a hesitant nod but continued eying her unwelcome visitor.

Dusty shifted uncomfortably in her seat.

After a moment, Marilyn said, "Well?"

Dusty felt uncomfortable with her disguise. But it seemed to be working; she would proceed as if it were.

Marilyn leaned back, folded her arms under her generous breasts and said, "I'm waiting."

Dusty still hadn't figured what her plan of attack would be. She hesitated before speaking: "Hi. I'm Miss Baker. I…I'm writing a story about—"

249

"I don't talk to reporters," Marilyn snapped back.

"Oh, I'm not a reporter. I—"

"Then what the hell do you want with me?" demanded Marilyn.

Dusty took out her new cell phone and placed it on the shelf in front of her. She looked at Marilyn Kantel through the chicken-coop wiring and said, "Do you mind? My father's in the hospital, and I'm expecting an important call. I may have to leave quickly."

Marilyn flicked her hand as if to say, *It's no big deal.*

Dusty nodded her gratitude and adjusted the phone so it wouldn't fall off the shelf.

Marilyn raised her chin and asked, "What the hell did you say you wanted?"

"I didn't say." Dusty faked a smile. "But I would like to ask you a few questions for the record."

Marilyn cocked an eyebrow. "What record is that?"

"Well, to be perfectly honest with you, Mrs. Kantel, I represent the insurance company that has an interest in the late Mr. Harry Thomas' assets."

Marilyn's forehead furled into wrinkles. "How the hell does that concern me?"

"He worked for your husband, Hans, didn't he?"

"They were partners."

"Were they equal partners?" asked Dusty.

Marilyn looked around the room before returning her attention to Dusty. "That's for the damn courts to decide."

"Also, weren't you and Mr. Thomas…um…quite close?" Dusty wanted to say "intimate," but that might clam Marilyn up.

"If you mean, were we friends? Yes."

Dusty was surprised Marilyn gave that up so easily. She decided to push the spade in further and dig a little deeper.

"Then you should also know that Mr. Thomas wasn't married, and most of his assets were placed in *your* name...as beneficiary, that is. Isn't that correct?"

Another disgusted look washed over Marilyn's drawn face. "That sounds more like a legal matter than an insurance issue to me."

Dusty faked a smile. "They sort of run together sometimes."

Marilyn nodded but said nothing.

"Also," continued Dusty, "Mr. Buddy Bowers was to receive part of Mr. Thomas' estate, if our records are correct." She hoped Marilyn didn't detect the flushness in her face that came with the lie she had just uttered.

Marilyn sucked in a deep breath and sat up straight. "Bowers had nothing to do with the Thomas estate. He didn't even know Harry. Why the hell would he be included in Harry's damned will?"

Ah-ha! Dusty had hit a nerve.

"Bowers must have known Harry Thomas," persisted Dusty. "He's been accused of killing him, hasn't he?"

Marilyn's eyes narrowed. "He did kill him. I saw him do it."

"Yes, that's what you told the authorities. However, we feel there are too many unanswered questions to establish that as fact."

"Like what?" retorted Marilyn. "The police seem convinced."

Now's the time, thought Dusty. "Well, like you and Mr. Bowers being intimate in the motel room and at the swimming pool later that evening—the same night Harry Thomas was killed."

"How do you know about that?" Marilyn sputtered, her face turning red from exasperation. "I mean, that's not what happened. I...I mean, we...we were never intimate. I only knew of Bowers when he was at the pool and...and tried to hit on me. Hell, he was so goddamn intoxicated he could hardly keep from falling into the damn water."

Yeah, intoxicated with you, thought Dusty.

Dusty said, "You mean to say Buddy Bowers was never with you in Harry Thomas' room?"

Marilyn glanced around the visiting room and breathed in a couple of times.

A prelude to a lie, thought Dusty.

"Never!" Marilyn retorted. "Like I told you, I only saw him at the pool."

"That's not what he told us, Mrs. Kantel. He said you, posing as Lynn Thomas, lured him into your room, and offered him sex and a very large amount of money if he would help you kill Harry Thomas."

"That's not true!" Marilyn snapped in a loud voice. "Bowers was hired by my husband to kill Harry so all of Harry's holdings would go to Hans."

What?

"How did you know that?" asked Dusty. "You just said you didn't know anything about Mr. Bowers."

Marilyn rubbed her hands together. "I...I...I didn't say that I didn't know him. I said that I saw him hit Harry over the head and toss him into the damn pool."

"No. That's not what you said, Marilyn. You said you were in the pool, and Bowers tried to hit on you. You even said he was so drunk he almost fell into the pool."

"He *was* drunk."

Dusty continued, "If he was that drunk, how was he able to overcome Harry Thomas and throw his body into the pool. I mean, Harry Thomas was one hell of a man...a linebacker in college, we were told."

"Harry was big, but—"

Dusty cut her short. "It was so dark that night, you couldn't see past the pool's handrail. Isn't that right?"

"I saw Harry bend over to talk with me," retorted Marilyn, talking fast; "and...and that's when Bowers surprised him from behind and hit him over the head. Harry fell into the pool right next to me."

"The police report said you were on your way back to your room when you saw Bowers hit him while they were in the shadows near the walkway."

"I can't remember exactly how it went," rejoined Marilyn, shaking her head in frustration. "That was some time ago, and I was upset over the whole damn thing."

"So, Buddy Bowers wasn't part of Hans' scheme?"

"That's not what I said, damnit!"

Dusty went for the jugular: "Didn't Harry Thomas catch you and Bowers in his motel room? And wasn't Harry so livid that he tried to kill both of you. However, you got the better of Harry and hit him on the head while he was wrestling with Bowers. You and Bowers then dragged him to the pool and dumped him in. Isn't that what happened?"

Marilyn shook her head violently. "You're twisting this all around, damnit!"

Dusty leaned forward. "And then you offered Bowers a portion of your insurance settlement to keep his mouth shut, right?"

"I didn't offer him anything. He...he was in on it from the damned beginning."

"In on what? The sex...or the killing?"

Marilyn's jaw tightened. "He was in on everything," she said heatedly.

Dusty could feel a knot tightening in her stomach. She wondered if Marilyn was really telling the truth about Buddy being in on their scheme. After all, Buddy did lie previously. Dusty felt like she had just been punched in the solar plexus.

Dusty took in a slow, deep breath before saying, "Yeah, but you lied about Bowers being at the pool, right?"

"He was at the pool, damnit!"

"And he was in your motel room, correct?"

Marilyn looked around as if to see if anyone was listening. "That's right," she snarled. "He was in there when Harry returned."

"So, who killed Harry? Was it you...or was it Bowers?" Dusty leaned back. "Or, was it Bruno Grimes?"

Marilyn's eyes widened in panic. "What?"

"That's it, isn't it?" pressed Dusty. "After you and Bowers had your little fling in the motel room, Bowers left. You then hit Harry Thomas on the head and summoned Bruno Grimes, who was waiting outside the room for your signal. And as big and strong as Grimes was, he had no problem carrying Harry's body to the pool and chucking it in. That's the way it went down, isn't it?"

Marilyn drew in a deep breath and glanced around again. "How do you know about Grimes?" she asked in a voice barely louder than a whisper.

"You and Grimes had this all planned out," said Dusty, moving close to the screen. "You and he killed Harry Thomas, and it was supposed to look like Bowers did it. Grimes also killed your husband, Hans, so the two of you would get both Harry Thomas' and Hans' money. However, you got greedy. Real greedy. You wanted it all, so you also killed Grimes, and then tried to frame Bowers for all three murders."

Marilyn's face was as brilliant as a red jaw-breaker. She lunged forward and grasped the dividing screen, trying to get to Dusty.

Startled, Dusty snapped backwards. Her green eyes widened behind her tinted glasses. Her heart stopped beating for a moment. She hoped the screen wouldn't collapse.

Marilyn's long fingers slithered through the screen like treacherous tentacles trying to get to Dusty's throat. She growled, "Why you little wench. I ought to—"

A guard hollered something, and Marilyn's clinging fingers slowly released the wire and dragged downward toward the shelf like slowly melting icicles.

Dusty swallowed hard.

Marilyn glared at Dusty like a crazed woman as she backed away from the screen. Her lips drew tight, and Marilyn continued staring as if she was contemplating her next move.

Dusty's stomach clenched.

Marilyn moved close to the security screen and said in a low, sneering voice, "I'm going to deny everything I said here today, so what I tell you means absolutely nothing other than I shut you the hell up, bitch!"

Dusty remained stoic. She said nothing; however, her pulse hammered in her ears.

Marilyn glanced around before returning her eyes to Dusty. After a moment of intense staring, she uttered quietly, "Bowers was a nobody...a naive john, who conveniently happened along at the wrong damned time—for him, that is."

Dusty's heart jumped in her chest. She said brightly, "You mean Buddy Bowers wasn't part of your scheme? He's innocent then?"

Marilyn nodded yes and smirked. "Yeah, honey... but he's still gonna fry for screwing things up for me."

"And Harry Thomas?" persisted Dusty. "He in on your little scheme too?"

"Nah. He was set up also. Harry gladly went along with the wig and contacts thing when I told him I didn't want Hans seeing us together." Marilyn eased out a bit of a smirk. "The dumb schmuck never saw it coming."

Dusty asked, "What if I tell the authorities what you just told me?"

Marilyn flashed a cockeyed grin. "You think they're gonna believe a sorry little nobody like you? I mean, you're just a—"

"And you're what?" interrupted Dusty, glaring and breathing quickly. "You're a good-for-nothing murderer, a swindler, and a...a jailbird who's about go to prison for life."

Marilyn said nothing. She simply pushed away from the screen and got to her feet. She nodded and grinned and winked at Dusty, then left.

Dusty also stood, picked up her cell phone, closed it and tossed it into her purse. As she watched Marilyn Kantel being escorted away, she marveled at how easy it was for her to change her looks and lose her back-country slang when she wanted. That thought, and the fact that Buddy was innocent, brought a satisfying grin to her lips.

Dusty gave one last look at the departing bleached blonde, then left the jail.

A lot remained undone.

FORTY-TWO

I, Buddy Bowers, was startled when Detectives Small and Biggs approached my jail cell. I sat up and peered through the bars.

Small unlocked and opened the door and said, "Get your sorry ass off that bed and outta this damn place."

I pulled back. "What?"

"You heard the man, Bowers," chided Biggs. "Get lost before we find something that will stick to your damn slippery butt."

I got to my feet and ran my fingers through my matted hair. My surprised stare darted from detective to detective. "You guys serious?"

"Serious as a damn heart attack," said Biggs.

My first thought was that the detectives had finally had enough of me and wanted to shoot me as if I had tried to escape. But that logic didn't hold water; it would be way too obvious in the city's public jailhouse. The next thing that flashed across my mind was that they were on to the money I had manipulated from Marilyn Kantel, and they were probably hoping I would lead them to it. But how the heck did they find out? It had to be the FBI. Or, maybe Marilyn Kantel knew about what I had done and had told the feds exactly what and how I had transferred the funds. Finally, a sickening thought weakened my knees when it smashed against the back of my brain: Dusty told the FBI she now had the money. I felt like puking.

I grabbed the bars of the open cell door to keep from falling.

"What's the matter, Bowers?" asked Biggs. "You gotten used to that jail cell and don't wanna leave?" He glanced at Small and snickered.

I blinked a couple of times to clear my head. I wanted to say something witty to the big man, but I couldn't come up with anything very clever at the moment; I wasn't exactly in a joking mood.

"Come on, Bowers," said Small, grabbing my arm and pulling me out of the cell. "Find some other place to freeload."

"I'm free?"

"Free as a finch," replied Biggs.

"How come? I thought you guys—" I cut myself short and glanced at each detective. "Did the FBI finally unpuzzle everything? Or did—?"

"Enough, Bowers!" snapped Small, jerking a thumb toward the main entrance.. "Get the hell outta here, damnit!"

I shrugged myself loose, straightened the sleeves on my blue shirt where Detective Small's hands had grabbed me; and, as soon as I pocketed my wallet, keys, and other possessions they'd taken from me, scooted out of the place as fast as I could. I wanted to be clear of the damned place before they changed their minds or found some other phony charge to pin on me.

I dashed outside onto the sidewalk and looked for a taxi.

A horn *tooted* from down the street. My head swung in that direction. The headlights on a shiny green Jeep flashed. I recognized the vehicle immediately: It was Dusty Diamond's new ride. My feet froze for a second while my brain attempted to sort things out.

Another *toot*!

I started walking in that direction when I saw a hand wave out through the driver's window. It *was* Dusty.

I waved back and quickened my pace. I was suddenly excited and delighted that Dusty was there. I didn't know how she was going to react after my telling her about the money. I wouldn't have been surprised if she had gone straight to the feds with the information.

The Jeep's passenger door swung open from the force of Dusty's kick. Her long, skinny leg dangled over the passenger seat. "Get in, Mr. B. I've got somethin' important to tell ya."

Dusty was back—again.

I climbed into the Jeep as Dusty's leg slithered back to her side. "Thanks for coming," I said to her as I shut the door and reached for the seatbelt. "How did you know I would be set free?"

She grinned as only Dusty Diamond can. "Oh, a little birdie told me."

I wondered if the bird was the same one as Detective Biggs' finch. I chuckled when thinking about those two clowns.

"Where to, Mr. B?" asked Dusty.

"I would like to see your father before I go home," I said, gritting my teeth. "I have some explaining to do."

"That's a noble thought, Mr. B, but you really don't hafta do that."

"I know, Dusty, but I think I owe him that much."

She glanced at her sideview mirror, then yanked the steering wheel, guiding the Jeep onto the street. She shot a glance at me and said, "It may confuse him…rather than clarifyin' thangs, you know."

I thought about that for a moment. Mr. Diamond may have been a darned good private investigator in his

259

time; however, he probably wasn't the most astute guy in town. Maybe Dusty knew more than she let on about the man. I wouldn't press the issue; I would follow Dusty's lead.

She gazed at me for a moment, her green eyes a-blazing. "How 'bout I explain it all to him...say, a little at a time. You know...so's he won't get so danged mixed up and all."

I grinned and nodded my concurrence.

"Fine," she said, returning her attention to her driving chores. "We'll go have dinner at some place nice."

Some place nice?

The thought of how much I owed her, and how much the Jeep cost, and how much I had borrowed from my golfing buddies—all flashed through my soggy mind.

She interrupted my thoughts as she added, "On me, of course."

I felt like a heel putting expenses ahead of her request. I shook my head at my silly selfishness. "That would be nice, Dusty."

She smiled. "Totally awesome, Mr. B. I mean like, way cool."

I loved it when she talked like that. It made me feel like a teenager again.

I smiled, and nodded and said, "However, Dusty, I'm going to pay you back when I get on my feet again."

"That's not necessary, Mr. B. I mean, you had to shell out a bundle of dough fer doin' nothin' wrong, and I don't thank that's right."

Doing nothing wrong?

The thought of Lynn and me in the motel bedroom flashed through my mind like stampeding stallions. Well, when I think about it, I really didn't do anything wrong.

Poor Harry Thomas saw to that, thank heavens. I shook my head at the close call.

Dusty must have seen that my thoughts were miles away because she said to me, "Dusty to Mr. B. Come in Mr. B."

"What?" I asked, blinking away the haze and gazing at her. "What is it, Dusty?"

"Mr. B, you've gotta understand and accept the fact that men tend to get carried away every now and then… especially when they've been drinkin' too much."

Well, I wonder.

I nodded my understanding to Dusty; however, it didn't help my guilt complex much. In fact, it felt as if my wife, Heather, was sitting on my shoulder listening to all this …and reading my mind. Sheesh!

Dusty continued: "You may have had thoughts of thangs, but you never went through with 'em. And, I know that to be a fact."

I twisted around to look at her. "And just how do you know that, Dusty?"

She peered at me from the corner of her eye. "Let's just say I have my sources." She turned fully to me and smiled broadly. "Besides, I tempted you myself, and you turned me down, dangit all."

She did? I did?

She motioned to the rear seat. "I've got yer suitcase back there. I'll stop at the YMCA so you can shower and change into somethin' nice fer dinner."

I nodded my acceptance.

Dusty pulled into a space in front of the YMCA building. She put the Jeep in neutral, gazed at me and said, "Don't take too long, we've got a lot to talk about this evening."

We do?

FORTY-THREE

As Dusty and I drove through the town of Gunter, I now looked at the place in a whole new frame of mind. It was a quaint little place with nice homes, interesting shops and a variety of fine restaurants. And, the people were as nice as any I had ever met anywhere. I wondered why I hadn't realized that before. Maybe my little stint in jail had something to do with it.

Dusty parked her Jeep, and she and I went into Oscar's. The amiable restaurant was supposedly the best Gunter had to offer; and since Dusty was buying, I thought nothing was too good for us.

What? Hey, don't get your nose all twisted out of shape over this…this money thing. This is not my style. You know for a fact they sucked all my money out of me, right? Besides, I'll pay the kid back somehow. You realize that, don't you? Okay, enough already.

Back to Oscar's: Low-hanging lights swung over each white-damask-adorned table, and a bouquet of fresh pink carnations blossomed in the center of each table. Background music wafted throughout the large dining area, trickled between the many varieties of plants and filtered into our brains without our realizing how pleasant it was.

Dusty and I were seated at a table near the window. A waiter quietly approached us. He was tall with dark hair and was wearing a black suit with a white shirt and a black bow tie. A white-linen towel was draped over his forearm. He appeared to be about thirty. He introduced himself as

Walter. He took our drink order and quietly vanished as quickly as he had appeared.

"Nice place," I said to Dusty, glancing around.

"I've heard it is *the* place in town for a steak," she replied, smiling.

"Great. It's been a long time since I've had a good bacon-wrapped filet mignon. A very long time."

"What's that?"

"Oh, my dear Dusty. You have so much to learn about life." I shook my head slowly at her charming ignorance. "It's a type of steak."

"Huh."

Walter brought our drinks: Jack Daniel's, from the distillery just north of Gunter in Lynchburg, Tennessee, for me; and a salted frozen margarita for Dusty. The waiter vanished without saying a word. I guess he would know when we were ready to order our meals. Class. Right?

I toasted Dusty on her efforts and wished her well in future endeavors. She blushed—I think—and then toasted to my future of staying out of trouble...and jail. Small talk followed, along with another round of drinks.

Dusty slowly rubbed her fingers around the rim of her glass. She said, "Doncha wanna know how I knew you was gettin' outta jail, Mr. B?"

I shrugged. "I figured you'd get around to telling me when the time was right."

A hint of a smile creased her lips. "Well, the time is right, Mr. B."

I assumed Detective Biggs told her I was being released. But there's the rub: Did he do that to have Dusty and me lead him to the dough? Or, was he trying to get something on the two of us, so they could put both of us away? I think not.

I said, "Okay, Dusty...lay it on me."

"You see, Mr. B, I went to the Huntsville jail to talk with Marilyn Kantel."

"You did?" I asked, pulling back slightly. "Didn't she recognize you from when she and Grimes abducted you in Atlanta?"

"Naw," replied Dusty, coyly shaking her head. "I had on this really cool disguise."

"Honestly?"

"Uh-huh," she said, nodding. "And you shoulda seen my fake boobs, Mr. B." Dusty made a cupping gesture under her petite breasts. "They were dandies!" She smiled proudly.

I smiled also. I then looked around to see if Walter—our waiter—or any of the other patrons were observing Dusty's antics. They weren't, thank goodness.

I asked her, "Didn't she notice your...your accent? I mean—"

"Naw. I spoke the same way I did when talking to Hans. Marilyn never had a clue."

I wondered why Dusty spoke her slang only to me. Maybe she felt comfortable and at ease with me. Or, maybe it's when she gets overly excited that she lapses into her Texas twang.

Is that good or bad?

I don't know. Whatever works for the kid, I guess.

"As I was saying," continued Dusty, lowering her hands to the table, "I met with Marilyn Kantel...you know, your little Lynn gal."

"Get on with it, Dusty."

"Anyway, she said you was in on their scheme right from the beginnin'."

"That's not true, Dus—"

She held up a quieting hand. "That was what she said at first. But when I pressed the issue and got her dander up, she spilt the beans." Dusty's green eyes widened and sparkled. "And I mean the whole danged can."

Here we go again. What does one have to do to keep this kid on track?

"Dusty, can you please get to the point."

She crunched up her nose. "I will." She shook her head at my impatience. "You shoulda seen her, Mr. B. She was like a caged-up crazy animal. Her eyes were large and red, and the veins in her neck…well, they bulged out like frozen water pipes. I thought they were gonna pop." Dusty shook her head at the thought. "Then, I was sure Marilyn was gonna rip the dang security screen down to git to my goldarn throat."

"You were lucky she was restrained, or—"

"I'll say," interrupted Dusty. "Anyways, Marilyn really lost it. I mean, she totally lost her composure along with… well, losing her cool."

"Really?"

"Yep," continued Dusty, "and when Marilyn couldn't keep a lid on it any longer, she blurted out that you had nothin' to do with any of it—their scheme, the murders—nothin'."

"See, I told you, Dusty. But how did you get that information to Detective Small? He wouldn't believe a thing you had to say in my defense. He'd think you were just making up something to get me the heck out of jail, and I'm sure Marilyn Kantel wouldn't admit to any of it."

"I didn't go to Detective Small."

"What? Who did you—?"

"I went to the danged FBI."

"And they believed you?"

"They had no choice, Mr. B."

"Why do you say that, Dusty?"

"'Cause I had a tape recordin' of our goldarn conversation."

My jaw must have dropped four inches. "You mean to say, Dusty, they let you have a tape recorder in the visiting room? I didn't think they were allowed. And if they did permit one, I'm sure Marilyn Kantel wouldn't talk to you, if she saw one."

"Well, I didn't exactly have one with me. You see, they lemme have my cell phone, and it was dialed to a friend of mine, who had a tape recorder goin'."

"Pretty slick."

She nodded. "Yep. I thought so."

"But isn't that illegal?"

"Yep. But the feds never had to use the danged thing," Dusty replied, grinning. "Just knowing she'd been hoodwinked made Mrs. Kantel 'fess up to it all."

I glanced around to make sure Walter, or anyone else, wasn't standing nearby. I leaned toward Dusty and said, "Did you or she say anything about the money? I mean, if the FBI got wind—"

"Nope," Dusty replied, cutting me short. "Nothin' was said about it. In fact, I honestly don't think Marilyn knows anything about you transferrin' the danged funds outta that account. Boy, is she gonna be pissed if and when she ever gits out."

"So," I said to Dusty as I raised my glass in a salute, "Congratulations are in order. And Dusty Diamond is now going to be a very rich lady, huh?"

"Naw." She shook her head slowly. "However, some deservin' charities are gonna have a lot of thangs they've been needin'." She smiled brightly. "But that's after I deduct the expenses Marilyn Kantel caused you."

I smiled back at the kid. I knew all along Dusty would do the right thing.

"Now," Dusty said, leaning on the table, "about *our* partnership."

Partnership?

About the Author

JOHN JOSEPH GRATTON has been writing for almost twenty years. He has written children's stories and picture poems; a Civil War tale; and several mystery/suspense stories.

John is a retired Air Force Officer and a registered Professional Civil Engineer. He loves to write, do artwork and play golf.

John and his wife, Ellie, have three children and five grandchildren in Florida, Texas and South Carolina. Ellie and John reside in Fairfield Glade, Tennessee, and Naples, Florida.

Printed in the United States
82485LV00002B/382-477